Why. Me.

A novel by Eric Toth

ISBN: 978-1-7369515-1-4

Published by Footpath Publishing

Cover Design by Brian James

Dedications

This book is dedicated first and foremost to my wife, Lauren. Since we first met, I have always known that you are out of my league. As the years have passed, you have consistently proved me right. I like to think this knowledge has helped me to be a better husband, father and person. You are the most thoughtful, kind and loving person I know. You also happen to be the funniest. All told, you are the total package, and I wake up and go to sleep each day knowing how lucky I am.

Specific to this book, it is an understatement to say that I couldn't have done it without you. You endured years of me talking about it, years of me writing, reworking and editing, and years of me letting it sit on the shelf. Said more generally, you endured years of me, and for that I am eternally grateful. Without your patience, support, editing and direct feedback, I would never have finished this novel, and I wouldn't be half as proud of it. Frankly, without your love, humor and insight, I'm not sure I would have even started. You have inspired and encouraged me. I love you, and I thank you.

I also want to dedicate this book to my three incredible daughters. Your creativity, intelligence, wit, and bravery impress me to no end. You floor me each day with all that you are. You have given me the courage to put this work out in the world. I love you. I love you. I love you.

Many people helped me along the way as I worked on this novel, providing essential edits, comments, and encouragement. In no particular order, I'd like to thank Nancy; Brian; Harriet; my parents, Christie and Jeffrey; and my mother-in-law, Lynn. Your time is precious, and you loaned it to me. You are the best!

Lastly, I would like to note that this book is a tribute to everyone I have known. If we crossed paths and spent time with each other, then you inspired some element of it. I hope you enjoy it and much as I have enjoyed knowing you.

What happened once upon a time happens all the time

-Abraham Joshua Heschel

Chapter 1

There are days when nothing happens, and there are days when everything happens. Sometimes the hard part is telling the difference. The only constant is that all days have to start, and they all start in the same place. That's why I like a rainy morning. Rain makes it difficult for dawn. Morning has no grand entrance. It comes on slowly. That is my favorite way for the morning to arrive: when you aren't even sure if it has. It lets the day figure out everything else for itself.

That's how it was this morning. I woke up before my alarm went off, and I could hear the rain drumming steadily on the skylight above. It's one of those big industrial skylights, like the ones in superhero movies that the hero comes crashing down through to save the day. But there was no superhero this morning, no one coming along to save the day. That was not a problem, I didn't need it right then.

I kept my eyes closed even as I woke up, which I usually do. I've always been good about waking up, and I like those moments. Sort of like what the rain does for morning, it helps me to cloud over the real beginning of a day. Lying there, I tried to piece together a dream I had during the night. I couldn't quite get back to it.

Something touched my stomach, and I twitched slightly.

"Hey," I heard.

A smile spread itself across my face. "How did you know I was awake?"

"Because you always make that face."

I stretched and yawned and pulled my feet back under the covers, curled up on my side and into a ball facing

Chance and opened my eyes. "Morning, babe." She was lying on her back and facing me, the covers up to her waist, her right hand behind her head. She was smiling at me. I love the way she looks in the morning. She has these little hairs along her hairline that stick up all crazy like a little poof of a halo. Her eyes were still puffy with sleep. She looked damn cute. I slid my hand up her shirt until my fingers rested in the scallop of her ribs. She was wearing an old T-shirt that she keeps at my place, a real thin one that is almost see through in places. I rubbed the bottom of her sternum with my thumb. "What face?" I asked innocently, "this one?"

She pushed my hand from her front and laughed. "Get off me. You should see what you look like when you do that," she said, curling up and facing away from me.

I jumped up and looked into the mirror above my bed. It's one of those convex ones that you can buy out of a catalog with a painted sunburst around it. Except this one had more of a nautical feel to it and was not out of a catalog. It was pretty old, an antique, and it had dark splotches on it where its reflectivity was peeling away. "Let's see," I said, searching my face in the mirror. It's funny to look at a mirror like that close up. If you pay attention you'll notice that even though everything reflected in the middle is distorted, everything around the edges can be seen in fine detail, perfectly sharp. Like when you are concentrating on something specific and a completely separate thought crystalizes out of nowhere, clear and true. I could see all the plants to one side of the room, my dresser and the opening to my closet behind me, even Chance where she was curled up below me, moving now.

"Jesus, Archer!" she yelled, laughing again but this time trying to pull the covers over her head. "Can't you let anyone wake up in peace?"

I looked down at myself, standing naked at the head of the bed. "It's not my fault you have to tear my clothes off every night before we fall asleep. I could ask you why you can't let anyone go to sleep in peace."

"You wish."

She was right. I sleep naked pretty often, and even though I was slightly blurry about the night before, I was sure it wasn't her who took my clothes off. I grabbed my boxers from the floor by the bed and pulled them on. "Okay, you're safe now." I sat on the edge of the bed. The rain was still beating on the skylight up above. My bedside clock said it was five to seven. Something didn't seem right. Then it hit me. "Shit," I muttered, "we overslept."

"Hmmm?" Chance whimpered from under the covers. She hadn't yet come out from under them. Most likely she figured I was still naked.

"Daylight savings. Spring ahead, you know." I'm usually up by seven. Turns out it was almost eight.

"It's friggin Sunday… what time did we go to bed?" It was easy to tell she was going to go back to sleep, so I went downstairs, grabbing some pants off the staircase railing.

The staircase is one of my favorite things about my apartment. It's a spiral set that my friend Pete salvaged from somewhere. We installed it together. I should say that he installed it, while I did essentially everything I could do to inadvertently mess up the project. I'm not super handy, but I sometimes have good ideas. The apartment was really just a raw space when I rented it. A loft in one of the empty industrial buildings just west of downtown Providence. On the other side of Federal Hill, as people familiar with the area would say. The upstairs is just a bedroom with a space I call my closet. From the edge of the bedroom you look down into the main living area and across to a large brick wall broken by five immense windows. Besides the skylight they are my only windows, but they face almost due south, so it's always bright, even on a rainy day. From the bedroom you can't see the kitchen because it is underneath you, open to the living space but separated by an island. The bathroom is next to the kitchen.

I picked the space for a couple of reasons. One, because of the loft style bedroom. And two, because the ceilings are soaring. Twenty-five feet, easy, more to the top of the sloped skylight. There are a lot of these lofts around this area; most are going to end up renovated and with much higher rents at some point, probably soon. But that was nothing that I was worried about.

Chance was right. It had been a late night. My friend Courtney throws a big party twice a year, at least at this point in our lives. When the clocks change. Last night was the "spring ahead" party. He promised everyone he'd make up for the hour we lost at the next party. He says that every year. Come October he'll be telling us that he's offering a bonus hour. He throws a good party. Food, music, lots of beer and often some sort of novelty. Last night it was fake mustaches. He claimed it was a great social equalizer. I couldn't help but agree, but the thing must have ended up in my beer a dozen times. The parties happen at his old apartment, which he still keeps even though he's since moved. It's also a converted industrial space, like mine, with a recording studio that he built across the hall. His building is on the other side of downtown from mine, at the bottom of College Hill on the east side of Providence. He keeps the apartment and writes it off as a business expense, I think, since he uses it for his recording business.

I pulled on my pants when I got to the bottom of the stairs and walked over to my stereo. It was already on, so I hit play. The music blared. I quickly turned it down and looked up towards the bedroom, waiting for Chance to holler at me. Nothing. I turned it up to audible and looked out the window. For some reason, listening to Bill Withers sing *Lovely Day* didn't seem out of tune with the weather outside. It was raining a little harder now, which made me think it wouldn't last. The coffee shop at the other end of the parking lot was open, and a few people were shuffling in and out, bent against the rain. The night before had been so clear, rain didn't seem like an option. April. But I love these rainy mornings. Like I said, it's hard to tell when they start.

Despite the fact that I am good about getting up and out of bed in the morning, I am slow as hell getting the day started. I tend to tinker around, do nothing, maybe read. I make elaborate breakfasts or start projects. Sometimes I just space out, and I always take longer than average showers. My mother could never figure it out. I was the first one up in the morning, waking her and my father up with the sounds of what young boys get into when no one is watching them. Yet I was never ready to leave for school. I was perpetually late for the first thing of the day, whatever it was and more or less whenever it was. When it comes down to it, it really doesn't make sense. I can't stand the idea of wasting the whole day in bed, but I can never get around to starting my day. But I try not to analyze it too much. Sometimes thinking too hard about something isn't worth it. Like figuring out why Chance was awake before me and then so grumpy about wanting to go back to sleep.

People are always inconsistent; it's one of the things we do consistently.

"I want soup for breakfast," I said towards the window, as if speaking to the coffee shop patrons across the parking lot.

My apartment is sparsely decorated. In the middle of the living space there is one large couch facing two overstuffed armchairs. This seating straddles a large coffee table. There is a long mirror along the brick wall to the left of the wall with the windows, and the wall opposite that one is simply painted drywall, extending large and blank to the high wood ceiling and steel rafters above. I have been trying to figure out what to do with that wall for a while. I can't seem to get to it. The seating in the middle of the room, though ample for six, seems dwarfed by the emptiness around it. I have a vision of putting a large spotlight in the rafters so that I can bathe it from above in a single pool of light. But I think it would make people uncomfortable. So, for now I make do with the highly offensive industrial lights high up on the ceiling that were there when I moved in and which I usually keep very dim.

I walked over to the mirror hanging on the brick wall to my left. It's one of those old bar mirrors, with a thick frame of dark varnished wood with pegs along the bottom. I try to keep them empty but I'm generally unsuccessful at it, right then it was the home for several jackets and sweatshirts, mine and Chance's. The mirror is an antique, one of the few items I've held onto over the years. It came from Ireland originally but hung in a bar in the Lower East Side of Manhattan for years. I'm sure there's a better story to it than that, but I'm unaware of it. It was a nerve-racking experience hanging it from the brick wall. I was sure that it would fall and smash to pieces within a day or two, but there it hangs, sustained by no less than six lead anchors pounded securely into the bricks. I'll admit that I had help with that project, just as with the spiral staircase.

My stubble was getting a little out of control, I observed, rubbing my face and stretching my skin down towards my chin with my hand.

It was my mother who taught me an appreciation for antiques. I can't remember her loving anything else as much, except for those times when I knew that she loved me. She had an eye for the value of things, but more than that, she seemed to know what people would want to buy. She had the angle, somehow, and I would guess that she never took a loss on an item, never misjudged the potential value of the pieces she found. She bought and sold things, mostly, but she also collected some items here and there. I remember clearly the time she came home with a handblown glass bottle she purchased at a flea market for two dollars. And my feeling of pride when she showed me that the stamp on the bottom matched perfectly the stamp on a bottle pictured on the dust jacket of her book on Colonial American glass. She kept that bottle for years on a shelf in the kitchen. I always wondered just how much it was worth in dollars, but I suppose it was worth something else to her.

When I was seven, I began attending a summer camp in New Hampshire. I loved that place. We hiked and went fishing and canoeing. The laid-back attitude of the counselors was something I hoped throughout my childhood to someday emulate. Still do. My first summer there my mother surprised me by picking me up by herself at the end of the session and announcing that I would accompany her on one of her hunts. She used these trips to scour the antique stores of central New Hampshire and southern Maine, to find deals, make connections, and purchase items. Antiquing. The word was like magic to me. It rang with a sense of the unknown, calling up the scent of dust and old varnish. In my mind, the next big find was always just around the corner. I relished in watching my mother's face as she leaned in close to inspect an item, in knowing that the questions she asked were always the right ones, in seeing how her lips would purse and hearing her breath come in and out in short bursts through her nose as she concentrated. I was rapt with attention for every second of those trips. My memory is crammed with the details of every shop, every shop owner, every inn and innkeeper we visited. I remember the splits in the roads, the names of the streets and of every antique dealer and their dogs. I was a willing student and a meticulous observer. I never touched anything, never asked any questions. My mother oozed with knowledge of things from before her time, and I absorbed everything that I could as if by osmosis. I felt special. It was like being a part of a secret society.

The things I learned during these trips ended up serving me well. I began to see how my mother saw and to get a sense of how she understood the appeal of certain pieces. I continued to attend the same summer camp for the next seven years, and while I loved being there, I could never wait for her to arrive on the last day of camp. On the steps of the farmhouse I would sit, all the other kids rushing for one last game of capture the flag, one last chance to pound nails in the woodshop, looking frantically for their lanyard bracelets and tie-dyed shirts. I would sit and wait, my bags having been packed since the night before, looking up the dirt road towards the cemetery at the top of the hill, watching for her car to come around the corner.

The time spent in those few short weeks every year came to be the only time I ever spent alone with my mother, and for that reason became my favorite weeks of the year. Even as a young teenager, I swam in the silences my mother and I enjoyed, and I felt close to her in a way I never felt with anyone else. In the quiet, I would stare blankly out the passenger window, trying in vain to keep my eyes from dragging along with the trees that flew past, wondering how many different trees a person could see in one lifetime. Listening to the creaks in old cottages and inns where we stayed, up alone late at night wondering what sort of haunts lived in the noises the buildings made. At meals, my mother contentedly reading her newspaper or poring over a road map to plan our next few stops, I would be lost in my toast or cheeseburger, picturing the next purchase she would make, nervous the shipping would get screwed up and the treasure would be lost forever. It never seemed odd that she would take me on these trips, though an outsider might have seen me as a tagalong. My mother was impenetrable.

I took one last look at myself and turned away from my reflection. "Soup," I echoed myself, this time to no one in particular.

Searching through the cabinets and refrigerator, I collected a pile of ingredients on the counter. Spring onions, rice noodles, vegetable bouillon, black bean paste, crushed chili peppers, a spicy brown sauce cryptically labeled entirely in Chinese characters, tofu. I put some water on to boil, rinsed the green onions and began to mince them. The tofu was already drained, I cut it into smallish cubes and scooped them into a pile next to the onions. Dumped the noodles into the boiling water and let them cook a solid three minutes, just enough time to go wash my face and use the bathroom. I drained and rinsed them, put them back in the pot, added about two cups of water, lowered the heat and added the bouillon, bean paste, chillies, tofu, mystery brown sauce and half the onions. I let it simmer, top on.

When I was growing up, I was a toast and cereal guy, straight up. I swear that I had that breakfast every single day until my late teens. Toast, either lightly buttered with jelly or just some peanut butter. And a bowl of cereal, usually Cheerios. It was after I moved to Manhattan for college when all that changed. The novelty of eating food not traditionally designated for breakfast has worn off at this point, but I just never got back into the mood for toast and cereal.

A folded scrap of paper on the counter got my attention. I peeled it open carefully and read it. *Music is life* was scrawled there, recognizably in my own handwriting. That's a funny thing about me. Sometimes when I drink, I wake up in the morning and find a little piece of paper where I wrote something I thought was meaningful the night before. Problem is, I can rarely remember what I was thinking about when I wrote it. *Music is life*. What the hell did I mean by that? I thought, scratching myself and then smirking like I had an audience. I rolled the paper up between my fingers. Even the times when I'm able to figure out the train of thought that I was riding, it never seems as deep to me as when I was under the influence. I hadn't realized I was quite so drunk the night before.

I stared at the tiny wad of paper trying to piece together my thoughts from the night before, but I couldn't get there. Frustrating. Kind of like with the dream I couldn't quite remember, like when the sky is a color that you can't name. Just out of reach for words.

Why. Me.

Seems like I forget most of my best ideas. And the ones I do remember I usually just jot down in a notebook, along with other useless tidbits. Over the years they've piled up but never been expanded upon despite my good intentions. It's a pathetic philosopher who sits on every idea. Of course, the most tragic discovery would be if, despite all these thoughts, there simply wasn't any revelation there at all.

My soup was ready. I was absentmindedly rolling the piece of paper between my thumb and forefinger. I flicked it into the sink and poured my soup into a large bowl. Allowing it to cool for a minute, I used the knife to push the remaining green onions from the cutting board on top of the soup in my bowl and dropped the knife and board in the sink. The ingredients went back to their places. I grabbed a pair of chopsticks and a soupspoon and perched on one of the stools at the kitchen counter, my back to the windows. I got up and set the microwave clock an hour ahead and sat back down. Not bad, I thought, sprinkling some more chillies on top of the layer of raw green onions and then stirring it all together. Looks good.

The college I attended was a small liberal arts school in the West Village, a division of a much larger institution. My first and, as it turned out, only roommate while I was there was a guy named Mark. Mark Rush. It was the two of us who came to love experimenting with different soups for breakfast. This recipe, if you can call it that, was our favorite combination. Before I left for college I can realistically say that I had only made four friends in my lifetime. Mark was my fifth, and we hit if off immediately. He was from a wealthy New York family, his father a lawyer, his mother a doctor, but their money was much older than their individual careers. You never would have known that he came from money. Sure, he was spoiled by his family, but he wasn't spoiled to the world. He never expected much from others.

We were both bored with college, unchallenged perhaps, or under stimulated. I grew up perfecting the habit of figuring out exactly what I had to do to get by in school, flying above the radar enough to have my teachers like me, but below it enough to hand in work that was just good enough to pass. The results were steady B's. My skill of regurgitation was fine tuned. I was always comfortable with that and nothing changed in college.

Mark was absolutely brilliant. He somehow picked up on everything in between, seeing the world in a way that anyone could understand but could never have noticed first the way that he did. In our mutual boredom with higher education we tried to create excitement, which meant we spent time focused on meaningless pursuits and sometimes did silly things for fun. What else?

While in class, I managed to do as I had always done, alternately swooping below and soaring above the radar, pulling down middling grades like I was picking apples. Besides that dubious skill, there was one other thing that I mastered while enclosed in the walls of academia: I perfected the art of doodling. Cartoon faces, invented animals, scenic vistas of mystical places, unintelligible designs, corporate logos, household items like teacups and doors. While my face was always studious, and my movements always implied religious note taking, my pencil was aptly creating doodle after doodle after doodle. Notebooks worth. You never knew there were so many ways to draw stick figures.

Fate was lining things up for me, characteristically without my knowledge, when I met Mark Rush. A month into our first semester, I was in the lounge of our dorm, hunkered over the microwave and busy at work on a new soup recipe when he burst in. His expression showed a vague annoyance that he had needed to search further than our shared bedroom.

"Bean paste?" he blurted, momentarily distracted from his main point by noticing a new ingredient I impulsively purchased earlier that morning at the corner bodega. He picked it up from the table.

"Thought I'd give it a shot." I replied.

He put it down purposelessly on the arm of a chair and looked out the window into the airshaft. "What a waste of space," he commented.

"What are you talking about?"

"Arch!" suddenly coming back to his dramatic entrance, "Dude, I found jobs for us. Check this out, we can work at this gallery place on the Upper East Side, my dad knows the owner or the concierge or whatever you call it. Did some legal work for the place. The curator. It's like an auction house." He rarely had time for complete sentences.

This guy never ceased to amaze me. I hoped to find some part time work. Mark never really had a job, never needed one. I didn't necessarily need one, but it kept me from having to ask my father for money, which I never wanted to do. I think it was the novelty of finding a place for us to work together that inspired Mark. And it was something new. I flipped through the pages of the brochure he handed me, quickly recognizing the eras represented by the furniture in their upcoming auction.

"That smells good," he said, popping open the microwave and pulling out the bowl.

"What will we do?"

"Can we split it into two bowls?"

"No, this, dumbass," chucking the brochure on the table and sitting down. The bean paste fell on the floor.

"Oh, yeah, it's perfect. We don't even really have to work for them. They just need some freelance sort of help with their new website. They didn't like their old webmaster, he was a dick or something, that's why my dad was doing something with them, arbitrating a contract or something. That's why they just want freelance work, I think. Anyway, all you have to do is write the blurbs about the pieces of furniture. You already know all that antique stuff. I can do the website design and coding, I know all that shit. It's perfect. We'll call ourselves a company and just charge a rate, no contract, no commitment, no set hours. This is good. Where did you find this stuff?" He picked the plastic jar of bean paste up from the floor.

"Ray Ray's place, on the corner." I said absently, reaching over to grab the brochure again. It seemed like a decent idea.

"What're you doing?" I snapped out of my reverie. Chance was standing at the top of the spiral staircase. She was wearing that threadbare shirt and pink underpants. Boy shorts, I think they are called, the ones that fit like a pair of spandex biking shorts but that would be few inches shorter than appropriate and a few threads thinner than practical for bike riding.

"Just thinking." My hands were clasped together and thrust between my legs, my elbows at my thighs, still perched on the stool. I stretched downward and then sat straight up. "Good morning sunshine."

"Did you shower?"

"Nope."

"I'm going to."

"Do your thing, ding-a-ling."

She held back a smile and sighed in exasperation. "You are such a loser, Archer."

I couldn't argue with that, so, having absentmindedly finished my breakfast, I put my bowl and utensils in the sink and went to stretch out on the couch. I watched as Chance gingerly picked her way down the steps, trying to peer over an armload of clothes to make sure her feet wouldn't miss one of the narrow stairs. It's an acquired skill. She looked good in her little getup, and I watched as she walked away from me and the stairs towards the bathroom. She disappeared as the door closed behind her.

★★★

Introductions always help. My name is Archer Why. That's my full name. Nothing in between. Believe it or not, my parents were not hunters or hippies. In fact, according to my father, my names, first and last, are shortened versions of my great-grandfather's name. My father's father's father. His name was Archibald White, and as my father used to tell it, he was so drunk when he arrived from England upon the shores of Ellis Island that his hiccups caused a no doubt weary immigration officer to incorrectly record his name, casting generations of potential Whites to be Whys. Perhaps the ordeal of immigration was so intimidating that he chose not to contest this improper and somewhat ridiculous surname. I like to think that he simply liked the originality of it. Either way, it stuck. And now I'm stuck with it, which isn't to say I mind at all.

My mother used to tell me that she liked the name Archer not because of the significance in my paternal family's history. Nope, she told me she had a different feeling about it. She always told me she'd get around to telling me at some point.

With a tag like Archer you'd think I'd never have the problem of turning around to answer someone calling my name only to find that said person was referring to someone else. Guys named John or Joe have that issue, I'm told. That being said, having a last name that's also a common question in a world where people love calling you by your last name means something quite the opposite. In my situation, you end up being the sort of person who never hears his name the first time someone says it. If I turned my head every time a person in my vicinity said "Why" then I would never have any spare time. No, I'm the kind of guy who suddenly hears, as if from nowhere and with zero prior warning, "Yo, Why, what are you fucking deaf? How many times do I have to call you?" Some people think I do it on purpose, and sometimes they are right. After all, like I said, I really can't waste time looking every time I hear the word "why." Some people have accepted repeating themselves. Some, if you can believe it, have taken to calling me by my first name. Imagine that. But the unfortunate nature of my name includes the fact that it is just plain fun for some people to call me by a common question. It could be worse. At least my name isn't "Huh." Good lord.

From where I was sprawled on the couch, I could hear the water splashing while Chance was showering. I decided to have mercy on her and not wash the dishes while she was in there. I figured she deserved good water pressure. I stretched again and stared at the skylight as if waiting for something to happen.

Bill was singing one of my favorite tunes from this album, and my eyes grew heavy as I listened to him sing of sunshine and smiles. As my eyes closed, I could feel myself lifting slightly, becoming lighter as I lay there. His voice was the rain coming through the skylight, which now seemed open. I was almost back to my dream from the night before when a sudden change in the air woke me from my doze. My head snapped up as the bathroom door opened. I stared at Chance standing in the doorway, her body and head wrapped as if bandaged in two fluffy purple towels.

"What?" she asked of my blank stare.

"Nothing, I thought I was remembering my dream."

"Come up with anything?" She asked, pulling the towel off her head and wringing her hair into it. "Is Bill helping you? You've had this album in all week."

"I think this might be the perfect compilation. He's got everything here. Love, family, friends, hope, god. The perfect album." I looked at her for a reaction. "I can't remember my dream."

"I guess that means we'll be hearing Bill Withers from now on?" She laughed. "You said the same thing last week about Pink Floyd's *Animals.*"

"Well, I was right then too."

"At least you're consistent." She hopped lightly up the stairs to the bedroom. I followed, taking the steps two at a time.

"Are you going to shower before you start harassing me?" She was still drying her hair, facing away from me. I grabbed her by the shoulders and wrestled her to the bed, making a play for her towel. She put up a good fight, which is easy against me. I'm simply too ticklish to wrestle well. We were both laughing and grappling when my cell phone began buzzing on the dresser.

"Damn it," I said, "You got lucky."

"Whatever. Answer your phone, sucker." I picked it up and glided down the stairs, much more quickly than Chance can do it.

Chapter 2

"Who was it?" Chance was dressed now, ready for the day in a pair of jeans and thin green hoodie. She somehow manages to look younger than her age. Which is younger than mine. Which is thirty-one. She looks nineteen.

"Jonas. He's on his way over."

Chance rolled her eyes. I could tell even while my back was turned while I was washing dishes. I rinsed the suds off my soup bowl and put it on the drying rack and put both palms on the counter as if bracing myself.

"What?"

"What, what?" Chance replied casually. "You know I don't like that guy."

That always frustrates me. "You don't know him, Chance."

"Yeah, and? You don't even like him, Archer. What's the friggin problem?" She was annoyed. She had a point.

"Yeah, but he's my friend. I know him, I'm allowed to not like him."

"You, my friend, are a weirdo, Archer. You are the only person I know who doesn't like his best friend."

"He's not my best friend, and I do like *him*. I just don't *like* him. I can't explain it."

"It wouldn't matter if you could, because I don't like *him*. And I don't *like* him. Either way. He's your friend, and I have to split in a few minutes anyhow. You guys can have fun with each other." I turned and looked at her. She looked at me and smiled. "I love you, Arch." I looked at her some more. Sometimes when I look at her for too long I have to remind myself that she is a separate person from me. I have to look at the situation as if I'm reading it in a book narrated omnisciently. Or like I'm hovering above it with a bird's eye view. The feeling from my dream started to come back to me and then disappeared. I smiled absently.

"What are you up to today?"

Chance shrugged. "Sunday dinner with the girls." By that she meant her usual Sunday afternoon meeting with the other women in her graduate program. She was studying architecture at RISD here in Providence. I keep telling her I want her to design me a better living room, and she hates that joke. She works hard and is good at what she does. She's more on the mathematical side of architecture, which I can never quite follow. It's all engineering and stuff like that. She has a couple partners in her program and the three of them always meet on Sundays to go over their projects, and right now they have a major one going. She'll be finishing school soon and it's her final big thing. I'm always excited for her when she gets excited about school, even though I can't really relate to that feeling. "I was going to go to the studio early to get some work done beforehand. You're working tonight." It was more of a statement than a question.

"Yup, Sunday shift baby." I wrapped her up in a hug and pushed my lips against her head. I inhaled deeply through my nose. Her hair still seemed hot from the hairdryer, and it was soft against my lips. It smelled delicious. "I love you, too."

There's a part of me, a continually smaller part, that is still scared shitless every time I say those words. It isn't the commitment of it. It's the letting someone else know you well enough for love to be a possibility. When someone else knows you like that, they own a part of you. And if they leave, they take it with them. I hadn't felt whole for a long time before I met Chance, there were too many people out there who had taken parts of me they didn't return. It is a terrifying feeling to realize you don't really know yourself, and somehow even more so to risk someone else looking too deeply. What might they find? What might they find missing?

"You seem out of it today," Chance said.

"Yeah, I'm cloudy. It's the rain. I can't figure out if the day started yet." But the rain had stopped. The skylight was silent. "I'm going to hop in the shower. Will you be here when I'm out?"

"Yeah, I'm going to eat something."

"There's soup in the pot on the stove."

"Thanks. Soup for breakfast. Someday I'll figure you out, Archer Why."

"Let me know what you come up with." I pulled off my pants and threw them half-assed up the spiral staircase. I danced a little jig in my underpants to show Chance I wasn't really starting the day off grumpy, prancing my way into the bathroom.

It's hard to say what really makes me take so long in the shower. I'm typically just daydreaming and enjoying the feeling of the hot water. I leaned my head forward and let the water run over the back of my head, dripping to the shower floor from around my face. My hair was getting a little bit longer, and the water pulled it together and ran off the ends of each clump in streams that looked like chains connecting me to the ground. I moved my head gently from side to side and watched the chains swing back and forth.

Growing up, my parents always harassed me to get out of the shower sooner. They complained I was using up all the hot water, that it was a waste of energy, or that it was simply unnecessary. Once I left home and went to college in the city, my showering was on my own terms. In my

Manhattan dorm room, the hot water was endless. I took showers that put my childhood showers to shame. It seems silly to go on about it, but I really like long showers.

Mark could never understand it, but he never seemed to have time to stand still for long, so it wasn't such a mystery that he wouldn't get it. It never ceased to amaze me how quickly he and I became such close friends. The four friends I had from childhood were the kind of friends where you simply can't remember a time when they weren't around. The five of us were basically inseparable, despite the fact that we didn't all attend the same schools. From kindergarten or earlier, we all knew each other in some respect, and spending time with them was easy. Jonas was one of these guys. If I met him for the first time today, I'd probably never want to hang out with him. But because of our history there was really no pressure there. Right or wrong, it always seemed to me that none of us ever really hid anything from each other and that everything was on the table. I was so used to having friends like this as a kid that I became no good at showing new people the kind of person I was. I either expected people to know immediately or I never expected them to get it, I'm not sure. But either way, for a long time it made it difficult to make real friends instead of acquaintances.

This became all the more apparent to me as I got to know Chance. She doesn't have really old friends, but she's able to make friends more easily than me, and she has many more friends as a result. I both envy and feel bad for her. She never seems to understand the closeness I have with my oldest friends, and the sadness of it for me is that I think she just might be on to something. These guys, these close friends of mine, have become not much more than a backdrop to my life than anything else. That closeness isn't any less real, but at some point, I stopped getting to know them any better. The relationships became a security blanket that I carried around for a little bit too long, one that kept me from picking much up from many of the new people I was meeting along the way, one that kept me stuck in the past. Which isn't to say that I needed to ditch the blanket. I just didn't need to cover myself with it so tightly. But I'm getting better at that.

With Mark, somehow it was my lack of openness to new friends that led us to becoming so close so fast. He seemed to have no friends from growing up and despite the fact that he grew up in the city, he only seemed interested in hanging out with me. And that's what we did. For some reason, I immediately felt at home with him, and we just clicked. I think he felt that I wasn't open, and that made him feel safe, which made me feel more open.

Things took off pretty quickly with the auction house gig. For my part, the curator was very happy with my work. The website was not only functionally crappy, but the descriptions of the items were mundane. They read like encyclopedia entries. He felt my descriptions were more personal, had more feeling or something. It is hard to give people a feel for antiques with a blurb on a website. There's something incongruous about reading a description of a nineteenth century schoolhouse desk on a computer monitor, but he liked it and that was fine for me. I felt like Mark was doing the heavier lifting with his website design, but he insisted we were fifty fifty partners. He knew all about web design, seemed to pick it up as he went along somehow, but I suspect he worked harder at it than I knew. Even though I knew nothing about the programming side of things, I helped him understand the type of interface customers of an auction house might appreciate. I suppose that together we made a pretty good team.

At that time, the internet bubble was in full swing. Huge companies were popping up as if from nowhere, and millions of dollars seemed to be flying around like nothing. Our small company had nothing to do with all that, and we happily provided a small niche service to the auction house Mark's dad connected us to. That work led us to connecting to some other houses and even a couple consignment stores, and we did the same thing for them. A part time job turned into a lot of work, but my passive attitude about school melded perfectly with the fact that I was busy with other things. Having too much to do helped me to avoid thinking about being away from Providence, about what being in college meant as far as becoming an adult, and about anything else for that matter.

"These auction dudes are pretty stupid," Mark said matter of factly while we were waking up one morning. Manhattan dorm rooms don't provide much elbow room, and Mark was talking to me from the bunk above mine. I had come to know every twist and turn of the grain in the flimsy piece of plywood that kept him and his mattress from falling on my face. I stared at the wood while I asked him what the hell he was talking about.

"Think about it, Arch. These places depend on suckers actually coming to their auction houses and bidding on shit. How many people are really going to do that?" He paused. "Actually, I mean, how many are going to keep doing that?"

"What do you mean? These places have been around forever. And people can call in, they don't have to go there."

"Same difference." I could hear him moving around on his bunk. The plywood bent towards me and groaned slightly. "People are already doing this stuff online. These places are missing out. Some jackass in Ontario may want their coffee table or something and they won't be able to bid, because they won't know about it, and won't feel like sitting on the phone long distance to make a bid."

"That's the point, Rush. Some people actually want to go to an auction, and that's who these places deal with. There's something for everyone."

"You're arguing my point, dipshit. These places can give something to everyone. It would be so fucking easy to just set up their website so they could have auctions over the internet at the same time as in person or not or whatever. They need to do things other ways or they are fucked. Go online, asshole, people are already doing it!" He had this way of cursing people out or calling them names as if they were right in front of him. "And forget this consignment shit, idiots. People will be selling their own crap online soon enough."

"So do it then, and see if they want to get on board." I was having a hard time getting on board with him myself, but I felt like he was right about something. In retrospect, things like long distance calling and the foreign nature of bidding on something you aren't sitting in front of seem almost as antiquated as the antiques we were helping to sell. At the time, not a lot of people were thinking about things the way he was. "But those places are institutions; they've been doing things that way since long before you were a scratch in someone's pants. Good luck changing that shit."

"Well all I'm saying is, the Romans were around for a long time too, you know."

"Rome is still there, dumbass. Let's go get some breakfast." I said, rolling out of bed. I'm pretty sure neither of us had a clue about Roman history, and it turns out that neither of us were exactly right in our thinking during our discussion, but the best part about it was that it all turned out not to matter.

★★★

"What are you doing in there?" It was Chance yelling at me through the bathroom door. I told her to come in the bathroom. "I have to go, you've been in there forever."

I ignored her comment. "Okay, can you come by the bar later and pick me up? I get off at midnight."

"Maybe I'll come earlier with Stacey and we can have a drink while you're finishing up."

"Cool, gimme a kiss." I said, craning my neck around the shower curtain.

She gave me a quick peck.

"What was that? Don't kiss me like you are drinking a martini. Give me some love." But I knew she wouldn't. I pulled her in the shower with her clothes on last week, and she was keeping her distance.

She smiled coyly. "Maybe later, I gotta go. Bye."

"Bye, babe." I shut off the shower as she closed the door.

"I knew you were done in there before I came in!" I heard Chance yell as she walked away from the bathroom. She knows I like to waste time in there.

I dried off and went up to my bedroom to get dressed. I made the bed and sat down for a minute on the edge of it. Not only had it stopped raining, but it looked like the sun was coming out. I could see the clouds getting brighter and some blue was showing through them. I looked at my plants that acted like a barrier to the edge of my loft. There was a spigot coming off a pipe poking up through the floor next to the wall. This was my first attempt at plumbing, which went fine until I turned the water on. Pete helped me to fix that, the same friend who installed the staircase, and mirror. I really wanted to be able to get a glass of water in my bedroom, and it worked out that it helps me to water my plants too. I filled up a measuring cup I kept for that purpose and watered a couple of them. I never tried to take care of plants until I moved into this place. I enjoy doing it. I particularly like the succulents and the cacti. There is something comforting about how slowly they grow.

Pete also made the headboard for my bed. That guy is amazing. He can fix just about anything that is broken. If he can't fix it then you can figure that it can't be fixed. And if he can picture something in his head, it seems like he can build it. He is meticulous and hilarious, with a thick blond head of hair that is about as enviable as hair can be. When I described the headboard I wanted, he said he could make it for me. It was exactly what I wanted. You might guess that being raised with antiques would make me dislike new furniture. That is not the case. I don't really buy old stuff anymore. I just have a few old things kicking around.

I like my feet to hang off the bottom of the bed when I'm falling asleep, so I didn't bother him to make a footboard. When I was a kid I used to get scared of monsters. I would convince myself I saw things in the shadows of my room, and I would stay awake with my eyes open waiting to fall asleep like that. My mother taught me to put one foot off the edge of the bed and count to twenty. She said that no scary things can resist a kid's foot for longer than that, so if I could make it to twenty I could feel safe.

Even as an adult I just never stopped doing it. Not the counting part, just the hanging of my feet off the edge of the bed. It's funny that the things that scare you as an adult are just as invisible as the things that scare kids. I guess I'm still hanging my feet out there for something.

I'm not sure if I heard the knock or if I remembered Jonas was stopping by first, or if they happened at the same time. I yelled that I was coming even though no one could have heard me from the door, went down the stairs, and slid on the floor in my socks to arrive at the front door, strangely out of breath even though I hadn't exerted myself. "Jonas, what's up kid?" I said. We gave each other a strong hug in the doorway. I felt something hit my thigh. "What's that, you staying over?" He was carrying a small, low slung gym bag. It was made of baby blue canvas and looked like it belonged to a high school basketball player from the eighties.

"No," he said seriously, his face was taut, "I was hoping I could leave this here for the day though, I have to deal with some stuff." I wasn't really asking if he was moving in, but he seemed so serious I didn't mention he wasn't getting the joke.

"Yeah, sure. Put it wherever." I closed the door behind him. He dropped the bag on the floor and slipped off his coat. It looked wet but was clearly drying. "You okay?"

He turned around and his face had softened a little bit. He seemed less tense already, and he ducked down in a boxing stance and jabbed at my body. I pulled him into another hug. It was no less strong than the first one. He didn't answer me but I didn't sweat him about it. "You want something to eat?"

"Nah man, I was sitting in the coffee shop having coffee and a roll when I called you. I saw Chancey leave so

I figured it was safe to come over." This was the whole weird thing with him and Chance that I didn't get. It bugged the shit out of her that he would sit there in the coffee shop and wait for her to leave. And it confused the hell out of me why he did stuff like that. Nothing ever happened to make either one not like the other, but she was uncomfortable around Jonas, and he seemed to avoid her, which made her more uncomfortable. It felt easier not to deal with it for some reason, even though I knew it would probably bubble up someday. I also didn't get why he had to call her Chancey, but whatever.

He sat down on one of the armchairs, and I sat across from him on my couch. We sat there in silence for a minute or two. I curled my toes around the knob on the drawer of the coffee table and pulled out the drawer an inch, then pushed it closed. I looked at him. His hair was kind of long, but not to his shoulders. The length of it looked less like a style choice and more like forgetfulness around having it cut. It was dark brown, as were his eyes. His skin was pale, like the paleness of someone who hadn't been outside much for the past few years. It didn't matter that I knew he could get very tan in the summer, his paleness made him look like a guy who'd been sitting in front of a computer for a decade. We used to call it the New York City tan. He fit that description perfectly. The features of his face were hard, sleek and tight. His nose was thin, his cheekbones pronounced and his chin slightly cleft. He looked like he could stand to gain a few pounds for sure. He looked like a character from a Dickens novel or something. He looked like shit to me.

Jonas was the only other of our group of five who left Rhode Island after high school, and he went to college in the city as well. But he went to school uptown and I went to school downtown, he immersed himself in school while I ran tight with Mark, and we saw each other more when back in Providence than we ever did in the city. Immediately after college, he got a high paying job at a Wall Street trading firm where he seemed to excel, getting promotions and earning more money than he knew what to do with. He became a real city guy, switching jobs from firm to firm, and none of us stayed in regular touch with him. But like I said, with old friends that stuff doesn't always matter. Sitting across from him, I was comfortable in our silence. It didn't matter so much that I didn't know what he'd been up to last night, when he didn't show up to Courtney's party, much less what he'd been up to for the past six months since I last saw him. And I didn't get the sense it mattered to him either. Not because neither of us cared, but because it wouldn't really change the level of our connection. There was a time when that would have felt like a special thing to me. Now it just felt like a hallmark of the past, calling out into high relief the fact that our friendship, though strong, was stalled somewhere just after high school. This was especially true with Jonas, who I rarely saw. All the same, I knew he was about to speak before he opened his mouth.

"So it's cool if I leave my bag here for a bit?"

"Why are you asking again, man? What do I care? What are you doing today?"

He looked up at the skylight. "I just have to take care of some stuff," he said vaguely. "I'll be around Providence for a few weeks, I think. I quit my job."

I wasn't all that surprised but was going to ask him what happened when someone knocked at the door. I got up and walked over to see who it was. I don't get a lot of unsolicited knocks. Probably Charlie, I thought. I opened the door and it was, indeed, Charlie, my hapless, hopeless neighbor. I shouldn't say hopeless, that's not entirely fair, but he's just one of these guys who fuddles through life with no real sense that most people actually do try for some sort of direction. Constantly starting projects and never finishing them, starting school, quitting school, working odd jobs, smoking pot. He was in high school with us, and we all knew him, but he ran with a different crew at that point. "Hey man, can I borrow your hammer? I'm still trying to build that bar in my apartment."

"I don't have a hammer."

"You don't have a hammer?"

"I don't anymore." I said flatly.

"You don't anymore," he repeated. He was so stoned it wasn't funny. I pulled my cell phone out from my pants pocket to check the time. It was about nine thirty.

"No, I had a hammer until you borrowed it around Christmas."

"Oh, right. Okay. Do you have a power drill?"

"Sorry Charles, I don't have one," I lied to him. I have one. I have a nice one, but I hoped to use it someday and that wouldn't happen if I loaned it to him. I started to feel bad. I caved. "Oh, wait, yeah, come in. I'll get it for you." Charlie was confused, but he came in and saw Jonas on the couch.

"Hey bro, Jonas, what's up?" He dragged out the *up* for about three seconds. "Dude I haven't seen you in so long." Jonas looked unaffected by this realization, but he stood up to greet Charlie.

When Jonas recognized the glazed look of Charlie's eyes, his own eyes sparkled. They shook hands and awkwardly gave each other a half hug, a 'brohug' if you will. "I'll go get the drill," I said, suddenly feeling like a

31

third wheel. I went to the closet on the far side of the room and waited for a second for the light to fully turn on. It took me a minute to recognize the case for the drill, and by the time I came back Charlie had left. "What the fuck was that?"

"That dude is one funny guy. I told him I'd stop by when I was leaving and he said that was cool and he left." There was a knock on the door.

"Why. Dude, I forgot the drill." He opened the door and peered around it. "Sorry man, I just ah… oh, cool the drill. Thanks, man, I'll get it back to you later." He left with the drill, and I just about laughed my ass off after closing the door.

Jonas and I sat around talking for about half an hour or so. The whole time he just seemed kind of distracted, but I chalked it up to his general way. I didn't feel so worried about it, but my gut said something was off. I started to feel antsy and was looking for an opportunity to leave. When he asked what I was doing for the day, I saw my chance. I told him I had to take care of some stuff at my dad's house, which was sort of true, and that I should probably be going. He stood up from the couch and walked over to the bathroom. I got up and picked up the loose change that had fallen from his pockets. Seems like every time Jonas stands up he leaves change in his wake. I slipped it in my pocket absentmindedly.

I snagged a thick, zippered sweatshirt off a peg on the mirror as I walked toward the door and waited for him as he made his way out of the bathroom. He looked at his bag in a funny way and looked at me again, almost searchingly. I thought he might ask me again if it was okay for him to leave it with me, but he didn't. We got outside the door and I locked it. We gave each other another hug and I couldn't help but notice that he didn't look at my face when we said goodbye. I could smell the faint tinge of marijuana in the hallway, and I knew it had to be coming from Charlie's place. I watched for a second as he walked towards Charlie's door and then I spun around and went down the stairs. As I descended towards the front door, I somehow knew there was no more chance I'd ever see him again than my hammer or drill.

Chapter 3

When I stepped outside, I still had it in my head that it was raining, but I found that the sun was already drying off the pavement in between the puddles. I walked straight across the parking lot to the coffee shop, turned around, walked halfway back and stood in front of my car. I looked up at the sky, back at my car and said to the world, "I'll walk it today." I went back to the coffee shop, bought a small cup of coffee, light on the cream, no sugar, made a point of saying goodbye to the baristas and headed out the door. I aimed east with no intentions other than walking straight through downtown Providence and hunting down some lunch on College Hill. The sun was in my face and the air was cool, a perfect spring day. I unzipped my sweatshirt so I could feel the air through my t-shirt and warm-up pants. I've taken a liking to this sort of outfit. I used to have a little more variety in my wardrobe, but I've grown to like this style, simply for comfort's sake really.

I saw a lighter on the ground and picked it up in stride. Stopping at a garbage can and balancing my coffee on the edge, I pulled off the metal top and pried out the round wheel used to make the spark. I dropped everything but the wheel in the garbage can and rolled the wheel between my fingers. I have a weird habit of collecting useless things like that. In my apartment I have an old wooden spice rack that has sixteen little drawers. I don't use it for spices. Almost every drawer contains a collection of small things that I've picked up over the years. One has lighter wheels, another has coins I've found on the ground. One is filled to overflowing with those little plastic things that act as a clasp for bread bags and one contains keys. They are essentially useless objects, and none are particularly beautiful. I suppose they are just the things that you overlook in your life, the sort of items you step on or over as you walk down the street, never realizing how many of them you see in your lifetime. For some reason, I started picking these things up, and in ten years I've amassed quite the collection of useless tidbits. It is one of those things you start doing and don't imagine you'll continue doing until the day you can't imagine stopping. Sort of a pointless habit, depending on how you define pointless, of course.

"Jesus Christ, Archer! You asshole! Are you fuckin deaf?" I recognized that piercingly shrill voice, but I swear I hadn't heard my name called at all until it was embedded in that string of profanity. Perhaps because she was saying it more like "Ahhchaa" instead of the way everyone outside of Rhode Island would say it. The way most of the world typically pronounces it, that is. Chrissy, for her part, was not typical when compared to the rest of the world, but she was fun to be around once you got used to her screeching.

"Hey Chrissy. What's going on, hot shit?" I asked as I walked across the street to where she pulled over. I leaned into her driver's side window. Her perfume was somewhat overwhelming, but at the same time it smelled sort of good. Who knows why, but I always like the way Chrissy smells, which is a combination of strong perfume, hair product, mint chewing gum and menthol cigarettes. There is something oddly appealing about that combination. She's fun to work with and is usually on for the Sunday night shift with me.

"Yup, I'll be there," she said after I asked for confirmation, "I'll grab you dinner, all right?" She was looking at herself in the rearview mirror while she talked, chewing her gum loudly with her mouth open and pulling at her hair. It was flaming red and fell in thick, moussed curls over her shoulders. Her hair was serious. I had been working at a bar called the Charter Club for the past few years, mostly part time, as a bar cook. The menu was about as simple as they come, and I liked the routine of being there. I felt like I was very different from most of the people who worked there, but I really liked doing it. I was friends with the whole crew there at this point, and Chrissy was a big part of that, even if she was a little nuts. Working there had come at just the right time for me.

"Dinner sounds good." I resisted the urge to say "dinnah" the way Chrissy said it. "See you at six."

"Alright," she said, turning to me and giving me a big smile while she pulled away from the curb without looking at all. She sped off, completely blowing the stop sign at the end of the block. Not that it really mattered. The entirety of downtown Providence is an absolute ghost town on Sunday morning. Nothing is open. No one is walking around. Few cars drive past. It is simply dead. In some ways, that is what I love most about walking through downtown on a Sunday, which tends to be the day where I just wander and don't do much at all. In other ways, it makes me miss living in New York.

In the city, there is simply no time or place when there is nothing going on. For people who have lived there, I might as well be telling you your name. For people who have visited, you might think you know it, but you don't. It could be four a.m. in Chinatown and two guys are standing on the corner with a brand-new mattress wrapped in plastic just waiting. Waiting for god knows what. A peaceful midday ride on the six train could be interrupted by a screaming match breaking out because someone decided to read out loud. At any given moment while walking down the street, you can't help but catch five or six words of each conversation you walk past, which might be hundreds on a simple walk from here to there, and if you pay attention you could make poetry from those sound bites. There is a constant barrage of stimulation on every sense, at every moment, at any time of day when you are outside in the city. It is wonderful and painful, uplifting and overwhelming, exciting and disgusting, all at the same time.

Mark and I used to have fun with the sound bite phenomenon by turning it on its head. We'd be walking down the street and right when we were passing someone, one of us would blurt out "so I had to stab the guy" or "it was a human toe" as if it was a just a part of the conversation. We never really knew if the passersby even heard what we said or reacted at all. It entertained us though, and that was pretty much the point. In all likelihood, no one was really paying attention. In a place like that, you have to try pretty hard to be noticed as unusual. The baseline for what is normal is simply nowhere near any other place I've ever been. Not that I've been that many places.

Very soon after moving there for college, I began to feel like it was my home. I felt instantly independent when I left for college. I started to see my father as just another adult, and I started to judge him in ways that were likely very unfair. I once heard the term 'unlikely hero' used to describe a character in a book, and I immediately pictured my father. That moniker stuck in my head, and I began to think of him as the unlikely hero who simply hadn't found his opportunity to prove himself yet. Again, this all isn't really fair. He is a smart guy, successful in business. I learned much later, once I became slightly less self-absorbed, that he'd engaged in a successful 'roll-up' of small security businesses, which after I left home was then purchased by another company doing a larger version of what he'd done in southern New England.

He recently moved to Florida with his wife. Florida. Of all places, I couldn't imagine why he wanted to move there. But his moving there was like the final punctuation mark in the sentence I could use to sum up my relationship with him: I just don't feel like I ever knew the guy. It's not that I'm mad at him, though I was for quite some time. It's not that I don't love him or care about him. I just don't really know him. I don't see myself ever getting to know him at this point, but since I never did, I don't feel much of a loss there. It's a strange thing to realize, but I don't think I have ever missed him once in my life. Florida. Go figure.

A month after I left for college, I came home for a weekend. It worked out to be the only time I returned to Providence while living in New York that wasn't for a holiday. It was the first weekend after our group of five was reduced to a group of four. It rained so hard that weekend that we could barely have the burial as scheduled. It rained so hard the water filled my father's basement, taking with it every childhood picture, kindergarten project, and item of importance from the first seventeen years of my life that I stored there before leaving for college. It rained so hard I don't have one memory of the weekend that doesn't involve the drumming of rain on a rooftop or being soaking wet. The memory of the first time I was convinced of the existence of a soul when I saw the body of my friend Quinn resting in a casket, peaceful but empty. The memory of how hard we all laughed while telling stories about him, drunk in the early morning hours in Courtney's new recording studio. The memory of Jonas being so hung over the next day that he fell asleep behind the wheel in the funeral procession and crashed his mother's car into a police motorcycle that was stopping traffic for the procession. The memory of being reminded of what it truly means to miss someone.

Nope. There is no other place like New York. Something new and weird is always about to happen, and sometimes you get to catch those unique moments. But it was finding the things that always happen that I enjoyed just as much, if not more. Finding that predictability amidst all the confusion was just as enticing as noticing the truly unusual. It was knowing that for a few days in July, you could see the sun drop straight down to the horizon when you look west on 8th from Astor Place. It was knowing that on any given morning on East 79th Street, around 7:30 am, you could see the same dog walker trailing behind a pack of dogs like an urban dogsledder, with a bouquet of meticulously folded newspaper pages fanning from his back pocket, ready for any of the dogs' morning movements. It was knowing that the downward breeze from the grate in my subway station would stop about fifteen seconds before the train came careening around the corner. These are the things that make you feel at home in New York, and knowing these things is what separates people who live there from those who visit.

★★★

As I walked through the Sunday streets of downtown Providence, the memory of Chance ridiculing my opinion of my favorite Bill Withers album and the fact that I left my stereo on hit me simultaneously. At that very same moment, I realized I was getting a little hungry. I was approaching the other side of downtown, and I figured I could stop by

Courtney's studio to assess the damage from last night's party. Courtney was an interesting dude, but for an interesting dude, you can sum him up in a few short sentences:

Immediately following high school, he opened a small recording studio in Providence. He got his high school girlfriend pregnant, she had an abortion and they broke up. During his rebound, he managed to get another girl pregnant. He has spent the past decade and change being a dad while trying to get back together with his high school girlfriend. His obsession with her runs nearly as deep as his obsession with Bob Dylan.

That's the nutshell, though we could get much deeper into it. He is a loving father and is hopelessly thoughtful and romantic. He is an incredible guitar player, yet he seems more enthusiastic about recording and promoting other people's music, an enthusiasm which has made him financially successful as well. He likes to throw parties, he likes to think of himself as young, despite having two daughters nearing high school (surprise, twins!) and a suburban three-bedroom house. He still runs that same studio, and he has kept the apartment across the hall to maintain his glory days. I was approaching his building now, which is a very old industrial space, occupied on the first few floors by a niche record store, a bar and restaurant, and a tattoo parlor. Courtney has the entire top floor. I thought I saw a shadow through one of his windows from down the block.

The door to the street was unlocked, so I ran up the stairs and just about scared the shit out of Courtney while he was coming out of the door, a piece of baguette sticking out of his mouth.

"Shit, Jesus." He said through the piece of bread, pulling it from his mouth. "You scared the crap out of me," he said, chewing. He looked at his watch.

"My bad. What's up, you want to get some lunch?"

"Can't dude, I got the girls. I'm already late to get them. You just missed Pete, he might have wanted to."

Just missing him didn't really help me out with company for lunch, but I didn't point that out to him. "Oh. Well. How did the place make out?"

"Fine, fine. I cleaned up a bit already. Are you staying? I really have to go, you can lock up if you want. Sorry," he apologized unnecessarily. He stroked his thin black goatee. I hate that beard, and I told him often. But he doesn't seem to care, or doesn't seem to believe that I genuinely don't like it. He is a shorter guy than me, the shortest of our group of friends at about five foot nine, five foot ten. He is slim and wiry and appears jumpy and quick. He has sharp features and dark hair and is a good-looking guy. His fingers are thin and pointy.

"Yeah, go, I'm going to hang for a minute if that's cool. I saw Jonas today. He was acting funny."

"He was here last night, late, after you and Chance left. He seemed aloof, nothing unusual."

"He seemed unusual to me, but maybe that's usual."

Courtney was distracted, which was usual for him. "Uh, okay, cool. I'll talk to you later, Arch. I gotta split." He was already going down the staircase. I picked up a few plastic cups off the landing and a couple empty cans.

"See you later, fuckface."

He was out of sight on the next set of stairs. "Later, asshole," he replied. All in good fun, of course.

I went inside and dropped the empties into a garbage bag by the front door. I walked around and picked up a few more items and tossed them out. He already did a pretty good job cleaning up. His theory was that you need to clean a lot before a party and that makes the cleanup easier afterwards. Judging from the way the place looked, he just might be right. I wandered into the kitchen, which was really just an open galley separated from the rest of the main room by several hanging window frames. The fridge was covered with those poetry magnets, the ones that provide a random assortment of words, prefixes and suffixes that you can use to write poetry. I looked to see if there were any quality lines from the night before. *Sausage is the last wisdom. A final rest for the grand piano. The mind walks a golder forest.* I liked that last one. It seemed true.

I opened the fridge in the vain hope that there would be some food in there, but there was nothing. No one lives here, so there is never any food here. But hope springs eternal. No coffee either. I suddenly realized my coffee was still resting on the edge of a garbage can on the other side of downtown. Damn it.

There was, however, beer. So I grabbed one and shut the door. I turned around and leaned against the fridge, looking through the hanging window panes into the living room area. It was always a little dark in Courtney's place during the day, there only being a series of narrow horizontal windows kind of high up along one side of the long room. There were several couches in the space, but it didn't feel crowded. Closest to the kitchen area there were two big couches on either side of a long coffee table, and on the far end of the room there was a large sectional couch facing a big television. And a swing. A jungle gym swing hanging from one of the rafters, placed so that you can get a good swing going without hitting the couch or the television. Courtney used to have a large punching bag hanging there, but working over a punching bag gets some guys a little macho feeling at times, and he didn't like that mood at his parties. The swing was a better choice.

Last night the place was packed, and the swing was going all night. The couches were full and a fair amount of cards were played on the table by the kitchen. The television played old movies on silent the whole night, movies I hadn't seen. It wasn't until late that Courtney pointed out that at least one of the main characters of each movie had a mustache. Always with the themes for his parties.

Sometimes when we had nothing else to do we would hang a large, white bedsheet from the middlemost rafter of this room and project a movie onto it. There was something odd about being able to watch the movie from both sides of the sheet as it hung there. Watching a movie you've seen before in a mirror image is a strange experience. Everyone is on the opposite side of the screen from what you are used to, people enter the room from the wrong way. It is disorienting and familiar, having everything backwards like that. Like a déjà vu that you don't realize until long after it happens.

The first time I ever saw Chance I was standing right here in this kitchen, leaning against this fridge and looking through these hanging windows. It was at one of Courtney's parties, and it was already somewhat late in the evening. It was fall, and we were going to be setting the clocks back before too long. There were always two different crowds at these parties. First was the old–school folks. By that I mean the people who were around our age, the people we knew from having lived around here for so long. The locals. They lent familiarity to things. Then there were the younger set. These were the fans of the musicians that Courtney worked with, a lot of RISD students or other college age folks. The people likely to hear about his parties even though Courtney had nothing to do with the college scene specifically. They were the unpredictable ones, and even though they really weren't that much younger than me and my friends, they seemed a lot different. But they were fun, and the parties were fun because of the mix. When I saw Chance through the windows, she seemed out of place. She wasn't a part of either set. And she was attractive to me regardless of that fact.

"Who is that?" Courtney was standing next to me, and I interrupted him to ask this question. I spoke much quieter than necessary, as the party was loud.

"Who?" he said, seeming unconcerned that he had to stop mid-sentence.

"That girl over there, the one on the swing. With the curly hair." I spoke a little louder. Chance was talking to someone who was sitting on the couch with her back to us. She was smiling and laughing and her hair was bouncing over her shoulders as she swung back and forth, back and forth on the swing. She was wearing dark jeans, white low top sneakers and a green sweater. She had large plastic earrings dangling from her ears, also green. As if she heard me, which she hadn't, she looked up from her friend's face and directly at me, back through the windows where I stood side by side with Courtney, us both looking at her. Like a kid caught with his hand in the cookie jar, I made like I was looking up at something on the ceiling, then down at the counter where I had rested my beer. I picked it up, took a sip, and turned around to face Courtney while leaning back against the counter.

"That was pretty smooth, Why," he said, raising his eyebrows sarcastically. "Pathetic, dude." Courtney shook his head, laughing at me. "Could you be a little more obvious? Sheesh."

"Cause you're so smooth?" I tried to protest in vain. But he was right. It was pretty pathetic. "So do you know who she is?"

"No, never seen her before. My guess? She's a grad student, heard about the party from someone. She's not from around here."

"How can you tell?"

"Because I've never seen her before. And you can tell by looking at her," he said.

Ignoring the implication that he'd seen everyone in Rhode Island and could recognize them by face, I couldn't help but agree that she looked out of place. "I want to go talk to her. Come over there with me?"

Courtney looked at me, surprise on his face. In all the years of him having these parties, I never approached someone like that. Truth be told, I have no game with women. Even thinking about going over there made my heart thump in my chest. Nerves. And Courtney knew it. "Wing man? Nah, that's not me. Where's Pete?"

Pete would be the last person I wanted to help me with this. I don't know much, but I know approaching a female with someone as confident and good looking as him could easily go the wrong way, even if he wasn't trying, which he wouldn't have. I love Pete, but I wouldn't have asked him for this kind of help. Not that Courtney is bad looking, he just isn't that smooth. We were on par with each other in that arena.

"Come on, dude. Is she still over there?" I couldn't tell why I decided I wanted to talk to her. But I didn't want to miss the chance. He looked over my shoulder for a second and back at my face.

"Yeah, she stopped swinging. Still talking to her friend. She's over there." He saw the look on my face, rolled his eyes and said. "Fine, let's go. Get her a beer, she's not drinking anything."

"What should I say to her?" I know. So pathetic.

"Dunno. You've got till we get over there to figure it out." He moved out of the way so I could grab a beer out of the fridge. I took two, putting my empty in the sink, turned and stopped. I opened the fridge and grabbed a third beer. Courtney looked at me, a question in his eyes.

"It's rude not to get her friend one too, right?" He nodded in agreement, and I started making my way across the room. I felt conspicuous but took care not to look up until I was about halfway through the crowd. She was sitting on the swing, not swinging, leaning forward and talking to her friend. I saw her eyes flash up towards me and she looked back down at her friend. She laughed.

I found myself standing in front of them. It was all I could do not to say "excuse me" and make my way between them to a couple people at the far end of the couch who I was moderately acquainted with. But I didn't.

"You mind if we join you guys? Things are getting crazy around here. Really aggressive women, they just won't leave me alone." I said, deadpan, panicked they wouldn't get my sarcasm.

"We?" Chance said.

I looked next to me and then across the room to where Courtney had stopped and was talking to a couple people. What an ass. I looked back at them. "The royal we. Just me, can I join you? Trying not to blow my cover here. Lots of people following me around, you know."

"You got jokes, huh?" Her friend said, kind of sarcastic, looking at Chance. She gave her a look I couldn't interpret.

I pulled up a chair from the wall behind me and sat down, so the three of us were in a triangle. I looked down at my chest to make sure you couldn't tell by looking at me that my heart was slamming against my ribcage. It was only obvious to me, apparently. "Okay, I'll come clean. I'm not undercover. Not one female has spoken to me tonight. I saw you two sitting over here, and I wanted to say hi. My friend Courtney over there," I did air quotes when I said friend, "was supposed to come over here so I didn't have to say hi alone. He flaked out on me, as you can see. But it's his place, so I guess I have to forgive him. That's all I got."

Chance's eyes got big, and she smiled a curious kind of smile. She had little dimples and large, dark brown eyes. Her face was more round than narrow. Her friend, whose name I would learn was Stacey, looked at Chance and smiled. I had a strange vibe, but not a bad one.

"Oh yeah, and I'm Archer. Archer Why." I extended my hand to Chance. She looked at me sort of funny. "Seriously, no more jokes. That's really my name." She reached out and shook my hand.

"Chance," she said. I looked at her blankly, not sure what she was saying. "My name is Chance." She smiled. "I guess we have that in common. We have to convince people of our names."

We were still holding each other's hands when Stacey said, "and I'm Stacey." I released Chance's hand and shook hers, saying my name again for some reason. I offered them each a beer from the three I placed on the floor in front of me. Stacey accepted, Chance shook her head.

"No thanks. I don't really like beer," she said. She had a nice voice, very even in tone, and with a very slight accent I couldn't recognize. Midwest or something? I couldn't tell.

I took at stab with Courtney's guess. "So, are you both in grad school somewhere around here?"

They took the guess in stride, telling me they were both in an architecture program at RISD. Stacey was from the south, you could tell even though her accent was subtle. Turns out Chance was from Chicago. Or the suburbs thereof. They asked me what I did, which was hard to explain. "I'm a cook at a bar," just didn't feel like a great explanation. But I left it pretty much at that. I knew it would either sound ridiculous, manipulative or pathetic if I went down the "trying to figure that out" path.

We talked about the band that was playing in the studio space across the hall, and the apartment in general. I told them about Courtney and what he did here, which they sort of heard about when they were told about the party. They asked about the temporary tattoo stations that were set up here and there throughout the space, so I had to explain Courtney's themes to them. The guys in the band playing there tonight were a heavily tattooed group, and two were actually tattoo artists themselves. Hence the tattoo theme. "And the bike on the table over there?" Chance asked, pointing at it behind me.

"The band is called Peloton." I said, feeling awkward trying to say the word as I was unsure if I should say it with or without a French accent. I hit it somewhere in the middle. "So Courtney is raffling off the bike. Did you get your tickets?" They both looked at each other and shook their heads no. "Oh, right. You wouldn't have gotten one if you didn't wait for a beer at the keg." They both shrugged.

I found myself feeling more comfortable, as did they. And even though they never really agreed to have me join them, it didn't feel awkward, so we were just talking like we knew each other.

"Did you at least get a tattoo?" I said, feigning incredulousness. They laughed. "C'mon, you need to get one." I jumped up, assuming they wouldn't want to lose their seats, and walked to the tattoo station by the bike. I always feel at home at Courtney's place, so I didn't feel weird picking up the small table that had all the supplies and carefully carrying it over to where we sat. I put it down next to Stacey along the arm of the couch and pulled out a stack of tattoos, handing a small pile to each of them. I flipped through the pile I was holding. There was quite an assortment. Superheroes, cartoon characters, shapes, odds and ends. "Find me one," I said specifically to Chance. It wasn't so direct, but I felt like it was clear that I was flirting with her. It was bolder than my typical self. Probably the beer talking, but I knew I liked her immediately.

"Okay," she said casually, without looking up. I saw Stacey flash her a smirk, but she didn't see her.

"Here's one for you," I said. I held it up for her to see. It was a big, cartoonish pencil with arms and legs and a big grin. "For the architect in training. You need your pencil." Corny, but whatever. She smiled.

"Okay, you pick, sailor." She held one out in each hand. In her left, an anchor. In her right, a heart that said 'mom' with a knife through it.

"The anchor."

"Guess that means you aren't a mama's boy. That's cool." She laughed at her joke.

I turned to Stacey. "Got one for you too," I said, holding up another pencil.

"What's with the wipes?" Stacey asked, pointing at the package of baby wipes on the table with the tattoos.

"For the tattoos. Here," I said. Stacey was wearing a short sleeve shirt, so I took her hand and turned it palm up. I peeled the backing off the tattoo, rested it on her forearm, pulled a wipe out of the package and placed it over the tattoo. I pressed it down firmly and waited about thirty seconds. The silence was a little awkward, but at least the rest of the room was noisy. I pulled the paper back carefully, revealing the shiny yellow and black tattoo. "There you go."

"How does someone learn that trick?" Chance said.

"I guess it is the kind of thing you know when you have kids," I said.

Chance gave me a funny look. "How old are your kids?" She asked with what seemed like genuine curiosity.

"Not me," I laughed. "Courtney. He has twin daughters." Maybe I didn't need to laugh. I suppose there would have been nothing funny to them about me having kids. To me it was a ridiculous concept. But they wouldn't have known that.

I turned to Chance and conducted the same process, sliding the sleeve of her sweater up gently and then applying her matching tattoo on the same spot on her left forearm. "Now your turn," she said, leaning forward from the swing and pulling my left hand forward. Her hands felt small on my arm, and her slim fingers were cold to the touch. I felt exposed with her holding my hand and arm while she applied gentle pressure on the wipe. It seemed all too obvious how much I enjoyed it. We made brief eye contact and I thought I noticed one eyebrow raise when she looked at me. She peeled it off carefully and revealed the black outline of an anchor on the inside of my forearm.

"Cool." I said, sounding uncool. "Looks like the Rhode Island flag."

"Is it an anchor?" Chance asked.

"The flag? Yeah. Except it has stars around it and says hope in a scroll below it."

Chance reached down and picked up her bag which was by Stacey's feet. She opened it up, dug around and pulled out a black pen. She popped off the cap and pulled my arm toward her again. And wrote "hope" in small capital letters under the anchor. "There, that's better then." She dropped the pen in her bag and pushed it back away from her with her feet. She started to swing a little bit. "I've never seen a swing in someone's apartment before." She had this way, even then, of alternately making me feel like the only person in the world for a moment and then that I was barely present in the next. It is hard to explain, but it wasn't that she was rude. She was just herself. I liked it.

We all talked for a while, and the conversation went this way and that. I was finished with the beer that I opened when I first sat down, and I eyed the one by my feet. It felt weird to open another one given Chance wasn't drinking beer. I had an idea. I stood up. "Will you guys excuse me for a minute?" They each looked at me as if to say: of course. "Okay, don't go anywhere." *Oh, Why, you sound so lame*, I thought to myself.

Courtney was still halfway across the room, chatting with some people. "Oh, hey, Courtney," I interrupted his conversation sarcastically, "I didn't realize you were still here."

He laughed. "Dude, you were better off without me. Looks like you survived. Did you get a number or something?"

"I'm still talking with her. With them. You still have any bottles of wine over in the studio?" I asked. "In the booth?"

"Yeah, go ahead. I guess I owe you." He smiled at me and looked over my shoulder. "She's cool?" He asked, genuinely interested.

"I think so." I slapped his shoulder and walked across the hall to his studio. Courtney had a sweet set up over there. It was essentially one large room, with space for musicians to set up their instruments and do their thing on one side, and plenty of seating and space for spectators on the other side. On a night like this, the area for the band became a stage of sorts, and people could sit and listen on the other. It was close quarters for the amount of people typically crammed in there, but intimate. It was usually kept acoustic on nights like these, given the size of the room. Tonight's band was a little heavy for my taste at full volume, but acoustic they sounded just right.

There was a booth along one wall, where all the recording equipment and sound boards were kept. It was locked and wouldn't get used during a party. I pressed the buttons on the combination lock, Quinn's birthday, 02-16, and opened the door. I sat at the chair behind the boards and felt the way I usually do when I'm in the studio: wishing I had musical talent. Then I opened the cabinet to the right and pulled out the first bottle of red wine I put my hand on. I leaned down to find the little corkscrew I knew was in there. There was a stack of plastic cups, so I took three. I pulled the door shut behind me and made sure it was locked.

When I got back into the apartment side, Chance and Stacey had switched seats, and Stacey was standing and leaning against the swing. They looked up at me.

"So, no beer, figured I could at least offer you a glass of wine." I looked down at the bottle and the cups in my hands. "Or a cup of wine," I corrected myself.

"I think I'm going to head out," Stacey said, fully standing up from the swing.

It was clear they had been discussing this. My heart started thumping again, like the bass line in my song of anxiety about this type of situation. I hate dating, and this wasn't even dating. It was just a party, but I didn't want to see Chance go. Not yet.

They were both silent, and I wasn't sure if I was supposed to say something.

"Just one cup?" I tried not to sound desperate. "It's technically an hour earlier than it feels like." They looked at each other. Stacey seemed resigned to go. Chance looked hesitant. Stacey gave her a look as if to say, your call.

"It's just that she's my ride," Chance said. I don't know what it feels like for a woman to be left alone, without a ride, with a guy at a party she just met. But it can't be anything less than uncomfortable. I wasn't sure how to solve that.

"Hey listen, I'm happy to walk you home. You already told me where you live, it's right around the corner."

Chance looked at me quizzically. "No, I didn't."

"Yeah, you said you found a sweet apartment near Benefit Street with a nice garden right behind a church. That's on Church Street. Behind Poe House." I didn't want to sound like a stalker, but I knew the exact spot. She was a little wide eyed, her mouth somewhat agape. "It's a small town," I said.

She smiled.

Stacey pulled her phone out of her back pocket to check the time. "Okay, here you go," I said. I pointed at

Stacey's phone, "can I borrow that?" She handed it to me. I swiped the screen, tapped the camera icon, and slid my driver's license out of my pocket. I always keep it loose in there, along with a credit card and my cash. I stopped using a wallet when I lived in the city, feeling like if I ever got mugged I could just give up my cash and keep everything else. I held up the phone, took a picture of my license and gave the phone back to her. "Now you know where I live, my birthday and my height and eye color. If she doesn't make it home, you know where to send the police." I couldn't tell if I was being smooth or creepy, or if I just seemed desperate. "It seems a shame to waste the bottle of wine," I said, looking right at Chance.

"You didn't open it yet," she said playfully.

"I'm going to open it either way, but I won't be able to drink the whole thing myself."

Chance looked at me. And she looked at Stacey. "It's cool, I'm fine with this guy. I can handle him."

Stacey gave her a raised eyebrow smile and a hug. She turned and shook my hand. "Nice meeting you."

"You too." She walked toward the door. I turned toward Chance as she was about to sit back down. "Wait, hold on. Let's go upstairs, I want to show you the roof."

"Cool," she said. I reached out my hand without thinking. She took it, and I felt my chest tighten. The rhythm section in my chest was back at it.

Chapter 4

Chance followed me through the main room, up the small flight behind the kitchen and to the second living area. It is a smaller space, though much louder up here, given the proximity to the bar area, and therefore the keg. I held her hand firmly, but not tight, as we slithered through the gaggle of folks crowded around the bar.

On tiptoes, I spoke loudly to the guy doling out beers from the tap. "Shane." I said. "Shane," a little more loudly when he didn't hear me the first time. He looked up at me. "I need a raffle ticket."

"Come on, Why. You're exempt. How would that be if you won?" He was taking his role very seriously.

"It's not for me." I nodded my head towards Chance, who was standing by my side now. Our hands were still clasped, but he couldn't have seen that. He looked at me wryly.

"She'd have gotten one with her first beer." Such a rule follower.

"She's not drinking beer," I said, holding up the bottle of wine and cups with my left hand as if to prove it.

"Fine," he said, reaching down, fumbling with something under the bar and then reaching up over a couple people's heads to hand me the ticket he produced.

I released Chance's hand and took the ticket. "Thanks, asshole," I said politely. I gave Chance her ticket, "don't lose it." She slipped it in her back pocket. "The window's through here," I pointed at the bedroom door, which was closed, as was the window. We made our way onto the roof. Courtney didn't love people being on the roof at his parties, but he didn't mind if people he knew were up here as they would respect it. The last thing he wanted was a hundred college students making noise and calling attention to the place from the roof. No one else lives in this building, so there was no one to complain about late night parties. He wanted to keep it that way, understandably.

We sat and I opened the wine. I poured out two cups into the plastic tumblers and held one up to swirl the wine. I stuck my nose in and inhaled deeply. "This'll do," I said authoritatively and handed her the other cup.

She looked at me sideways, "you've got a lot of corny uncle jokes, don't you?" She took a sip of her wine and took in the view of downtown Providence. "No kids. Any nieces or nephews?"

"Only child." I replied. "You?"

"Me too."

We were quiet for a couple minutes, sitting side by side with the bottle between us. I saw her turn to look at me.

"You don't do this very often, do you?"

"Sit up here? I don't know. I like it up here, actually. But I'm not over at this place that much really." I didn't understand why she asked me that.

She laughed. "No, this, like meet a girl at a party. Walk up to her and her friend like that. You don't do that very often."

"Never," I said. There was a moment of silence.

"So why tonight?"

"How could you tell?" I asked at the same time she asked me why tonight. I looked at her. "You just stood out, I guess. Felt like I wanted to talk to you."

"Do you always do what you feel like, exactly when you feel like it?"

That was a funny question. In a way, my entire life for years was exactly that. I did what I wanted, when I wanted.

But that isn't what she meant. "No, not in the way you mean."

"In what way, then?"

I wasn't sure how to answer. "Not sure how to answer that." I looked back at downtown. "I guess you could say I have a lot of spare time. I do what I want with it."

"A man of leisure." She said. It wasn't a question.

"You could say that." This was one of the strangest conversations I'd had in a while. "How could you tell?" I asked again. "How could you tell I don't do this much?"

"You can just tell."

"How am I doing at it?"

"You stumbled a bit at first. Still not sure about these corny jokes. But you're doing alright." Her frankness was impressive.

"Thanks, I appreciate the feedback."

She smiled at me warmly and took a sip of wine. "No problem," she replied.

The silence was entirely comfortable for several minutes, and we moved past this portion of the interview into more specific talk. She told me more about where she was from, a little about her family, about college, about Stacey, her first friend here in Providence. I asked questions, and listened. I didn't know her at all, but I could tell she was different than most people. Comfortable with herself, but not self-assured. Honest but not oversharing. Balanced. That was the only word I could come up with. I don't know many people like that.

I topped off both of our cups with another splash of wine. "So, you're an engineer."

"I studied engineering in college," she said.

"Doesn't that make you an engineer?" I asked. This was a foreign topic to me. The idea of having a career was beyond my scope entirely. I wasn't even really able to ask the right kind of questions, I was suddenly painfully aware of my own lack of direction.

"I guess so, in a way. But I only studied that to become an architect. I've been working at a firm in Chicago since college, it's been years now. Saving up so I could come here."

"So you'll go back when you're done?"

"Not sure. Hard to say."

"That's brave of you." It sounded patronizing, so I tried to clarify. "I mean, just leaving where you've been all that time, and coming to a new place. Seems like a big deal."

She looked over at me. "Didn't you go away to college?" We hadn't covered that aspect of my life yet, so it was a true question.

"Yeah. But at eighteen. It just seems different."

"So which part is brave, you think? The leaving? Or the coming?"

It was a good question. "I don't know. Both, maybe?" I looked back out at downtown Providence. There were so many lights on in the buildings across the narrow river. There couldn't possibly have been so many people doing things in there.

I heard my name from behind me. "Why, come on in here. I need your help." It was Courtney.

"I wonder what that's all about." I looked at Chance. "I guess we should go in." Nesting my cup in the one intended for Stacey, I picked them both up and the bottle of wine. We'd only gotten about halfway through it. I reached out my hand to Chance and pulled her to her feet.

We climbed back in through the window, following Courtney through the crowded area by the bar, down the short flight of stairs alongside the kitchen and into the main room. He walked over to where the bicycle was perched on the table by the wall in the middle of the room. He picked something up off the table and started tapping the end of it. Nothing happened. He looked down at it, which was when I recognized the object as a microphone. I hadn't realized there was no music playing until he started speaking into it.

"Hello and good evening everyone!" his voice boomed across the room. It must have been wirelessly connected to his sound system. "Welcome to Daylight Savings Time! That's right, it is almost the precise moment when our clocks will be set back and we can all begin making better use of daylight for the next six months or so. The extra hour tonight is free, folks, so don't hold it against me when I take it back this coming spring." He looked up at the landing above the kitchen, where Shane was working his way through the crowd carrying what looked like a cylinder the size of an oatmeal container.

"The time has come for our raffle. The raffle of this vintage beach cruiser. Note the gleaming chrome. The metallic mint green paint job. The banana seat. They don't make them like this anymore, folks. Or at least I thought they didn't, till I found this one online." Chance and I were standing at the front of the group that formed around Courtney. He loved being the center of attention, which was not my favorite thing at all. Which was why I rolled my eyes when he waved me up to join him, just as Shane made his way up to the front as well. He handed Courtney the container, and he placed it on a small metal frame that was sitting on the table in front of the bicycle.

"Spin it," he said, off mic. I realized it was a miniature bingo drum or whatever you call it. It was full of raffle tickets. I took the handle and spun it slowly. Chance was looking at me and smiling.

"Please give my lovely assistant, Archer Why, a big round of applause, folks." Everyone cheered, a deafening chorus of more than a hundred drunken hopefuls, clutching their tiny red tickets. "Okay, let's do it." I stopped spinning the thing, fumbled with the little latch and then finally got it open.

"The honors go to the host," I said. Courtney reached in and selected a ticket.

"If the person with the winning ticket already went home, then we call a new number. You have to be here to win," he said, then looked down at the ticket and began calling out numbers. "Seven, eight, one, two, one, four!" He belted into the microphone.

The room got quiet while everyone read their ticket, and then started looking around to see who won. No one came forward. Courtney read the ticket again. I looked over at Chance, and noticed she wasn't holding her ticket. *No way*, I thought. We made eye contact and I raised my eyebrows, mouthing the words: where's your ticket? And pointing to my back pocket. She jumped and reached into her pocket and pulled out the ticket. She looked at it in shock, then looked at me. She smirked and raised her hand.

"I've got it."

Everyone roared. Courtney looked at me and then at Chance, he was silent for a moment. Then, "WE HAVE A WINNER!" He shouted.

After the din died down, and the crowd thinned out a bit, the excitement over, I approached Chance, who was standing alongside her new bicycle. "Pretty sweet." I said.

"If I didn't know better, I'd say you set me up." She looked at me, a sparkle along with some suspicion in her eye.

"Not sure how I'd have pulled that off," I said. She still had that look in her eyes. I couldn't help but laugh. "Seriously, how could I have set that up?"

She shrugged and looked down at her prize. Courtney approached us. "Hey, congratulations," he said, and gave Chance a big hug. I felt strangely jealous, which was odd. "Listen, if you can't get it home tonight, just let me know and you can leave it here. We'll get it to you somehow. No worries."

"Oh, thanks. I think I can get it home though. It isn't far."

"Hey, your call. Good work, hope you enjoy it." He wandered off, probably to find a bigger crowd. He was not always one for one-on-one pleasantries.

Chance yawned.

"You ready to get out of here?" She nodded. "I can walk you and the bike home. It's no problem. And I don't want your friend sending the cops after me."

She willingly let me take the bike from her hands, and we made our way to the door. Every couple feet Chance was congratulated by another person, but we eventually got to the landing at the top of the stairs and made our way down to the street.

The walk to her place was less than fifteen minutes, and it was a nice night. It was uneventful, and the streets were very quiet. We were about a block away when she asked, "why do they call it Poe House? The house on the corner up there?"

"He lived there, I think. Edgar Allen. Or maybe it was his fiancée who lived there. I can't remember the entire story." I thought for a second. "Yeah, it was his fiancée. She lived there, and he couldn't stop drinking or something. So she broke it off. Pretty sure that's it. He used to hang out at the library back that way a couple blocks. The Athenaeum. The one with the fountain out front. You've seen it?"

"I think I've walked past it."

"They say if you drink from that fountain, you'll never leave Providence. Or maybe you'll leave, but you'll be back."

"Seems like there's lots of interesting things about Rhode Island."

"It's a small place, but there's a fair amount to take in."

"I haven't even been to the beach yet."

"Not since you've been here?" I said, probably a little too loudly. "I guess it's only been a month or two, right?"

"No, never. I've never been to a beach. Not by the ocean. Not ever."

"Never?"

"Never."

"Hm." I said. We were in front of her place now. We walked through the garden to the steps leading up to the apartment. "You need help with this?" I asked. I was trying not to make her uncomfortable. I didn't want her to think I was trying to get in her place.

"No. I'm just up this flight. I got it." There was a moment of silence. This wasn't a date, but it felt like one. And I got that awkward feeling of wondering how to end it. She handled it for me. She got up on her tiptoes and gave me a tiny kiss on the cheek. "It was nice meeting you. I'm glad you came over to talk." How is it some people just know what to say?

"Me too."

Why. Me.

She pulled her bag up in front of her and rested it on the banana seat of her new bike. She dug around for a moment and pulled out the black pen again. She took my hand and pushed my sleeve up past my anchor tattoo. She used her mouth to open the pen, and with the cap between her teeth like a cigar nub, she wrote a ten-digit number with an area code I didn't recognize right under the four capital letters of the word "hope" she wrote there earlier.

"Stay in touch," she said after taking the cap out of her mouth.

I tried to think of a witty comment, something about the ink being permanent or something, but couldn't. I just smiled at her. "Sure thing," I said.

She slung her bag back over her shoulder, and I watched her carefully carry the bike up the small flight of steps and made sure she got inside before turning around and starting my long walk home.

★★★

I smiled at the thought that I was standing in the same place where I summoned the nerve to go talk to her that night. It was probably one of the smartest things that I ever did, at least one of the smartest things I ever did on purpose, anyway. I turned to leave the kitchen, thought better of it and went back to the fridge. I put the first beer in my sweatshirt pocket, grabbed another, and made my way up to the roof. From here, in the daylight, you could see across downtown, looking west and north, all the way to the horizon above North Providence. It's not a majestic view, but it is sort of beautiful in its own way. I sat on the tar roof, put the second beer down next to me and cracked open the can that was in my pocket. It was a run-of-the mill light beer, but it was very cold and it tasted good. The day had really opened up, and the soon to be midday sun was making things very warm. At this point, you wouldn't have known that it was raining earlier, except for the faint haze clinging to the horizon in the distance. I heard a car pull up four stories below. It raised my interest.

I walked towards the edge of the roof, and then got down on all fours to crawl to the edge, which had no railing or raised sides. I'm not scared of heights, but I'm not stupid. The closer I got to the edge, my body got tense and tingled a little bit. A foot from the side and I pretty much laid down completely to worm my head over the edge. I could see Pete's light blue pickup truck parked about forty feet below me. The driver's side door opened and his blond mop appeared. He pulled on a faded red cap. "Shithead," I called down to him softly. He shut the door and walked toward the front of the building. "Hey shithead," I called a little louder. He kept walking to the door. I heard the noise of it closing behind him as it echoed off the building across the street along with my third and loudest call: "Shithead!"

Pete, as I have mentioned, is the kind of guy who can do just about anything with his hands. He is also an incredible guitar player, but he rarely played since Quinn died. Pete was from Little Compton, a small Rhode Island beach town with a handful of year-round residents, a badge of honor that he could claim as his birthright. We Providence guys knew him as a result of Quinn's parents and grandmother, who summered there. Pete and Quinn knew each other first, going back to before kindergarten. In first grade, Pete started the commute to Providence for private school, the same one as Jonas. Courtney, Quinn and I all went to public school, but since we all lived in the same neighborhood as Jonas, and since Quinn knew Pete previously, we all ended up running together at a very early age. It seemed like Pete was in Providence all the time, but that was because he spent a lot of nights at Quinn's house. In high school, he moved in to live permanently with his own grandmother, who also lived in Little Compton. His parents had some issues, which he never talked about but which we got tidbits of here and there. Around that time, they disappeared and we never really heard what happened to them.

It occurred to me that Pete came inside about ten minutes ago. I didn't want to miss him, so I walked over to the window to make sure he didn't leave before knowing I was there. Before I got there, I saw one of his boots come swinging out the window, followed by his leg and then his entire self. He stood up, and we were standing chest to chest in front of each other. He gave me a big bear hug, picking me up off my feet. I'm six feet tall or so, and he's an inch or two taller than me, but he is friggin strong and he picked me up like a rag doll. "Hey bro," I said, trying to peel myself out of his embrace.

"Hi shithead," he replied drolly, dropping me effortlessly.

"Oh, you heard me then." I said, taking a deep breath to replace the air he squeezed out of my lungs.

"Of course I heard you. You think I'm deaf, shithead? It's getting friggin hot out here, the sun is scorching my nuts." He has this way of talking that is almost impossible to describe. At times he seems to speak his own vernacular, making up sayings as if they were common colloquialisms. He can be prone to exaggeration and curses at a lot. "Fuck Why, how long are you going to let this shit sprout up?" He rubbed my head as he said this, implying my hair was getting too long. He pulled off his coat and dropped it on the roof next to my second beer. He squatted and rocked back on his heels, looking across downtown.

"Have that beer," I instructed him, "I took two." I ignored his question about my hair. I scratched my chin and realized I forgot to shave.

"No thanks, I'm driving." He rolled off his heels and landed on his butt. He kicked out his legs and lay out fully on his back. I sat down next to him. Rolling over, he used his foot to drag his jacket over to him and began searching his pockets. He pulled out a pack of cigarettes and a pack of matches. He lit one and offered one to me. I waved him off; he knows I don't smoke. I looked at the view and thought again about what a nice day it was turning into. The haze was all but gone at this point. I heard a beer open, and looked at where I left my second one, which was still there. I looked at him, now sitting up again and holding a beer to his lips. He was wearing a blank expression. I looked next to him and saw another unopened beer.

"Driving, hmm." I should have known he was full of it. That guy drives as drunk as he wants and has never refused a beer in his life. He was taking a long, long sip of beer, and he followed it up with a hiccup. He took another sip and tossed his empty can towards the window. It rattled along the roof. He cracked his second beer and fell back to a prone position once again. I heard his cigarette crackle as he took a deep pull. The smoke came out of his mouth like out of a chimney. Two wisps plumed out of his nostrils and joined the torrent of smoke pouring from his mouth. Nasty habit, but somehow he made it look appealing.

"I thought you left. Courtney said I missed you."

"I did leave, and you did miss me. Like you always do."

"Why are you here then, asshole?"

"I realized I left my keys."

"How did you drive your truck then?"

"My other keys, to my house and bike. I always leave my truck keys in my truck, so I don't lose them."

"So it's okay if you lose your house keys and motorcycle keys?"

"Yup."

I had to ask. "Why?"

"I don't lock my house."

"What about your bike?"

"Oh yeah, I wouldn't want to lose those."

Did I mention that he was a little bit of a strange guy? "If you don't lock your house and you don't want to lose your motorcycle keys, why did you even bring them here if you drove your truck?"

"Because I have a bottle opener on my keychain."

"That makes sense," I said sarcastically.

"Get off my nuts, Archer. Stop sweating me, seriously, I'm hung over."

"Is that why it took you ten minutes to get from the front door to the roof?" I was messing with him now.

"I guess so." He was lying on his back with his hat over his face, an open beer in his left hand resting on his stomach. With his other hand, he was flicking the wheel of a lighter repeatedly, something he often does. I was never sure why he always used matches for his cigarettes when he always carries a lighter.

"So what's the plan, you want to get some lunch?"

"No thanks. I have to get back to the house to do some stuff and then I'm going to go for a ride."

"Nice day for that."

"I guess."

"Not sunny and clear enough for you?"

"No, I just got nerves."

I looked at him, but his face was still hidden. "Nerves? Like nervous?"

"Yeah, just nervous."

"I thought you liked riding it. Why ride if you are nervous?" I was confused. I kept looking at him as if the hat was going to tell me something. "Seriously, what are you talking about?"

"No. I like riding." He knocked the hat off his face and sat up sideways, resting on one elbow and facing me. His blue eyes were piercing, the color of a pool of water on polar ice. His blond hair swept across his freckled forehead. Even his eyelashes were blond. A grown man, totally blond. He should be in California surfing or something with that look. Unbelievable. "You know what I mean, nervous. Like, I feel nervous." His eyes were searching my face, trying to make sure I understood.

I didn't. "Sorry, dude, I don't know what you mean. You like riding, but you are nervous about the bike?"

"No, it's not about the bike. Forget I said that. I guess I'm just feeling nervous. It's like that a lot. It always has been. Antsy, like I'm forgetting something that I can't remember." He took a small sip of beer and looked away from me.

I was shocked. Absolutely shocked. Pete. The guy seemed fearless. Nothing ever seemed to faze him. His confidence was legendary in our circle. He could talk to anyone, anywhere, anytime. He rode a motorcycle, went tuna fishing, built his own house. I mean, he did repairs on his *own* car. I once bought a new car because I didn't trust my mechanic to fix my old one. He could build furniture, weld. He had those steely eyes. My whole frame of reference shifted. Where was this coming from?

"Don't look so crazy, Archer. What the fuck?" He was looking at me again. "Don't take it so seriously, fuck face."

But I was still confused. It didn't matter; I stayed confused. He flopped down on his back again and pulled his hat over his face. He started talking about a recently soured relationship, one of a long string of intense but short lived affairs. It was baffling how he managed to always be in and out of some sort of a relationship, while the circle of people he was in seemed very tight. He was going on and on about it, down to the last unnecessary detail, but my mind was stuck on his nervousness. Was he talking about anxiety? About something specific? If you asked me ten minutes ago: who is the most confident person you know? Who is the least preoccupied person? Who seems to have the least of a care in the world? I would have answered: Pete Jones. Now I wasn't sure what to think. It didn't matter though, because he was on to the next thing.

We kicked around a conversation for another half hour or so. At this point we were both flat out on the roof, soaking up the sun. Two beers on a more or less empty stomach pushed me to a sweet and powerful state of relaxation. My body was heavy against the tar of the roof. There was a moment of silence; I heard him sit up.

"Okay brostink, I'm leaving. Gotta go get my swerve on." We both stood up. I yawned and stretched, my stomach full of beer. I caught a brief head rush from standing too fast. We climbed through the window, a task made more challenging by the fact that I was carrying four empty beer cans. Pete didn't seem to care to clean up his mess. He lit a cigarette while we walked through the main room. The sulfur from his match burned my nostrils. We trooped single file down the several flights of stairs. When we got outside the front door I realized it was ten or fifteen degrees cooler in the stairwell. I shivered as I stepped out into the sunlight.

"See you later kid."

"Yeah, later." He replied unceremoniously, climbing into the cab of his dusty old pickup. Dusty old pickup: sounds like a cliché, right? Well, this pickup wrote that cliché. It was dusty, old, light blue and it made more noise than it needed to. But that's just Pete. That's his style. He pulled off and gave me the finger as he drove away. It made me bust out laughing. *Thanks for offering me a ride up the hill*, I thought as I turned to continue my walk.

Getting to know other people is a lot like getting to know yourself. You think you know yourself and then you do something, act some way, that you never thought yourself capable of. Sometimes you can see yourself doing something that you know isn't like you, and even as you do it you are surprised with yourself. I always assumed that Pete never questioned anything, because those questions evolve into worry and then they take on a life of their own. He always seemed impervious to that, in his actions and his personality. Now I was questioning the fact that I missed something about someone I knew so long and so intensely. And I wondered if he was more like me than I thought.

All of this questioning is probably why I seem to go through life so slowly. Too much thinking, too much process, not enough living. There is a line in a song by Pink Floyd that describes years and years going by while you're sitting there waiting for the starting gun. It is a song you've probably heard before, but maybe you never paid much attention to the words.

A few years back I heard that line for probably the hundredth time in my life, and I caught the words in a different way for some reason. That's when it hit me. Ten years of my own life had slipped past me. I couldn't account for much of them. It had been ten years since I left New York. I had liquidated my life. I picked up some hobbies and dropped them just as quickly. I got fully in and then out of shape two times. I landed a job as a bar cook. And I thought about stuff a lot, and about a lot of stuff. But not much else happened. That is to say, I didn't do much else.

I wouldn't say that I had an epiphany that day. I didn't get my shit together, write a novel or buy a one-way ticket to some exotic place. But I stopped thinking and only thinking. I started thinking about what I could do next, which was an entirely different approach for me. It has been a few years since that moment, but I've finally gotten to a place where I can actually start planning and almost start doing. I was almost there by today. That day when I heard that song again, for the one hundredth time, it had been ten years, almost to the day, since Mark died.

Chapter 5

I was wired after my walk home from Chance's place, even though it was the equivalent of nearly three in the morning. For the record, this was rare for me. I was being honest with Chance when I told her I never do this sort of thing. As some people might put it, I have essentially zero swagger. It had been months since I'd been on a date, and years since I was enthusiastic about someone new. This felt different already.

I carefully copied the number from my arm onto a slip of paper, double and then triple checking that I got it right, and then saved it on my phone. I stuck the paper into a clip that hung on my fridge, but that somehow seemed too eager. I took it down and put it in a drawer. Staring out the windows from the island in my kitchen, I felt totally sober. I had a few beers and a little wine, but I didn't feel like I'd be able to sleep. I pulled a bottle of scotch out from the cabinet and poured myself about an inch in a wide glass. I took a tiny sip and let it roll around in my mouth, such a small amount that it basically soaked into my tongue, the rest evaporating behind my soft palate, the smell of it wafting into my nasal passages. I took a larger sip and swallowed firmly. It was hot in my throat yet cool in my mouth at the same time. There was ice in the freezer, so I put a couple cubes in my glass, circled the kitchen and saddled down on a stool at the opposite side of the counter. I took a third sip and rested the glass carefully on the counter. I swirled the glass around, watching the ice and the scotch chase each other around the edge of the glass.

The night replayed itself in my head. It made my heart start pounding again. I took another sip. I wasn't sure why I still felt nervous, remembering some of the things I said, wondering if I handled myself well. "She gave you her number, Why." I said out loud, reassuring myself that I'd at least get another chance to hang out with her. Alongside the replay of my own participation in the evening, I thought about Chance. The things she said, her manner, the way she held herself. I couldn't put my finger on it, but there was something very appealing about being with her. She was attractive, sure. But that wasn't really it. There was something special about her, different. I got up and walked across the room to the windows. The streetlights were on, but that was the only sign of life in the world. The streets were quiet, there was nothing happening. I drained my glass and walked back to the middle of the room. The ice clinked in the glass when I rested it on the table. I leaned back on the couch.

The lateness combined with the jolt of warmth from the scotch relaxed me. I closed my eyes and thought about the beach. It seemed like only minutes later when I opened my eyes, but the ice cubes were all melted in my glass. There was a ring of condensation on the table when I picked it up. I wiped it with my palm and wiped my hand on my thigh. I put the glass in the sink, brushed my teeth and washed my face, and went upstairs to bed.

My alarm went off at seven, but since I forgot to set my clock back, it was actually only six. My eyes felt hot around the edges, and it took me a few minutes to cut through the cobwebs. I went downstairs and took a long, long, hot shower. That helped. I made myself a bowl of soup. That helped a little more. I fell asleep on the couch for about half an hour, and I was feeling pretty good, all things considered. It was still only about eight thirty, and I was working with only a few hours of sleep. My body was slow, but my mind was working.

I was sitting on a stool at my counter when it hit me. I knew what to do. I spoke out loud to myself, as I'm likely to do. "Fuck that." My face showed confusion and disbelief, despite the fact that there was no one there to see me. "Never been to the beach?" I grabbed my phone, keys and cash, took a sweatshirt off a hook and slammed the door behind me.

When I pulled up in front of Chance's apartment, I got nervous. Cold feet. This was not a good idea. This was stalker behavior. I pulled up my sleeve and looked at the tattoo from the night before, and the letters of the word hope and the digits of her phone number, faded now from my shower. I summoned some courage, if you want to call it that, and said it to myself again. "Fuck that." I got out of the car, walked through the garden, up the steps and knocked firmly on the door. Then I rang the bell. I waited.

The window had six small panes of glass, covered from the inside by a small white curtain. I saw a shadow on the curtain and then a hand pushed it to the side, revealing Chance's face. The curtain dropped back, and she opened the door. She just looked at me. Her eyes looked puffy and her hair was pulled up loosely in a ponytail, kind of high up on the back of her head, curls pouring out of the elastic like a geyser.

"Morning," I said.

"Morning," she replied.

"I woke you up?"

"It's nine o'clock, I didn't go to bed until four." She laughed. "You don't call?" I could tell she was being sarcastic despite her sleepiness.

"Right, yeah. I was probably supposed to wait a day or two to play it cool, right?"

"Or at least until noon."

"I couldn't relax. Get dressed," she was wearing flannel pajamas, her feet bare, "we're going out."

She stared at me blankly.

"How could I relax knowing you've never seen the beach?" I said, as if this was a normal thing to say. As if this was a normal thing to do. "Come on, I'm taking you."

She continued to stare at me. "Really?" she finally said.

"Yeah, unless you were busy. Or going to be busy," I wasn't being sarcastic.

"Okay," she said after another moment. "Okay, just give me a few minutes." She turned around, leaving the door open behind her.

"Chance," I said.

She turned around and looked at me.

"I brought you a coffee," I said, reaching towards her with a paper cup. I pulled two small plastic cream containers from my sweatshirt pocket, a couple packets of sugar and a stirrer wrapped in a napkin. "I don't know how you take it." She took the couple steps back to the door as I handed her the coffee and supplies. I remained on the outside of the threshold of the door. She held the coffee in one hand and looked at the items she was now holding in her other hand. She looked up at me. "I'll wait in the car, I'm right out front," gesturing with my thumb over my shoulder. I pulled the door shut behind me and walked back to sit in my car, sipping my coffee while I waited.

The drive to Little Compton was uneventful. Chance was quiet for the first half of the drive. She ate one of the bagels I picked up from the coffee shop, choosing cinnamon raisin over plain. The radio was turned low on a classic rock station. I drummed my fingers on the steering wheel to a familiar song. She was so quiet that I wondered if she was asleep. I looked over at her, and she turned to me. She

75

smiled, looking sleepy. It was very warm in the car, mostly due to the sun, which felt nice against the somewhat chilly morning. It was early November, after all. An unusual time to go to the beach.

"So, what is it about me never being to the beach that kept you from relaxing?" She finally asked, right around the time we exited the highway, near Tiverton.

"Don't know. Just seemed wrong for you to have been here, in Rhode Island, for a couple months and not to have seen it. And to never have been in your life? I don't know. I love the beach. It's one of those things that's always perfect even though it is always different. Not a lot of things like that."

She looked out the window. "Are we close?"

"Pretty close. There's beaches right around here, but a lot are private. We'll go down a little ways. To Little Compton, to South Shore. I love the beaches down there."

We sipped our coffee in relative silence as we passed a scrap yard, a marina, the turkey farm.

"This is Tiverton," I said, like I was a tour guide, when we got to the four corners. "Best blueberry ice cream at that place," I pointed to my left, "but not open this time of year." The lazy hub of civilization here was a ghost town this time of day on an autumn Sunday. We continued on our way, winding along gently curving roads buttressed by golden leaved trees and stone walls. I cracked the window on my side. It smells so good around here.

After passing by the small cemetery in the town of Little Compton, we were on the final approach to the beach. "Here we go," I said, as we pulled down the last stretch of paved road and past the entrance booth, now closed for the season. The parking lot was empty, no one here for a mid-morning walk even on such a beautiful day.

Why. Me.

I parked the car at the far end of the lot, and I resisted the urge to say something as we got out of the car. Chance walked ahead of me and stopped when she got close to where the sand became smooth and damp from the water's reach.

"I see why you like it here," she said about a minute after I stopped to stand next to her.

"Yeah." The location spoke for itself. There really wasn't anything to add.

"I've always seen pictures of beaches, or beaches in movies. They never look like this." That has never occurred to me. "The air is different here. It's clean. Like, it doesn't have a smell or something." The place was so familiar to me. I wished I could experience it for the first time, even if simply to be able to understand what she meant.

We stood there for a few minutes. The wind came along in gusts. The waves crashing softly on each other and on the shore were the only sounds.

"Should we walk?" I suggested in the form of a question.

"Yeah," Chance said, sounding and smiling like a kid. She bent down and started untying her sneakers, the same white tennis shoes from the night before. "I want to walk barefoot."

"It gets a little sandier up ahead, maybe leave them on till we get past the rocks up here."

We walked about fifty feet, past the rockier sand, and then we both took our shoes and socks off. She stood up, holding her shoes in her hand. I put mine down, about ten feet from where the sand was wet. "The tide is going out. No one is going to mess with our shoes. You can leave them here." I reached out my hand and took her shoes, placing them neatly next to mine. They looked tiny.

"How do you know the tide is going out?"

"The way the lines in the wet sand are. See, look here. Look at this line, and the area in front of it is really dry. Then you have this one where a wave came up to here, and the area inside that is a little wetter. Then you see where the waves are still reaching," pointing at the wettest part of the sand. "If it was coming in, there would pretty much be just one wet area with a line in the sand from the most recent wave." I didn't feel like I was making sense at all, but she nodded.

We walked along the drier part of the sand, where it was smooth and hard. The distance between us and our shoes grew wider and wider.

"So, do you do this a lot?"

"Come to the beach? Or show up early in the morning at the homes of people I just met to bring them out here?" I laughed, knowing she was referencing her comment from the night before.

"Both," she smiled.

"I get down here pretty often. My friend Pete lives in this town. We all grew up coming here a lot." I'm still in the habit of referring to my group of boyhood friends as *we* even though each of us has our own adult life. It can be hard to let go of a *we* like that.

"And the other part of the question?"

"I've never brought anyone down here. I mean, I've been to the beach with people, but not like you mean." At least I thought I knew how she meant it. "And I've never been to the beach with someone for their first time." I looked over at her and asked, "so, how am I doing at it?"

"You are better at this than you advertise yourself to be."

"Unfair advantage, using the ocean to do the heavy lifting."

"That's true," she teased.

I stopped and picked up a round, flat stone from the ground in front of me, turned and threw it sidearm into the water. It skipped a couple times before disappearing into a wave.

"Oh, a challenge?" She said, scanning the ground for a stone. She found one and turned to the water. She flung the rock, and it skipped several times.

I raised my eyebrows. "Not too shabby," I complimented her.

"We have lakes in Illinois," in case I wondered where she learned that skill.

We walked for about twenty minutes, past the narrow inlet where I showed her a pond on the other side of the dunes. We were following the long curve of shoreline that ended at a point which is just over the Massachusetts border. "Let's sit," I said, taking a few steps away from the shore and flopping down on the soft dry sand. There were only a few tiny wisps of clouds in the sky. You couldn't have asked for a more perfect autumn day. Chance sat down beside me. We sat and looked out at the ocean. There was some kind of boat pretty far out. It floated along lazily from west to east.

I spoke first. "I was thinking about what you said last night. Or what I said." I stumbled off the blocks to make my point, a habit I have. "About the coming or the leaving, and which one is brave." I stopped for a long moment.

"And?" she said, patiently pointing out my pause.

"Yeah. I guess I don't really know your situation, but I don't think it's the leaving that's brave. The coming is the brave part. A lot of times staying is the hard part." I felt like

I was losing my point. "It's the arriving at the new place, that's what I mean when I say coming."

She thought for a minute. I leaned back on one elbow, resting on my hip to face her. I slid a few inches further away, trying to be subtle, so it wouldn't feel to her like I was crowding her. She was sitting cross legged and had to turn slightly towards me so she could look at my face. "I think it depends on what you are doing. Or what you are looking for."

"What do you mean?" I asked.

"Well, I haven't really thought about this, but it seems like if you are looking for something in yourself, or about yourself, you can do it anywhere. Stay put, leave, whatever. It doesn't matter. But if what you are looking for isn't something that's inside of you, then you gotta go. You have to go find it."

I thought for a minute. "Then I guess that means one of two things."

She looked at me, her expression telling me to continue.

"I guess it means you know what you are looking for, or you are all set on yourself."

"Makes a person sound overconfident on both fronts."

"I think it just means you know yourself pretty well. And maybe that you know what you want." I looked back at the ocean. "You seem pretty comfortable with yourself."

"So do you."

I looked at her and laughed. "Not to betray anything too serious, us having just met. But that's pretty far from the truth." I laughed again at myself. So untrue. "So, does that mean you know exactly what you are looking for?"

"No. I just know that it wasn't in Chicago." She said, looking over me and down the stretch of beach ahead. "It wasn't at home."

Here I was, sitting on a beautiful beach, with a pretty girl, on a picture-perfect day. We had just met. I liked her. I knew it. And I knew this was different than anything that I ever felt with a new person. At this moment, on what amounted to our first date. And all I could think was: what am I looking for? If she was right, and I suspected she was, then what I was looking for was something about myself. That's why I'm still here, in Rhode Island, close to home, with the people and places that had surrounded me for most of my life. So what was it? And why was I spending so much time thinking it was something out there? I forced myself back into the moment.

"Why not?"

She looked me in the eyes. "I just don't have much in common with the people there. My friends. My family. I love them. I miss them. But there was nothing much left there for me. It was clear." And it was clear that was all she had to say about that. "What about you? What's your deal?"

"My deal?" That was a huge question. "I guess I have probably too much in common with my friends, which is why my circle is sort of small." I picked up a handful of sand and let it fall slowly out of my fist. "My family?" This was a tough one. "My dad and I don't have much in common. He splits time between Providence and Florida. We don't see each other much. He's retired." It would have been clear to anyone I was leaving something out.

"And your mom?" She addressed the exclusion.

I looked down at the small pile of sand I created below my hand. I dropped my fist onto it gently and looked up at her. "Maybe another time," I said.

She looked at me, not breaking eye contact for what seemed like an eternity. "Sure," she said, very gently. As if she knew being gentle might have been necessary.

This was getting a little too deep for the circumstances. I got up and said, "Okay, I've got a game for you." I walked to where the sand was damp, about eight feet, and squatted down. I found a piece of straw-like dune grass that washed up with the high tide. It was about ten inches long, and I stuck it in the wet sand, pushing the sand against the base so that it would stand straight up. Standing halfway up, I made my way along the shoreline, bent over and searching till I found what I was looking for. A small shell, beige and about an inch long. Walking back to the newly erected straw pole, I slid the open part of the shell over the top of the grass so that it hung there, suspended about six inches above the sand. I walked back over and sat cross legged next to Chance, well aware of the fact that my leg was almost touching hers. It was as if I could feel the energy from her knee even though it was about an inch from mine, like when someone puts their hands on either side of your head and you can feel it in your ears. It almost tingled.

I ran my fingers through the sand between us, catching a couple small stones in my hand. I gave one to Chance. "Here, you go first."

She took the stone. "What do I do?"

"Try to knock the shell off the straw." I gave her a look like this was something she should have known, and that we were embarking on a serious endeavor. "What do you mean what do you do?"

She held the stone lightly and overthrew by about two feet.

Why. Me.

"The first one is always hardest," I said, feeling like a know-it-all, wishing I hadn't said it. I took my turn, missing to the right.

We went back and forth, laughing at ourselves and at each other, picking stones up from the sand around our feet. A stone I threw hit the straw and the shell spun around on its perch but didn't fall. "Oh!" I moaned, rolling on my back in the sand. "So close!" When I sat back up my knee was touching Chance's, but I didn't slide over. Neither did she. Our knees rubbed against each other as we leaned to pick up stones and threw them at the shell. This was harder than it looked.

It took many more attempts, but eventually Chance succeeded, the stone making a clear click against the shell and the shell making a soft sound as it landed on the sand. "Hah!" She said triumphantly, I put my hand up and she gave me a high five. I rocked forward and crawled on the sand to the shell, picking it up and shimmying myself backwards to where she sat.

"Your prize." I said, handing her the shell. "That and the enduring glory of your victory. You just beat the best."

"You were the best, you mean," she threw back, smiling and looking at the shell in her palm. "It's so pretty."

"We called them sea slippers when we were kids. Some sort of a snail, I think. You see the shells more than you see the snails. You used to see a lot more of them," I said, trying not to sound philosophical, because I wasn't trying to be. It was true. The humor of the game had broken the serious track of our conversation, and our silence was comfortable, easy. I was, once again, laying on my side and facing her, supporting myself uncomfortably on my elbow.

"I know this wasn't your plan for the day," I finally said. "We can hit the road if you have things to do."

She looked at her watch, and back at the ocean. She didn't answer right away. "This was so nice of you to bring me out here. It's beautiful here." She wrapped her hand around the shell.

I looked up at her from where I rested, "Yeah, it is." She looked down at me. "The beautiful part, I mean. Not that it was so nice of me." We smiled at each other.

"I do have some work to do. Maybe we should get going." I stood up and pulled her to her feet, using both hands. Once up, she didn't let go with her left hand, so we walked back to our shoes hand in hand along the shoreline. We dusted our feet off as best we could on the sand and put our shoes on for the walk back to the car. I opened the passenger door for her and then walked around to the driver's seat. The tires rumbled as we rolled through the parking lot, and then we quietly glided onto the pavement.

We talked the entire drive back to Providence, which takes about forty-five minutes if you are driving the speed limit. This drive took about fifty, because I was driving slowly to make the most of my time with her. She told me more about her school program, about engineering, about Chicago. I told her about living in New York, a bit about Mark, Pete and Courtney. We talked about Providence, and I spoke about how different it was from when I was a kid, but also the same.

We were almost back when I noticed it was a little after noon. Lunchtime. "You hungry?" I asked. I knew she had things to do, and I never have things to do, which wasn't fair. But I really did not want the day to end. Not yet.

She answered quickly that she was.

"Don't worry," I said, turning the wheel against the steep curve of the off ramp, "I'll have you home by one.

We're going to get you the best sandwich you've ever had. Promise."

I miss living in New York, even though I'm not one of these people who thinks it is the only place to be. What I sometimes miss is the *everything* that is always happening, the things you see and the things you don't. I miss the exquisite beauty alongside unimaginable ugliness. I miss the way New York simultaneously hits both ends of pretty much any spectrum you can imagine. And I miss the food. But there is one thing I have to say. It is true that in New York you can find Icelandic cuisine at three in the morning if that is what you are craving, and you can eat at the same Italian restaurant where Miles Davis once snorted coke off the back of the toilet, but the single best falafel place on the Atlantic seaboard is on the east side of Providence.

Chapter 6

Things happen quickly in New York. Everything seems the speed of light, and the way things went down for me and Mark was no exception. I had been in the city for almost two months when he found us our so-called jobs. By the end of the semester, we were doing work for several other small auction houses and high-end consignment shops. We worked through the winter break, and the same week classes started in January we were contacted by an internet company that specialized in online auctions. Mark had decided to do what I had more or less dared him to do. He designed a simple software program that allowed the auction houses to let potential buyers bid on the web in real time with the live auctions at the houses. Only one agreed to use the software, and they only tried it out once.

It is worthwhile to note that we were pulling in what felt to me like wads of cash. I only had one real job in my life up to that point, which was working at the summer camp I attended when I was a kid. Not including room and board, I earned about six hundred dollars during the second summer I worked there. Keep in mind that if you wanted spending money on your days off, you had to draw against your salary. I think I made it home with about a hundred bucks that summer. At the end of my first summer, I actually owed the camp money, but my boss called it even. Regardless, the auction house gig gave me way more cash in my pocket than I was used to. I was clueless about business, and so one day I found myself sitting in an office with Mark and his dad after we were contacted by the online auction company.

Why. Me.

It was his father's office, and since it was his dad, the lawyer, who arranged our little business, he called us in to discuss some stuff. It had something to do with the software Mark designed. It wasn't that online auctions were entirely new at that point. What they were interested in was something about the code he wrote, something about the way companies could use his software. It was something I really didn't understand, and I kept insisting that I didn't design the software. As far as I was concerned, it was up to Mark to do what he wanted with it. He kept insisting that it was our company, and that it was somehow my idea, and that he wouldn't have come up with it if it weren't for me. "Fifty-fifty," he kept saying. Meanwhile, his dad was trying to explain something to me, but I didn't fully understand what he was talking about.

"So, let me get this right. They want to give us the option to buy part of their company? And for that option, we let them use the software?"

"Half right. Yes, they are offering you options, but they would own the software," his dad said.

"But aren't we already making money with this software, can't they just pay us to use it? Why do we have to pay them to own their company? I mean, I guess I don't really care. It's up to Mark. He built it."

This got Mark animated. "I.. we'd have to *give* them the software? Yeah, can't they just pay us to use it? What is it worth for us to have the right to buy some of their company? Can't anyone buy stock?"

We were way over our heads. His dad basically told us that, yes, they were giving us the option to buy stock, but to buy it at a certain price. If the company's stock went up, which it had been doing, those options would be worth money even if we didn't actually buy shares. Apparently, this stuff was very clear to some people, but I didn't know a stock option from a stock clerk. His dad was sure it was a good deal, so we let him and his firm do some paperwork, we signed some contracts, and we were the proud owners of some options. Lots of options, it seemed.

The problem was that now we no longer had jobs because we didn't own our company anymore, so to speak. So we fiddled around, made new soups, went to class and two months later, in March, we once again found ourselves in the Fifth Avenue office of Mr. Rush. I couldn't believe what he was telling me. The company's stock launched through the roof, and those options were now worth some money. A lot of money. Mark and I were near midtown anyway, and we stopped at his dad's office to see if he wanted to take us out to lunch. He didn't, but he asked us to sit. I don't think either of us ever thought about the options much since the weeks after we signed the paperwork. We figured his dad would fill us in if anything important was going on.

"Are you kidding me?" I still didn't really understand what an option was. I didn't get how they could be worth that much. I tried again to understand. "So we own the option to buy part of this company at a certain price, but because the price is now higher than that, we don't actually have to buy the stocks at that price? We can just sell the options?" I think I grasped the concept previously, but I was trying to re-understand it. It all seemed sort of surreal.

"That's right. But this company's stock is going up like crazy. It could be worth twice that in a month. Or more at this rate." His dad beamed. Money was nothing to this guy. He was genuinely proud of us, and I felt that he was happier for me even than his own son, who needed for nothing but had nothing really of his own. Until now. Mark and his dad kept talking along this line of thinking, that this could get even bigger. But I was on a different train of thought. I remembered something my mom told me once while we were sitting at breakfast during one of our trips.

I was up before her, always the early riser. It was the last summer that I would go on one of her hunts. I was thirteen. A little immature for a teenager, but life would speed that up soon enough. Sooner than I expected. I remember the way she looked that morning, even more beautiful than usual. Her long black hair, slim aquiline nose, dangling turquoise earrings and wrap skirt combined to make her look like some sort of princess. To me, she never seemed old enough to be my mom. My father used to say she looked like a gypsy. But that was just one of the annoying things he said.

I was eating toast under the watchful eye of the Maine innkeeper, suspicious of anyone my age no doubt. My mother came downstairs looking immaculate and gracefully crossed the room to where I sat. She didn't say a word at first, just picked up her paper and began glancing over the classified section. The print option was the only option in those days. I was looking at the map, tracking where we had been and wondering where she'd take us next. I felt something was off and looked up. My mom was staring at me.

"Look at you, Archer. You look all grown." She smiled. She was distracted.

"Yeah?" She never talked much when we were on these trips. I was more of a sidekick, but I loved it. She looked distant. "You know Archer, you're going to be a man soon." She was the sort of person who could get away with talking like this. I've never known anyone who could do that without sounding cheesy. Even seeing it written, it looks cheesy.

I didn't respond.

"You're a smart boy, but you should know something," she paused for a moment. "I want you to remember something. There's going to be times when no matter how hard you try to understand something, it won't come to you. I want you to remember that if that happens, you need to move on. Find a way to settle it and stop worrying about it. I see worry in you. If you just can't wrap your mind around it, it isn't worth it. If it's worth it, if it's understandable, you'll get it. Okay?" She smiled. Her smile, in retrospect, seemed to hide another emotion. "There are things in this world that no one can understand. Your job isn't to worry about them."

I was embarrassed. I felt like the whole room was looking at me. Which was true in a way, since my mother and I were now alone and she was looking at me intently. She put her hand on mine. I looked at it. "Just try not to worry." Many years later I thought about that morning. I didn't know it then, and I wouldn't really ever understand why, but it was my last time making that journey with my mom. I have alternately taken and avoided her advice since that day. I use it more often these days, and that day on Fifth Avenue I decided to.

I snapped out of my reverie. "Wait," I was interrupting Mark and his dad who were deep in conversation. "I don't get this." His dad was patient. He started to explain options again, but that's not what I didn't get. "Why is this company's stock going up?"

"Because they are going to make a lot of money." His dad replied, ever patient.

"But they didn't have any money two months ago, isn't that why they gave us the options? Are they making money now?"

"Yes, but they were making money then too. They just didn't have any cash. What's your point?" He wasn't asking in an aggressive way.

"Well, I don't get that either. They are making money, but they don't have cash. They don't even really sell anything either? Do they make anything?"

His dad seemed to be searching for a way to explain this to me. But I couldn't wrap my head around it. I was trying.

"It's about expectations," he finally said. "It is about how much money they expect the company to make. They have revenue now, and they will make a profit in time. So the stock is growing in value. Does that make sense?"

I thought about that for a minute. I didn't get it. *How did people know they'd make money?* I looked at Mark. I'm not sure that he got it either, although he always seemed to get things. I felt like he was looking at me and waiting. He was waiting for my move, I suddenly knew it.

"Sell them." I realized I sounded like I was giving an order. I rephrased: "Can we sell them?"

"Well, yeah... but selling your options now... you boys could make a lot more money."

"I'd rather sell it. Money I understand. This company, these options, I don't get it. Can we sell them?"

Literally, by the end of the day those options increased in value by over fifty thousand dollars. The next day his dad began arranging the sale. They were worth another hundred thousand by the time it went through. One month later, they would have been worth close to fifty percent more. Two months later, and they were totally worthless. I don't like to talk about money, but we walked away from that deal with a lot of it. More than two million dollars. Each. Not bad, considering that I really didn't do shit.

★★★

After saying bye to Pete, I made my way up to the top of College Hill and stopped in at my favorite falafel place where I'd taken Chance after our first date, if you can call it that, at the beach. Once finished, I began to make my way towards my father's house. It was true when I said I had to take care of some stuff over there. The house was being sold, and I wanted to grab a couple of things before the closing. It wasn't a long walk. There really aren't any long walks in Providence.

Walking through my old neighborhood, it seemed like every block, every driveway, every nook and cranny carried some memory of my childhood. As little kids, we rode our bikes block by block, knowing which houses had cranky occupants or nasty dogs. As we got older, we played manhunt through the backyards of all our neighbors, the crankpots, the dog owners. They would all complain to our parents about destroyed property or emotionally disturbed dogs. As teenagers, we snuck around corners and found spots in which to hide while we smoked cigarettes and other things, stashed beer for weekend parties in neglected garages.

I walked around the back of the house where I grew up. The grass seemed freshly mowed in the front yard, but around back things had gotten a little out of hand. My father hadn't lived here for quite some time. The front was cared for. Curb appeal, the realtor said. The garden in the back was always something my mom dealt with. Now it looked like crap. I walked to the cement step at the back door and bent down, searching intently with my eyes, and then with my hands, in the weeds to the side of the step. I pulled up a rock, tossed it away, and reached back down to grab a small copper turtle about the size of my palm. I smiled without thinking about it. I pinched the figurine between my thumb and fingers, grabbed the head with my other hand and pulled. It was stuck. I pulled harder and it just flew open. The turtle's head acted as a handle to a tiny drawer that slid into the body of the thing, and it shot out of my hand and fell ten feet to my right, something else landed a few feet short of that. "Fuck. The key." Five minutes later I finally fished the key and the little drawer out of the tall and weedy grass, opened the door, pocketed the key, and rested the turtle pieces on the kitchen counter. And, suddenly, I was fourteen years old again.

The house was quiet and still like it always was when I came home. This time more so. I dropped my bookbag on the floor by the back door, hung up my jacket and went straight to the fridge. I pulled out the orange juice and drank from the container. I looked around the kitchen. Something was not quite right.

I went through the kitchen and up the back staircase, decorated generously with dozens of family pictures. I walked past my mom's office, past the master bedroom and went straight to my bedroom. My pencils and pens were neatly arranged in the mason jar on my desk. I hadn't left it that way. My dresser was always littered with piles of junk. Toys, rubber bands, bracelets, books, loose change. It was a mess, but it was my mess. I knew where everything was. My change was now neatly piled, items were either missing or organized into categories, assorted bracelets that were the style at that time on one corner. Sunglasses in their case.

Three matchbox cars were lined up in a row. I turned around again, and saw my bed was made. It was never made.

Quickly, I went down the hallway and started down the back stairs, feeling oddly panicky. That was when I saw an empty nail on the staircase wall. I looked at the picture to the left. Me and my father on the beach, I was nine. I looked to the right, my father's parents' wedding picture. I looked at the nail where my second grade class picture had been hanging. Where I smiled at the camera with missing front teeth and a white and green striped Izod shirt with the alligator logo. I ran back up the stairs and threw open the door to my parents' bedroom. But I was no longer fourteen.

The bedroom was empty, and I stood there staring at it. All the furniture was gone, the kitchen was empty, the bedrooms were empty, every closet. Empty. It had been a long time since I had much stuff in this house. Friends of mine and people I knew had all sorts of furniture from their parents' homes, and they had things like their old baseball card collections, boy scout uniforms, stuff like that, still stored in the attics of their childhood homes. Everything from my childhood was gone, lost underwater. Everything else, I didn't want. I left it for my father. He never even asked if I wanted it. I think he knew what I would have said if he asked.

I closed the door behind me and walked down the hall. This house was quiet. Quiet like the mornings when I'd wake up before my parents and creep down the stairs to watch television. Quiet like the nights when I'd sneak in, late for curfew, to creep up the stairs to my bedroom. Quiet like the day my mother left. Quiet like the way my mother left.

Why. Me.

My old bedroom was at the end of the hallway, and as I approached the doorway, I half expected my bed, dresser and personal belongings to be there. But it was empty too. The sun was shining through one of the windows, bright and hot. Dusty particles floated through the rays, stirred up by my opening of the door. I remembered that night, when my father returned from work. He came home earlier than usual and went straight to their bedroom as if looking for something. Like he knew something would be there. He came and found me in my room.

"Archer, I need to talk to you about something. Can you come downstairs?"

I didn't turn around from my desk. I hated him. I blamed him. "We can talk here."

He paused. He knew. I knew. And he knew I knew. I had found the note. I had taken it. I never wanted him to read it. "Archer..."

In retrospect, I know that there was nothing that my father could have said. There was nothing he could do. I almost feel badly for him now, but my anger, my confusion and my age combined to dig a deep foundation for the wall that had always been there between me and him. "It's your fault. You called her a gypsy. You made her leave." I didn't yell, which probably made it worse for him. I talked to him calmly, channeling the calm that defined my mom. I was furious inside. I hated him. But I stayed calm. "Get out of my room."

The house was silent. It had never been a boisterous home, but it now seemed lifeless with her gone. I didn't say another word, just to see if he would break the silence. To see if he would share a good memory of her. If he could act like a parent at all. If he would even ask me for the note, the note I knew he was looking for when he came home that day. He knew. Maybe he'd been told that day. Maybe weeks, months, years before. He knew; I was always certain of that. I could never forgive him for it. Because I was the one who had to discover it.

I sat down in the square of sun where my bed once was. I sprawled out in the sun on the carpeted floor, like a cat in its favorite warm place. I remembered the first time Courtney and I got stoned, after school in ninth grade. We lay down on my bed right here, holding sticks of incense and watching the smoke spiral up into the sunlight. I let my eyes close, almost feeling them roll into the back of my head.

Alone in the empty house, I imagined myself on the beach. The hot sand below me and the sun up above. I was in a memory now, the day from the picture at the beach that used to hang by the stairs. I was lying on the sand in my swim trunks. The sand was stuck to my entire body and I was rolling around in it like a dog. The waves were coming just high enough to reach my feet and lower legs. My parents were sitting in chairs on the dry sand, some thirty feet or so from shore. I looked up at them from where I lay on my stomach. As an only child, you get used to playing by yourself on family outings. I watched them as they sat there. They were having a conversation. Years later, it occurred to me that this was one of the only times I remembered seeing them deep in conversation. It was also years later that I realized the odd nature of memory. What should have been a meaningless moment, and it felt meaningless to me at the time, was actually quite special. For some reason, my brain locked in on that moment, decades before it meant anything to me. My father took off his sunglasses, and my mom leaned her head back and to the side. She was laughing and he was smiling at her. In my memory, they were happy. And so young. I'd guess that I'm almost as old now as they were then.

A sudden wave covered me from my toes to my head, and I rolled over, a beached whale or a shipwreck. I rolled myself down with the gentle undertow, stood up and capsized into the water. Floating now, staring up in to the bright blue sky. And I was floating. The sun heavy on me like syrup. Melted butter. It wrapped around me. I felt a tingling on my leg. It was dark behind my eyes. The dream flitted before me. The faces, the darkness. A tingling on my leg. A vibration. My body twitched violently and I sat up with a deep breath like coming up from underwater. My leg tingled again. My phone was buzzing.

I waved my hand in front of my face as if swatting at a gnat. I pulled my phone out of my pocket. It was Courtney. "'lo?"

"Arch. Did I wake you up?"

"Hey, yeah, what's going on?" I was still cloudy.

"Are you still at my place?"

"No, no," more awake now, "I'm at my dad's place. My father's house. I guess I dozed off. Remember when we got stoned here that time. The first real time? With the incense?"

"Yeah, that was nuts." He said hastily. "Listen, was I a dick earlier?"

"No, why?"

"Nothing, I just felt like I was a dick. Did you see Pete?"

"Yeah he came by just after you left. You weren't a dick, you just seemed late."

"I saw his truck while I was going to get the girls. It looked like he was heading the wrong way, so I thought he might have left something." Courtney had it bad for Pete.

97

Don't get me wrong, we are all closely knit. But he seemed to hinge on him in a strange way. Pete would get annoyed by it sometimes, but then he was closest with Quinn, and the three of them used to always play music together. I think when Quinn died, Courtney took all that hurt and looked to Pete to soothe it somehow. Meanwhile Pete took all that hurt, and it disappeared way deep down inside.

"Yeah, his keys."

"But he was driving."

"Yeah. Don't ask, too confusing."

"Anyway, we cool?"

"What are you talking about, are we cool? Haven't we always been cool? Nothing's changed. Because you were in a rush? You think too much you bread-eating freak." He was always eating bread.

"You're one to talk. I'll speak to you later." We hung up.

That was Courtney. Man, that guy is thoughtful. It hadn't even crossed my mind that he'd been short with me. I don't even think that he was. Funny how people are.

***

When you get something without really trying, it doesn't feel real. As I walked through the hallway of the house I grew up in, I thought about how hard my parents worked for it. My mom, always treasure hunting, always wheeling and dealing, a dervish in the slow-paced world of antique commerce. My father, buying businesses, combining them, wringing out the efficiencies, and then selling the whole thing for one lump sum. They both worked hard. My father stayed at it; my mom walked away. They bought this house and worked for it. I ran my fingers along the nail pocked wall of the back staircase as I descended to the kitchen. This house felt so real to me. I hadn't been here for any meaningful amount of time in quite a while, but I already found myself missing it.

Being rich in New York carried certain advantages. And being rich and eighteen years old was like being in a perpetual playground. I finished what would turn out to be my final semester in college, because I felt it was the right thing to do. On my last day of classes I went to my advisor's office and informed him that I would be taking a leave of absence. I went to the registrar and unregistered for my fall courses, then walked across the hallway to the financial aid office. There was some paperwork to fill out, but when I left the office I owed no money to the school, to the bank or to the government. More importantly, neither did my father. It wasn't vengeful, and it wasn't because I didn't appreciate that he wanted to pay for my college education. I just didn't want to feel like I owed anyone anything.

I stepped outside onto Fifth Avenue and watched all the people walking by on the sidewalk. It was a crisp May afternoon in Manhattan. When the weather starts getting warm in the city, all the beautiful people appear. The temperature goes up, and the amount of clothing goes down. I stood and watched all the pretty people go by. Nothing felt real for the past couple of months. It would be a while before it did.

The dawning of the fact that we had to leave the dorms was like a door opened for us. Where to go? The answer seemed clear: Brooklyn. For me, coming from Rhode Island, something about Brooklyn seemed magical, probably the coolest place on earth. For Mark, a Manhattan boy, it was like moving to another country. As it turns out, neither perspective was correct. But, man, could you get some square footage there.

As had been the case up to that point, things happened quickly. We rented a crappy (but huge) loft in the DUMBO neighborhood of Brooklyn. People liked to say it was up-and-coming. I hate that term, but so be it. Within a month of signing a lease, the landlord began the process of attempting to evict everyone in the building. It turns out he was in a bit of a financial mess. The apartments were zoned for residential, but they were far below potential, not to mention code. Empty apartments meant he could fix them up for a higher rent. The problem was he had no money, no cash. I still couldn't understand how revenue didn't equal cash, but that was this guy's problem, not mine. I don't think he planned ahead very well. Without enough time to get people out, since we all had leases, and without the money to fix things up anyway, he couldn't even get the building into a state where he could sell it for what he wanted.

Back to Mr. Rush's office. More advice. We bought the building. As it turned out, the adjacent lot was part of the property, so we ended up owning that as well. When you get something without really trying, it just doesn't seem real. The day we closed on the property, reality still hadn't hit us. The income from the rentals already in place allowed us to break even or better on owning the buildings, and we had a healthy amount of cash that could cover things if need be. We weren't enrolled in school, we had no jobs, no apparent responsibilities. It was midsummer. We were eighteen.

In a medieval text, an author once explained how the story he was about to tell was like the flight of an arrow. In order to make its mark, an arrow must first take the path of an arc. The story would be the arc. The target is the meaning. Given the distance to the target, an archer must aim high above this mark, and the arrow then follows a long curving arc to reach its target. In other words, the author informed his readers that the story may seem to go off point, but would eventually come back to its purpose. The further an archer aims in the air, the higher the arc and the further the arrow will drive into the target, despite travelling in the wrong direction for half of its flight. Mark and I were launched fast and well off target. But reality would come on quickly, and would drive its point home, deeply. And unreal would become very real quite quickly.

★★★

I stopped in the kitchen and picked up the pieces of the copper turtle from where I left them on the counter, sliding the tiny drawer back into its place with some effort. I looked around the kitchen a final time and walked to the back door which I had left open. Standing on the single square concrete step, I held the turtle tightly in my hand and then threw it into the far corner of the backyard. I imagined that it would settle in the tall grass and get buried by leaves, and that some kid might one day dig it up and imagine he found some buried treasure. The grass was already green and starting to over grow. Low bushes were beginning to sprout tiny green leaves, and the several towering deciduous trees, though still bare and gray looking, held thousands of tiny reddish buds ready to explode into leaves. The neighbor's dogwood tree was already in full bloom. I fingered the key in my pocket.

Second guessing my decision to leave, I went back inside and found myself face to face with the basement door.

I went down to the cellar. This was one of those nasty, unfinished basements typical of homes like this. It was dusty and dirty and full of cobwebs. I used to freak myself out down there as a kid. It was now a place that made me angry, as I remembered my father telling me about the water, the flood and the mold. I was angry I never got to salvage anything from my childhood, angry I couldn't see it go. Angry that strangers came with thick gloves, vacuums and dumpsters to unceremoniously dispose of everything. In the far corner of the basement was a yellow door. To be accurate, it had been a yellow door, which sectioned off a small storage corner on one side of the basement. It was now a patchwork of peeling yellow paint, showing the white primer and bare wood underneath, dingy and gray and rotten on the bottom corners. This was the door that used to really scare me as a kid, wondering why there was a door down there, what lurked behind it, and why did it need a deadbolt? I tried to open it, but it was locked.

Impulsively, I gave it a kick. Dust, paint chips and dirt fell from all around it. I kicked it again, harder this time. I heard the frame groan and crack. I kicked it again, and again, and again, until it flew open. The upper hinge snapped off the frame and the door swung towards me. I flinched as it almost hit me in the face. I hit the light switch and a single bulb burned in the middle of the tiny storage room littered with basement style junk. A few flower pots, a stack of nasty looking newspapers, half a bag of potting soil, a rusty shovel head with no handle. But there, hanging by a hook from the ceiling where it evidently escaped much damage was my old BMX bike. I laughed out loud. I had completely forgotten about this bike. It slipped my mind when I thought of all that was lost from my childhood. I pulled it off the hook and put it on the ground. The tires were totally flat. I looked up and there was my old pump, hanging next to where the bike was hanging. It took a few minutes to get the tires pumped up, since the pump was nearly rusted solid and not quite air tight. I carried the bike upstairs, shutting off the lights and closing all the doors behind me as I walked out to the back yard. I took a better look at the tires in the daylight, the outer tires showed evidence of some dry rot, but the tubes miraculously seemed to be holding air.

Down the hill from the house, there was a service station. I walked the bike down the hill, used their pump to get a few more pounds of pressure in the tires, and asked the attendant for some grease for the chain. It must have been a slow day for the shop, because the mechanic came out with some oil in a can and he greased the chain and single gears with a rag. He was my age and seemed to be working there alone. I thanked him for his help and got on the bike, which was a few sizes too small for me. Peddling cautiously at first, I stood up on the pedals and bounced up and down. The tires seemed to hold, the chain stayed in one piece. I peddled faster and turned off the main road to a side street and down a hill.

I was flying now. My sweatshirt, half zipped, filled with air and ballooned behind me. I came to the bottom of the hill at the long boulevard that cut across this side of Providence. I skidded to a stop with the handbrake. It squeaked loudly. I hadn't even thought to check it, so I was relieved to find that it worked. I was oddly out of breath given I'd been riding downhill. I walked with the bike to the middle of the boulevard and aimed myself along the dirt path down the middle. I hopped back on, going more slowly now, feeling good in the fresh air, feeling good to be moving along slowly. Taking my time.

Chapter 7

When Quinn, Pete and Courtney used to play guitar together, it seemed like the world stopped. Time took on a whole new meaning. Watching them was one of my favorite things to do when we were teenagers. I am not musically inclined at all. I have little rhythm, and I can't even really hear tone. But I'm an avid music listener, and I'm envious of, and enthralled by, the talents of great musicians. For my part, the best compliment I've ever received as a musician is that I can play a mean air guitar. I can really rock at that.

The last time I ever saw those three guys play together was during the summer after we graduated from high school. It was a fun summer, the end of an era. An end that none of us saw coming. We all had some little odd jobs, but we mostly spent a lot of time hanging out, alternately in Providence, mostly at my house where we could get away with most anything, and in Little Compton, at Pete's house, where the same held true. Towards the end of the summer, we had one last big party out on the beach near Pete's.

It was the quintessential beach party. An early evening football game on the beach. Lots of beer. Lots of young, tanned bodies running around and getting into trouble. And, of course, a bonfire after dark. We spent a bit of time collecting firewood up and down the beach, particularly along the rocky areas where the driftwood and other detritus would get caught up, and we had quite a pile by the time it was ready to light things up. Driftwood has a special way of burning, and I found myself lost in the flames while listening to my boys jamming together. I'd been watching them for quite a while, their smiling faces lit by the fire, flashing and popping.

Why. Me.

Their hands moved easily up and down the necks of their acoustic guitars, their fingers picking at the strings. Each of them had a very specific look when playing. Pete's gaze was always far off, and it seemed as if there was someone else in charge of his hands. His play seemed effortless. He was the most gifted of the three of them, and he seemed to try the least. It appeared to come out of him as easily as a breath. Quinn was usually in the middle, smiling so big he seemed to be laughing. He'd look back and forth at Pete and Courtney, raising his eyebrows and making all kinds of expressions as if he were conducting an orchestra with his face. He had the most fun with it, and for him it seemed truly like play. Courtney was always watching his hands in great concentration. His lips pursed and forehead slightly furrowed, he worked the hardest at his craft, practicing daily for hours on end. Even when jamming with Quinn and Pete, he made it seem like it was work.

Knowing these guys my whole life, watching them create music, create sounds that would impress and then disappear forever, was a treat for me. I could watch them for hours, and they would often come through on their end. But tonight, I was lost in the fire. I looked to my left, and Jonas looked over at me. We both made an expression as if to say, *you seeing what I'm seeing?* And then we both turned back to the fire.

Just before dark, the five of us had wandered back to Pete's house from the party and split about a half an ounce of mushrooms. We made tea with them, which was not my favorite way to do it. I never felt like it truly masked the taste enough, and I really, really don't like the taste of them. I don't like mushrooms at all, regardless. Making tea with them means they get all slippery and foul and trying to gag them down is as bad as finding one in a calzone. It's like eating slugs. No thanks. But my vote for peanut butter and mushroom sandwiches was nullified when Jonas dumped them all in the teapot on Pete's stove with a few bags of apple cinnamon tea. I drank down the tea and then choked down my share of mushrooms, and I was happy that I didn't get sick. That was about two hours before sitting by the fire.

An hour or so after the tea, I was enjoying a beer in Pete's kitchen. The five of us were playing some cards around the kitchen table, getting ready to head back down to the beach, waiting for the mushrooms to kick in. Pete came back to the table after going to the bathroom and sat down to my right.

The mushrooms were coming on a little bit at this point, and the yellow Formica table top seemed brighter than usual under the kitchen light. The silver border of the table appeared sort of wobbly around the edge. I suppressed a laugh and smiled to myself. Here it comes.

"Arch, are you drinking my beer?" Pete asked.

I knew he wouldn't really care if I drank his beer. I knew he wasn't mad. "You can't *own* a beer, Pete, you know that." Trying to be funny.

"No, but, did you pick up the beer I was drinking? It was here." He pointed at the table, as if it could have been somewhere else. He looked right at me, I could see the sliver of blue wrapped like a halo around his widely dilated pupils. "Here." He said again, laughing a bit.

I looked at Jonas who was sitting on the other side of him, whose eyes were equally dilated, and who was sort of smiling an odd smile. Not such a strange thing. Was this the mushrooms, or something else happening? I looked in front of me at the two beer bottles there. I picked one up in each hand and looked at them. "I guess this must be yours," I

said about the one in my right hand. "I drank a little, sorry."
I was confused but chalked it up to the mushrooms. I
handed it back to him, and he held it up to the light. Jonas
looked up at the bottle too. Why were they looking at it?
It was about half full.

"Yeah, it's mine. Don't worry about it Arch, it's cool."
He smiled, but it didn't hide the strange look on his face.
"Arch." He paused. "Me and Jonas. We... uh... we put a
couple few tabs of blotter in that bottle. We were sharing
it. You'll be feeling that a little bit I think."

My heart skipped a beat. Dropping acid was not
something I planned to do again, at least not tonight. "How
much?"

They looked at me sort of blankly. "How much what?"
Jonas asked.

I looked around the table at Quinn and Courtney.
Their wide eyes reflected the look that must have been on
my face. "How much was in there?" Knowing Pete and
Jonas had a habit of overdoing things.

"Four tabs." Jonas said. Pete nodded in agreement.

I made an attempt to do some quick math in my head,
but that got me nowhere. I really wasn't sure how much I
drank from their bottle. The table pulsed under the lights. I
drummed my fingers on it. "Okay, I guess it's on then."
Pete smiled and put his hand on my shoulder. I heard him
think, *we got your back, Archer.*

The fire was dancing, drawing my eyes away from the
music, away from the three faces that were glowing like
masks over their guitars. My face was hot from the flames,
my skin tight. I yawned. Mushrooms always make me
yawn. I closed my eyes and I could still see the bright yellow
faces there, floating in a red orange hazy background from
the fire on the other side of my eyelids. When I opened my

eyes, the yellows and oranges and reds were dancing again in the fire. The sand, a hot yellow under my feet. Were my flip flops melting? Was I sitting too close to the fire? I kicked them off. The sand was cooler under my feet somehow. The acid was coming on strong now, and the fire was feeling too intense.

I looked at my friends with their guitars. I looked around quickly for Jonas, but I didn't see him. There were other faces around the fire, illuminated too brightly by the flames. They appeared like grotesque masks, their movements followed by the blur of melting skin. I yawned again. This was a little too much. Standing up suddenly, I looked up at the sky, watching how the thousands of golden sparks were trailing up to the sky followed by long tails of yellow. The stars above that. *Would they get that high?*

I turned away from the fire, and almost tripped over a large cooler behind me. *Had I been leaning against that? What's in there?* My internal monologue felt jumpy and rapid fire, yet soothing. *Open it, what's there? Dig in the ice, what's under it? So cold. Get a beer. Is that an orange? Why is there an orange in there? Whose is that? Just take it.* I grabbed a beer and the orange, closed the cooler and started walking down to the water's edge, about forty feet from the fire. I left my flip flops up there, but I was happy on the beach in bare feet. The moon was high up in the sky, and I could see that the water was pretty calm. Some really low waves were rolling in, reaching almost to where I stood on the hard, cool, damp sand. A boy, a beer, and his orange.

"Should we walk?" Quinn asked.

"Yup," I replied as if I'd known he was standing next to me. I wasn't surprised for some reason.

"Let's do it," he said. We both turned west and started walking along the shore. Like it had been the plan all along.

We'd been walking about ten or fifteen minutes before either of us spoke, and when we did it was both of us simultaneously.

"Why'd you stop playing?" I asked.

"You feeling that acid?"

I answered first. "Yes."

"You peaking?"

"Maybe. The mushrooms are throwing me off a bit. I can't judge."

"Judge." Quinn repeated.

I felt the orange bouncing off my thigh with each step from where I put it in my cargo shorts pocket. It only took a minute or two to walk far enough away to where we couldn't hear the guitars or the laughing or the carrying on. The colors changed from the yellows and oranges of a fire lit party, to the blues, grays and silvers of a moonlit beach. I was instantly calmer and felt ready for the rest of the night.

"Did you take some too? Some acid?" I felt almost hopeful, like I'd have a partner.

"Nope. I ate a few more mushrooms though. Maybe an hour ago. Maybe less." He said. "Judge. That's a good word."

"Yeah." For a moment, from the outside looking in, I could tell this was ridiculous. I yawned again. Damn mushrooms. My ears felt like they were popping. I opened my mouth really wide and forced another yawn. It was like bubbles were coming up through my neck and pushing out through my ears. *It'll pass*, I told myself.

We were still walking along the shore close to the water, and the firmness of the damp sand was stabilizing under my feet. I practiced focusing on the ground about twenty feet in front of me, letting my feet remember where I'd seen rocks or piles of seaweed ahead of me. I tried to open up my full range of sight, concentrating on everything in my peripheral vision while keeping my eyes centered ahead of me like that. I could see my hands down there below my forearms, the toes on my feet popping into my vision with every step for a split second. The low waves rolling in from the ocean to my left. Quinn walking to my right. It was like being in a fishbowl. Everything was in focus.

We had been walking for a while when I realized we reached a recognizable spot. The rocks were a little more frequent, the sand a little more pebbly. I broke the concentration I was holding on my field of vision and looked at Quinn. We both stopped walking.

"You won't be able to keep walking with bare feet," he said. He read my mind.

"Yeah." I looked at his feet, clad in tennis shoes, and then looked back at the direction from where we came. Even though we walked around a large crescent of beach, you couldn't see where the fire was burning back at the party because we passed a small point between here and there. The beach here stretched along a large marsh where we used to throw rocks in the wintertime, listening to the bizarre echoes in the ice while the stones ricocheted across the surface.

Looking back at the distance we'd come, I knew I didn't want to walk back. "We have to keep going, though." I said it like it was meaningful, even though it wasn't. But Quinn was in agreement.

"Yeah, I think so," he said pensively, "you can't go back."

I turned and looked at the water, the tips of the waves painted silver in the moonlight, coming towards me like a series of icicles rolling on a black table. I looked down on the ground to my right, and saw something over there, about thirty feet away. It looked out of place, not like a rock or driftwood or an old buoy. *What is that?* I thought. When I heard Quinn say, "What?" I realized that I must have spoken out loud. Whatever it was, it intrigued me and I walked over and stopped in front of it.

"Shoes," I said.

"Shoes?" Quinn replied. He was squatting back where I left him, looking at the sand. Standing up, he said again, "shoes?" He ambled over.

I leaned down in disbelief. There, at my feet, placed perfectly next to each other was what looked to be a nearly new pair of leather docksiders. This is the kind of thing that only happens when you are tripping. I looked around, suddenly nervous that we weren't alone. But my vision hadn't fooled me. There was not a soul to be seen. One at a time, I brushed the sand off my feet and slipped them into the shoes.

"Perfect fit." Not really my choice of footwear, but beggars can't be choosers.

Quinn arrived at my side. "You know that's fucking crazy, right?" he said in a matter of fact tone.

"Yup."

"No, like, that's insane. That's the kind of shit that only happens…"

"… when you're tripping." I completed his sentence.

"Yup."

"I guess we can keep walking then."

"You can't go back."

I nodded in agreement but more to myself, and we continued on our way.

It's not that the walk was strenuous or that we were scrambling over treacherous terrain, but I found myself stuck on the four words Quinn said when we set out on the last leg of our journey. *You can't go back*, I was repeating to myself while carefully making my way through this stretch of beach with rocks that ranged in size from small boulders to cantaloupes. I imagined myself a giant crunching boulders underfoot. A minion of hell, walking over the skulls and bones of the damned. A tiny ant clambering across a pile of sand.

We only stopped once more on the walk, to admire the plumes of bioluminescent plankton shimmering in a small tide pool. We tossed a couple rocks in, one at a time, and watched the shimmering of the tiny creatures in the water.

"Wait, is that the stars?" I asked, thinking I was seeing a reflection.

"Bioluminescence" Quinn replied, in a sage voice.

You can't go back, I said to myself, and turned to keep walking.

You could see the lights of a house now, just inland from the beach, which meant we were coming closer to Warren Point. We were both familiar with how to cut across the point on the small road here, which would bring us straight to Warren's Beach Club, a small private beach where we were always able to gain access as a result of Pete's grandmother being a member. At night, no membership was needed, just the willingness to trespass past the padlocked gate. We were willing, and we slipped under the bar and walked along the edge of the small parking lot down to the soft sand of the beach club.

Why. Me.

We both took a beer with us when we left the fire, and we both carried them with us, unopened, for the walk this far. Quinn pulled a lighter out of his pocket and used it to pop the top off of his, then handed it to me while I handed mine to him. He opened that one and took a long sip. I looked at the beer in my hand and tipped it back. It was the same temperature as my mouth, which made it so I almost couldn't feel it going down. It wasn't refreshing, but not altogether unpleasant. I took another long sip, sat down on the ground, and rested it in the sand next to me. Quinn sat down too.

"Why'd you stop playing?" I asked him again.

"My hands wouldn't do what I wanted them to do. It was like they didn't belong to me. And I couldn't stop yawning."

Him saying that made me realize that my yawns had gone away. "I didn't know other people got the yawns from mushrooms. Thought that was my own thing." I said.

"Me too."

I leaned back on my elbows, and then, realizing that was uncomfortable, I lay down flat on my back and looked up at the sky. The moon was bright, kissing the edges of the wispy clouds in the sky. The stars appeared to be squirming around in the sky like bacteria on a microscope slide. My field of vision seemed imprinted with a fingerprint pattern, a giant swirl of faintly colored ripples covering the entire sky. I was past the real peak of my trip, I could tell, and I was enjoying the visuals. The fingerprint patterns turned geometric, and then like static that melted the stars away and then thrust them back out, like pinpricks in a black sheet held up over a bright light. *What's behind this sky?* I wondered. The clouds were handfuls of cotton candy, then smudges of paint. I closed my eyes and watched the

113

patterns form there, on the backs of my eyelids, like millions of jellyfish swimming in a red sea. I opened them again and sat up.

Quinn walked down to the water, and was standing there, staring out at the ocean. He was doing his own thing, as was I. I tipped my beer back and drained it in a series of gulps. It went down like water. I stood up and kicked off the docksiders, pulled off my t-shirt, dropped my shorts and boxers, and started to walk along the beach over to the so-called bluffs, a natural stone jetty that thrust out into the water at the edge of the beach. I wondered if I'd be brave enough to jump into the water off the rocks. Out at the end, at one of the highest points, a diving board was attached to the stone. It was only about twenty feet, and I'd jumped it a million times. But never at night. And never while tripping. Just before the end of the sand I spotted a stone on the ground that looked out of place. I picked up what was perhaps the world's most perfect skipping stone. I looked at it in my hand for a moment, and then, wrapping my fingers around it, I headed out onto the rocks, choosing my steps carefully and navigating my naked body away from the shore.

The tide was low, which meant there was no water to walk through to get to the bluffs, but that also meant the jump would be further. The moon offered plenty of light to find my path across the rocks, and I finally reached the diving board. I had that feeling of being too close to the edge as I made my way out to the end of it, but once I got out there, I felt myself in perfect balance. Shimmying slowly to the edge, I hung all ten of my toes over the end of the board, and I wiggled them a little bit. I watched on television how divers stand at the edge of the platform before a big dive, sometimes even doing a handstand there.

It never made sense to me how they didn't ever fall while standing there at the edge, their balance so perfect.

The board seemed solid and strong below me. And I realized it wasn't so much about trying not to fall, it was about knowing you wouldn't. I opened my hand and looked at the stone I'd picked up. I couldn't skip it from here, I was too high up from the water. It had a nearly perfect egg shaped outline, slightly more rounded on one side than the other, and was perfectly flat on the top and bottom. In the soft moonlight, the surface appeared almost powdery, and I could see tiny reflective flecks in the sediment that made up the stone. I tried to look closer, but the moon was suddenly covered by one of the small clouds up there, so I wrapped my fingers around the stone and looked down at the black water below me.

That's when I heard the patter of footsteps behind me, a high pitched "whoop, whoop" and then the smack of flesh on flesh. My head jerked back and then forward, and I felt myself suspended in midair and then falling down towards the water, which rushed up to meet me quicker than I could have expected. I hit the water sideways, but mostly feet first. I let my body go limp as I landed, sinking down under the water, but then quickly pushed myself up to get my head above the surface. There was no chance to hold my breath before Quinn tackled me, and I needed some air, which I got.

"Oh, you fucker," I said once I was treading water comfortably. I could hear Quinn howling in the distance. He had gone further out, I could tell. It was hard to do a body check while in the water, but it seemed like I wasn't hurt at all. I started to swim toward the bluffs, but then remembered the story we were always told about the kid who drowned trying to climb the ladder at low tide. He'd allegedly been pulled under the rocks near where the ladder hangs down, where there is an underhang in the rocks that you can't see under the water. I got a little nervous, and even felt like an undertow was pulling me towards the rocks as I tried to swim away. But I was fine, and got myself a good thirty or forty feet away from the bluffs before even starting to swim back towards the shore.

I was able to float effortlessly in the salt water. I closed my eyes and let the water rock me, my arms outstretched, my feet dangling just below the surface of the water. I opened my eyes, but my ears were just under the water and the quiet under there was deafening, so I started to tread water, a bit more vertical in the water now. Straightening my body, I pushed my arms down quickly and then allowed my weight to pull me underwater, pushing my arms up now and propelling myself downwards. I slid down quickly, quite aware of the water growing colder and colder on my feet as I sank. The darkness enveloped me, and even with my eyes open underwater I had no frame of reference to know if I was still moving down or simply floating below the surface. For a brief moment, I wondered if I could breathe under here, I felt unaware of temperature, of pressure, of my body. A strange numbness surrounded me, a blackness, a deafness. And then a wave of panic, like I was dying. Or dead. I frantically swam to the surface, with no idea exactly how far down I had gone. It wasn't far, but I came out of the water with a sudden burst and deep inhale. I gasped a little and then heard a cackle of laughter and another howl in the distance. Quinn was out there, somewhere. I got my bearings about me, and I could tell that he was swimming further out rather than going in to shore or back to the bluffs. I resumed floating on my back, and gently kicked myself towards shore. It wasn't until I was back on dry land that I realized I was still holding the stone I was looking at when Quinn slammed into me.

I found my way back to where I left my clothes, spread out my t-shirt and sat down on it carefully so as not to get my wet body covered in sand. If it was anyone else, I'd have had a hard time not worrying about him swimming out there, alone, at night, tripping. But not Quinn. That guy was like a fish. He could have swum along the shore the entire walk to here from the fire, which was probably at least a couple of miles. He was the last one for me to worry about out there, even though he was a touch reckless. So I wasn't surprised to hear, a bit far off but then closer and closer, the barking of a seal, followed by the hoot of an owl, followed by a wolf's howl. And then I saw what looked like his head pop up from underwater about forty feet from shore, and then again about twenty feet from shore, and then his entire body rose up from where he floated in to about a foot of water. His naked body was silhouetted by the sea. He walked up to where I sat and flopped down directly on the beach next to me, unconcerned about being covered with sand.

Remembering the orange, I reached over to my shorts and pulled it out of my pocket, leaving the stone in my shorts for safe keeping. In the moonlight, it seemed like the only thing out of the blue-gray scale on the entire beach. I admired its roundness and weight before beginning to peel it. The feeling of the peel under my fingernails was somewhat unpleasant, but the smell of the thing was so enticing. I felt like I'd never eaten fruit before as I ripped back its magical peel and got down to the wedges below. I ripped it in two, and reached half of it over to Quinn, who was watching like he never saw an orange before.

"Where'd you find that?" he asked incredulously, as if I found it while swimming in to shore.

"In the cooler back by the fire." I said, missing a terrific opportunity to fuck with his head, which he would have deserved after the whole tackling off the diving board maneuver.

"Oh," he said, somewhat disappointed.

I was immersed in eating the orange, which somehow seemed to be giving my body an extra bit of energy. When I finished, I looked over at Quinn and saw that he had, for some reason, crushed his half in his hands and was rubbing in on his face, and then on his chest. "Aw, shit. That feels good," he said, rolling over and laughing on the sand. He then jumped up and sprinted down to the shoreline, ran a few high steps to the deeper water and then dove in. He appeared about fifteen seconds later quite far out from shore. That dude could swim. I followed him down and used some sand and water to scrub the orange peel off my fingertips, and then walked back up and started to pull on my clothes. Quinn was suddenly beside me doing the same. "Let's go find those other guys," he said.

"Yeah, let's do it."

We walked off the beach, out to the parking lot, and started off down the road instead of heading back the way we came. I told Quinn to wait up and ran back to the parking lot. I took off the docksiders and left them right by the opening of the footpath to the beach. I wasn't going to need them for this part of the walk, and someone else might need them if they were going that way, I thought. After all, you can't go back.

It took us well over an hour to make our way to Pete's grandmother's house. We stopped at Quinn's family's house along the way, which was really close to Warren's Point, and stole a six pack of beer from the fridge. The walk was pretty quiet, the both of us winding down from our trip. By the time we got back to Pete's, we were both on our third beer, and I was carrying a six pack with four empty bottles in it. We walked around the garage and through the gate up onto the porch on the far end of the house.

Pete's grandmother was away a lot, and this night was no exception. His room was almost like an apartment, separated from the rest of the house by the garage. Even when she was home, she treated this as his space, and never really came out to his room. She mostly left him alone, even though it seemed she was the person who did the most to raise him.

I left the bottles on the table, tipped back my beer and drained it, and slipped it into the six pack. It looked oddly complete even with the empty place for the sixth beer. I looked at Quinn as he finished his beer. He put the empty bottle on the table and looked at me. I guessed he must have agreed.

Inside, Courtney and Jonas were sitting on the couch, and Pete was sitting on the floor with his back to the fireplace. There was a smoldering fire burning, mostly down to the embers. Jonas was laughing and telling Courtney he was going to lose, which told me they were probably playing gin, which was their favorite game that summer. Pete was intently working away at something on the low coffee table. They all three looked up at us when we came in through the sliding door, which was wide open.

"Oh man, we thought you guys were gone." Jonas said with a big smile. "What happened to you guys?" Courtney smiled like he'd just seen a miracle. Pete looked up at us and smiled as he turned back to his work.

"I knew you fuckers would turn up," he said. A cigarette burned almost down to the filter in his right hand, and in his left hand he held a small knife that he was using to carve a large cylindrical candle, one of those wide ones with three wicks. It was burning, and based on the pool of wax, it had been for some time. I bent down to see what he was up to while Quinn started telling the story of our walk. Listening out of the corner of my ear, it sounded like he was telling a story that happened to someone else. But, then, that was also the case.

Pete looked at me sideways and smiled. He turned the candle so I could see better the face he carved into the dark red wax. It was hard to imagine he started with a simple round candle, the detail and expression of the smiling face was stunning, and the light from the burning wick above seemed to call into high relief every wrinkle around the eyes and mouth of the jester like face he carved there. He continued to carve it, delicately holding the pen knife and wielding it with ease and precision. I squatted down and watched him work for several minutes.

"Now watch this," he said. And he stuck the knife into the mouth of the face and gave it a quick twist. When he pulled it out, hot melted wax poured out of the mouth in a steady stream, running over the teeth and lips, down the chin and then began to pool up on the table. As the wax drained out of the candle the wicks burned brighter and then the wax started to pour off the table onto the carpet by Pete's knee. He put his cupped hand out under the stream, and I saw his face wince slightly and then go taut. Using his other hand, he put the cigarette into his mouth, picked up the candle, turned and tossed it right into the fireplace. It would take me a month to carve something like that, and it would never have looked so nice. It was just like

Pete to make something beautiful and then destroy it. The smoldering fire popped and flared as the wax melted and burned. Pete peeled the wax off his palm and tossed it into the fire as well, which slowly, slowly tampered back down to just a smoldering pile.

He turned to Quinn and said, "that sounds like some walk."

"Yeah, it was."

At this point, it must have been four in the morning. I was well past the peak of my trip, and standing back up I realized my body was feeling tight, my feet sore from all the walking. I slipped back out onto the porch, not feeling much like being inside. There was a pack of cigarettes on the table next to the six pack of empties we left there. I slid one out of the pack and pulled the matches out from where they were tucked into the cellophane packaging. The match flared up bright when I struck it, and I watched as the flame pulled into the end of the cigarette as I lit it. I shook out the match and tossed it away, taking a long drag and looking up at the sky. I exhaled deeply and watched the smoke spread out above my head.

"Some walk you guys had." Jonas said from behind me, echoing Pete's comment.

"Yeah, I guess." It seemed mundane now to talk about it, though it seemed like such an adventure at the time. He gestured at the pack in my hand. "These yours?" He nodded and I pulled one out and handed it to him along with the matches. I saw the flare of the match and the glow of his cigarette and then the trail of red from the match he tossed toward the edge of the porch. I flicked the cigarette towards where he threw the match. I wasn't much of a smoker, but it seemed like the right moment to have lit one up. I watched it make a long red arc through the air, a second one seemed to trail behind the first. I was still seeing trails, somewhere in the middle of the long tail of an acid trip. "I'm gonna go take a shower," I said to Jonas.

"Yeah?" he said. "Yeah," he repeated quickly, "yeah, that sounds good. I'm going to go get into some trouble, I think." That's what he always said when he decided to disappear. It sometimes meant he was going to go find a girl, but a lot of the time he'd just take off and show up later. It was summer, and there were lots of people in town for the season, lots of families and lots of kids. We spent a good deal of time running around with people from around there for the summer, and Jonas probably knew where some might be hanging out, even this late. But you never really knew what he was up to. He gestured again at the pack of cigarettes I was holding, which I handed to him. He walked to the edge of the porch, said "see you in the morning" over his shoulder and then disappeared behind the bushes as he headed towards the road.

I took another look up at the sky, and walked to the other side of the porch, down the two or three steps to the yard, and then around the side of the house to where there was an outdoor shower. I dropped my shorts to the ground, pulled my shirt over my head and went into the stall. Pushing the shower head to the side, I turned on the water and waited for it to warm up a little, which didn't take long. I let the water run over my head, and rubbing my hair I was surprised to feel how salty and even sandy it was. I didn't realize how much of the beach was still stuck there. There was a small, hard piece of soap on the ledge inside the shower stall, and I worked it up into a lather over my body, carefully scrubbing every inch of skin as if I could wash the trip off of my body, cleanse myself of the acid I'd not intended to drop earlier that night. My body had a strung out feeling that I didn't like, and the heat of the water was releasing it a bit, but not enough.

The shower valve squeaked loudly when I shut off the water. I used my hands to rub the water off my body, first my face and head, then my arms, followed by my chest, thighs and calves. The cool night air rushed in to fill the shower stall as soon as the water turned off, and I felt clean and lighter. I was covered in goose bumps. My head was a little cloudy, which I could chalk up to the beer, but I didn't feel drunk. When I looked up in the sky, I could barely see the stars. It was going to be light out soon.

I walked around the other side of the house, carrying my shorts and shirt, and went in through a door by the kitchen where we played cards earlier that night. It was dark and quiet, and I thought about getting a bite to eat, but opted just to drink a big glass of water. I drank it quickly, and I could feel the cold water sloshing around in my empty stomach as I crept upstairs to the small guest bedroom next to Pete's grandmother's room. The bed was made perfectly, with several large fluffy pillows, a deep comforter and stiff cotton sheets that felt cold and rough when I climbed in between them, but then soft and warm as I sunk into the featherbed and became immersed in the thick down comforter over me. I wedged my head between two pillows, lying on my back as if in a coffin, my arms crossed over my chest. My eyes closed almost involuntarily, and I somehow felt the sleep pull me further into the bed, the silence deafening, my ears covered by pillows, my eyes burning under my lids as I slammed into sleep like a car door shut in anger.

It seemed like seconds later when I felt someone jump on top of me, I awoke suddenly and the fierce daylight burned my eyes. Quinn leaned up on one elbow, his face less than a foot from mine, a big shit eating grin spread across his mouth. I let out an unintelligible noise.

"Wake the fuck up, Why. C'mon." He started pulling the covers off me.

"Shit, get off me, asshole." I couldn't tell if I'd been sleeping or what, my rest had been so dark and dreamless.

Quinn cackled. "C'mon, hurry up. Let's go." He jumped up and sprung out of the room. I heard him crashing his way down the stairs. I sat up in the bed, my eyes still adjusting to the light. Not sure how long I slept, I looked for a clock but didn't see one. I slid out of the bed and saw my shorts and shirt where I left them on the wooden chair in the corner. I looked down at my naked body. I yawned.

When I got down to the kitchen, Quinn, Pete and Jonas were all sitting around the yellow table where we sat the night before. I sat down with them, plopping in the seat forcefully. There was a cup of coffee in front of me, and I picked it up and took a sip without thinking whose it was.

"You sure you want to drink that?" Jonas smiled mischievously.

"Get the fuck out of here." I knew there wouldn't be anything slipped in there at this point, but you never really knew with Jonas.

He smiled and laughed. "Don't sweat, Arch. That cup's for you."

"I told you to hurry, didn't want your coffee to get cold, and we gotta get going," Quinn said excitedly. "And Courtney's making waffles."

As if on cue, Courtney dropped a platter full of waffles in the middle of the table, followed by a measuring cup full of steaming syrup. "Oh snap," said Pete, "what're you guys going to eat?" He grabbed a waffle in each hand and put them on his plate, dropped a huge blob of butter in the middle of the one on top, and poured about enough syrup for everyone all over his plate. "Shit, that's good" he said, his mouth full of food.

"Damn," Quinn said, "Courtney, you're the best mom I've ever had." I saw Jonas shoot him a look and they both looked at me and then away.

"Me too," I said, helping myself, not wanting him to feel bad on my account for the joke. Pete laughed and chewed. I wondered what he was thinking.

Courtney loved to make big breakfasts, and he was always good for being up first, or not going to bed at all, making omelets, French toast, waffles or whatever else he could come up with. He liked to take care of people, and we loved his breakfasts. So it all worked out. He sat down at the table, putting a plate of toast down next to the waffles. He took two pieces and put them on his plate. No one else was going to eat the toast.

All through breakfast I felt like there was some plan I wasn't aware of. It was clear everyone else was up all night, so I missed out on something. Quinn seemed to be in a rush, and everyone had their heads down eating. I didn't think much of it. People aren't particularly talkative at breakfast when they haven't slept.

After we ate, we moved as a group without anyone giving directions from the table to the back porch. Quinn, Pete and Jonas lit up cigarettes. Courtney was never much of a smoker, and I really only smoked occasionally. You could tell it was going to be a hot day. There was a thin shield of clouds over the sky, but it was bright. That would all burn off soon enough. Another August day. "C'mon, let's go," Quinn said. He bounded off the porch and walked around the side of the house to the driveway. From where we couldn't see him, his voice carried back to us, "Come *on*, you fuckers."

We all followed behind him, he was sitting in the shotgun seat of Pete's jeep parked in the driveway and was waiting there for us. The gravel crunched under my bare feet. Courtney, Jonas and I squished into the back seat, and Pete hopped in the driver's seat, turning the key that was hanging in the ignition as he sat down in one fluid movement. He pulled out into the street without looking either way, gravel flying out from under the tires, his cigarette hanging casually from between his lips. I leaned forward from where I sat behind Pete, gripping the back of his seat to hold myself steady.

"Where we headed?" I asked.

"Beach," he replied, the cigarette bouncing between his lips as he answered.

I leaned over a little towards Quinn. "What's the rush, Q?"

He answered with a big smile, looking straight ahead, "We don't have many days like this left."

I sat back in my seat and slouched down to avoid the air whipping around. I closed my eyes against the sun and wind. It seemed like a reasonable enough answer.

★★★

The boulevard stretched out ahead of me, and I was feeling more and more comfortable on the little bike. I knew that the long slow downhill ride meant that I'd be making a long uphill trip whenever I decided to turn around. But for now, I was taking Quinn's advice. Sometimes, you just can't go back.

Chapter 8

I am fortunate enough to have had more than my fair share of days where I can wake up and plan the day as I go along. I understand that makes me lucky, although it is also the engine that drove me in no particular direction for quite some time. A few years ago, I woke up one morning and it was exactly one of those days. It was summer. It was hot. I spent a couple of hours fiddling around my apartment, then I got in my car and drove north.

Even though it had been over ten years since I made this drive, it was nevertheless familiar. The wide sweeping curve nestled in a thick evergreen forest as you cross from Massachusetts into the state of New Hampshire. The lazy tollbooth. The exit to the secondary highway, the turn to the tertiary road. The general store, the steep hill and the cemetery at the top of it.

As I turned left onto the dirt road in front of the ancient graveyard, a million images of summer camp flashed through my head. The songs we sang in the camp vans heading to and from the lake, the after-dinner games of capture the flag, the sneaking out at night to dodge counselors and play pranks on other cabins. I remembered my time as a staff member there, up all night drinking underage, losing my virginity in the shower house, chasing campers while on night duty. The dirt road down the hill and through camp seemed shorter to me this time, and as I pulled into the gravel parking lot along the side of the road, I half expected to see myself, a boy, waiting on the steps in front of the farmhouse. I wondered why I drove here.

I got out of the car and stretched. I heard a screen door spring strain as it opened and then snapped shut. I turned around and saw a man in his forties with a scruffy ponytail and a thick beard walking towards me from a building that I remembered to be the nurse's station. I was somewhat in disbelief as the man approached me.

"Ken?"

"Yup," he replied, looking at me from where he stood across the road and on top of a short retaining wall, a stack of three railroad ties. His eyes searched me.

"Ken, it's Archer. Archer Why." I felt ridiculous. I felt like the little kid and teenager that he'd have no reason to remember, having known hundreds and hundreds.

"Archer Why. How the heck are you?" He broke out in a big grin and lumbered off the wall and across the road. Again, I felt awkward when he reached out to shake my hand. I wanted to give him a hug.

"Ah, I'm good," but I didn't sound convinced even to myself. "I guess I just felt like going for a drive." I kicked my toe into the ground, harder than I intended. A small shower of gravel shot towards Ken's feet. I waved away a cloud of black flies that appeared and started to bite my neck. It was futile. A cloud circled his head as well, but his ability to ignore them seemed to keep them away. I tried to ignore my cloud too, but they were still out for blood.

"Not the first time for that," he said, smiling at me. "So you drove here." He stressed the word 'here.'

"Yeah, well I figured camp was over. I thought I'd just drive through. I didn't think anyone would be here." The damn flies were killing me now. And I realized it might have sounded like I was planning to arrive while the place was empty. I still didn't know why I was there.

"Come on up." He gestured to the farmhouse, and I followed him up over the railroad ties, up the stone steps and through the front door.

Why. Me.

This wasn't the first time I showed up there unannounced, Ken was right. The summer after my mom left would have been my first summer not attending summer camp. I was fourteen years old, too old for camp. I spent the first half of the spring wondering if my mom would still take me on her trip, and I spent the second half of the spring and nearly the entire summer knowing it wouldn't happen. Being a kid often means that your days are planned for you. But at certain times of the year, your days are your own. It was my first summer in years that I hadn't gone to camp, and I didn't have a job. I was fourteen and had nothing to do. I'd been running with the guys all summer. Days at the beach, nights up late watching movies, eating junk, smoking a little pot, acting stupid.

One particular morning that summer, with nothing to do, I found myself in the kitchen after my father had already left for work. It had been Courtney's birthday a couple days before, so I happened to know the date and even the day of the week, which was not usual for me at that age in general, but especially not during the summer. I knew it was the last day of camp. I saw my dad's extra set of keys hanging by the back door. I saw the second car parked in the driveway. I saw an opportunity, and without a thought I drove north. I knew every turn by heart. I suppose I was lucky the car didn't need gas because it never once crossed my mind to check, being two years too young to drive and more or less clueless about such matters.

As I drove up the steep hill to the cemetery, turned left and drove down the hill, I watched the steady stream of oncoming cars, looking for familiar faces as they drove away from camp. I pulled slowly into a space in the gravel parking area, stopping suddenly and conspicuously. I stepped out of the car and found myself face to face with Ken, who was seeing off families from this, the central area of camp. I felt sheepish but tried to stand up taller to make myself look old enough to be there.

"Archer Why, who are you picking up?" Picturing his face now, his smile expressed a combination of confusion, concern and care. I stared at the ground and kicked the gravel. I had no idea what to say. He put his arm around my shoulders and walked me with my head hanging low to the office alongside the parking area, a small wood building no larger than a shed. Behind silent tears, I listened to Ken talking on the phone from the bench outside the office where he sat me down.

"…just showed up… seems fine, a little upset…" there was a long pause. Ken was listening. "Don't think there's any way to get here without you having two cars to get back to Providence." Another drawn out pause, "Tell you what," I could see through the screen door that Ken turned and was looking at me, "let him stay the night. We'll keep an eye on him. A few of the staff are driving together back down to Rhode Island tomorrow. I'll have one of them drive your car and Archer instead of catching a ride with someone else." He listened, "I don't think he'll mind, most everyone knows your son from last summer." There were goodbyes and few more reassurances. He hung up, left the office.

"You heard?"

"Yeah, I can stay here tonight." I tried not to sound pleased. "I'm sorry."

"You just keep that in mind. I'm sure you'll be sorrier when you see your dad tomorrow."

I doubted that. This guy, this father of mine. His fourteen-year-old son steals the car and drives three fucking hours away, and he lets him stay the night. Trusts another teenager he's never met in his life to drive him home. It wasn't that I'd never hear the end of it. I'd never hear anything of it. He didn't even ask to get on the phone with me? Come on, be a *dad*. Even at fourteen I knew it wasn't right, this lame ass reaction. This non reaction. But it wasn't that I was testing him on that. That's not why I did it.

But Ken didn't know about all that. "Yeah," I agreed, acting penitent. Inside I was excited to be staying the night here. I hadn't realized how much I missed this place.

I was told to go in the kitchen and get some lunch. I went into the farmhouse, through the small rooms set up with tables and chairs for everyone to eat, and into the kitchen. Jen, the cook, made me up a big plate of bacon, lettuce and tomato and I created a massive, mayonnaise laden, artery clogging sandwich and washed it down with a tall plastic cup of orange drink. She brought me an ice cream sandwich. I enjoyed being babied a little by her. I felt younger than I had in a while. She gave me a big smile. I couldn't tell if she knew the circumstances of my being there, but I milked her kindness.

Just about everyone was gone when I left the kitchen. A handful of kids were playing a last-minute game of kickball and I joined in. Remembering me from last summer, they asked why I was there. I acted old and told them I was just visiting. I felt like they were jealous of me, and, again, I nursed that feeling. One by one, all of their parents came to pick them up, and I was left sitting on the front steps of the farmhouse, just like I sat every summer for half of my life up to that point. Waiting, but this time I was just waiting, and not for anything in particular.

"If you're here, you're gonna have to help." Ken's voice rose over the sound of the screen door slamming behind him. He was leaving the farmhouse behind me, a couple of staff members trailed behind him. In reality, most of the counselors, the maintenance guys and kitchen staff weren't really that much older than me. Some were campers with me only a couple of years ago. I felt young though, but somehow older that I'd be helping out. I followed the lead of a couple guys I liked from previous summers. We covered the lines on the tennis court with lengths of scrap wood, carried canoes into cabins, screwed the plywood shutters down on the screen windows of the cabins, turned the dresser drawers upside down to keep the mice from nesting all winter. Others stacked firewood by the nurse's cabin, which was the only year-round structure, I'd learn years later. Like ants, several dozen staffers swarmed the camp, shutting it down for the winter. At the end of it all, Ken ordered everyone to spread out and each bring him five pieces of trash from the ground. "And you smokers," he said, "bring me ten."

Once that was done, everyone piled into vans and went to the lake. I rode shotgun with Ken in his truck.

"Shoot, I don't have trunks." I was feeling more comfortable now, less nervous about what I'd done.

"Guarantee you that someone will have left some at the lake. I'll bet you." He reached out his hand.

"Bet what?" I smiled.

"Gentlemen's bet."

"Deal." We shook. He won. There were no less than three boys' bathing suits hanging from wooden hooks in the changing house. Everyone got into their suits and jumped in the lake. It was a gorgeous day, not a cloud in the sky. The lake echoed with the shouts of teenagers and young adults horsing around in the water. I couldn't believe how many of them smoked. They did a good job hiding that from us as campers. I jumped in the water, but even surrounded by all of them, I was alone. They were a part of something all summer and I wasn't a part of it. I started to feel foolish for being there.

I got out of the water and dried off in the sun. I entered the changing house alone, changed back into my clothes and hung the bathing suit carefully on the hook where I found it. I sat on a split log bench watching everyone enjoying themselves. Ken came and sat down next to me.

"Can I work here next year?" I asked. "I want to work here."

"How old are you? I don't think old enough."

"How old do I have to be?" I was looking at the staff swimming. Some of them I knew were only a couple years ahead of me in school.

"Sixteen to be on the maintenance crew." That was a glorified term for the guys who cleaned up after everyone all summer. "Seventeen you could be a counselor."

"Oh. I won't be sixteen till right after next summer." I looked at Ken and smiled a smile I figured would be persuasive. "You could round up, I'll be over fifteen and a half." I gave a shit eating grin, sitting up straight to appear taller.

"Hm. Not sure about that, Why." But he smiled and messed up my hair. "Let's get going."

He stood up and yelled over the noise. "Softball at four, troops. Get it together."

Back in the truck, windows down, Ken drove smoothly around the curves in the road. He'd likely driven this road thousands of times, could probably do it with his eyes closed. "Okay Archer, we're going to set you up in the cook's quarters tonight. Jenny's leaving tonight so it'll be empty. I've decided I'm going to let you watch the staff softball game. I'd reckon no one has ever seen that game who hasn't worked here before. But your move today earned you something, I suppose. You'll eat with the staff and then that's it. You're upstairs in the farmhouse, understood?" When Ken decided something, you somehow knew it was a certainty. He wouldn't change his mind. When he said "understood" it was more of a statement than a question.

"Understood," I said.

"The staff have a party tonight, and it's not a thing for someone your age to witness." He chuckled. "Nope."

We went on in silence for a minute or two. I looked out the window. In the silence and surrounded by this scenery, I imagined that I was with my mother. The last day of camp, and she'd just picked me up. Me proud to show her off to my counselor from the summer. We would spend the first part of the drive with me talking and her listening to all my stories of the summer, and then the late days of August would stretch out in delicious silences like these. I closed my eyes and I was with her again. The clean air rushed over my face, my hair danced on my forehead. I expected to hear her voice.

"Why are you here, son?" Ken asked. And that was it.

I broke down in tears. I told him everything. I told him about my mom, about the trips, about her antiques. I told him about how she left, the day she left, the note. I told him about my father, his silence, his absence. I told him about how angry I was, how alone I felt. I told him everything. He had pulled over at some point in my tirade and was looking at me with concern in his deep hazel green eyes. I spent seven summers in his camp under those watchful eyes. I saw him cradle his dog in the throes of a seizure until she relaxed. I saw him handle the injuries kids get at summer camp all in stride, calmly pinching together inches long gashes and carrying young boys with broken ankles to the infirmary. But I don't think Ken knew quite what to make of this. Here I came, one fine August afternoon, to drop my life at his feet. He said something that I would never forget. He said just what I needed to hear before I told him everything. He called me son.

★★★

Watching the staff softball game, I quickly understood why Ken made such an issue of someone watching it who was not a staff member. I'd seen people drink before, and my friends and I had been dabbling in this arena. This, however, was serious drinking. This group was absolutely plastered an hour into the game, and what started out as a fiercely competitive softball game turned into a hilarious mess.

The game over, I was the only sober person during dinner. This taught me two early lessons: being the only sober one in a group is an isolating experience, and people say some really dumb shit when they are drunk. I felt at once invisible and the center of attention. I was asked the same questions by the same people repeatedly. I heard utter nonsense stated with an air of authority. I had beer spilled down my back.

After a couple of burgers and a hot dog, I was lingering near the grill trying to chat with some of the female counselors when I felt a tap on my shoulder. Ken glanced at the farmhouse and tapped his wrist where a watch would have been, if he ever wore one. I caught the drift.

"Sure thing. Good night everyone." No one looked, but I didn't take it personally. Ken winked at me and turned away. I smiled at his back. I was almost to the farmhouse when I heard him call my name from close behind me.

I swung around. "Yeah?" I said, hopeful for something, I don't know what.

"The keys. Why don't you give me the keys?"

"Keys?" I was confused.

"The car keys. I'd like to hold onto those if you don't mind."

It hadn't occurred to me that the keys were still in my pocket. I fished them out and tossed them to him.

"Goodnight Archer."

"Goodnight."

I walked through the back door of the farmhouse which also acted as the door to the kitchen. I walked along the long Formica countertop and into the first dining room. There were cases of beer stacked on the table there. I looked around and grabbed a beer out of one of the six packs. Thinking better of it, I slipped the beer back and grabbed the entire six pack and clambered up the stairs to the cook's quarters without any stealth whatsoever.

It wasn't late, and I wasn't tired. Being it was the end of August and only just after eight, it wasn't even dark yet. Once upstairs, I realized that the beer I grabbed was not twist off. There were two rooms upstairs in the farmhouse, I found out quickly that the one to the left was storage, to the right was a bedroom: the so-called cook's quarters. There was a big bed which turned out to be two twin beds pushed together, a dresser, a rocking chair and a desk. I saw a piece of paper on the desk with a note written on it. I picked it up and read it: *Archer, ballsy move kid. I like your style. Jen.*"

I found it odd that she wrote that note, which I folded and put in my pocket. Rummaging around the desk, I found a lighter and a bag of tobacco, the kind you use to roll cigarettes. I opened a beer using the lighter against my thumb, a trick I learned recently that I was proud to have mastered. I was only fourteen, but this summer brought with it my first drinking experiences. We were a little young for it, and we approached it recklessly, the way teenage boys can do. I polished off that beer very quickly and opened another one. The desk drawers held no more interest. There were a few pens and pencils, a couple of old pictures of people I didn't recognize but in recognizable parts of camp, the tobacco, and a random assortment of sewing instruments, buttons, craft supplies and other garbage. I added my two bottle caps to the mess and closed the drawers. I was bored.

I rolled a bunch of cigarettes, another talent I was proud to master as the boys and I were smoking pot a bit that summer as well. It was only a few months before that when Courtney and I had stared at the incense smoke floating through the afternoon sunlight in my bedroom at home. I lit one of the cigarettes and took a deep drag. It tasted disgusting. Letting the smoke waft up towards the ceiling in the waning daylight, I lay back on the bed and thought about my dad. I wondered how a woman like my mom ended up with a guy like him. How could they have met, decided to get married, had me? Why did she leave, and where did she go? Why didn't he seem to mind, and what the hell was I supposed to do now? I hadn't given myself much time to think about this stuff. In fact, I actively avoided it.

A lot of people say that the high school years are your glory days. They say the same thing about college too. For me, being a teenager sucked. I couldn't wait to get out of my situation, to something. I considered running away. Just saving some money or stealing some stuff from my dad to sell and disappearing. I wondered if I could make it. If I could make it to someplace warm I could sleep outside, panhandle maybe. Could I erase myself from being Archer Why? Would I be able to adopt a new identity, find the people who could make things like that happen? Join some group of homeless wandering teens, or find myself in some great situation, get rich, show up back in Providence to my friends someday and tell them amazing stories about what I'd been up to. Would I find my mom in my travels? Would she have been waiting for me? Would she have known just where to wait for me?

But even at fourteen, I knew I had too much of my dad in me. That type of adventure wasn't for me. I like my home base. I like to take things slow. I think too much about what's happened before and what's happening now. I can't always think about what's next. I knew that even then, on that bed, in that room, in the farmhouse, at camp, somewhere in New Hampshire, where I showed up hoping for something but I couldn't say what.

It was almost dark in the room now. Sitting up, I put the cigarette into the empty beer bottle, and opened a third beer, slipping the lighter in my pocket. I found the switch to the bare light bulb hanging from the ceiling and turned it on. I opened the dresser drawers, but they were all empty. Now I was really bored.

I wandered across the hall and into the storage room. I was hoping for something exciting, and I was greeted by boxes of paper plates and plastic cups, napkins and cases of generic powdered orange drink. There was nothing happening in here. It was almost completely dark at this point; the light from across the hall was the only light into the storage room. There was a window at the far end of the room. I walked over and sat on a cardboard box, looking out into the night. It was darker inside than outside, so I could see pretty clearly. Down the road a short stretch there was a parking lot where the camp vans were usually parked. I could see that a big bonfire was going. A couple male staff members were walking down the road, sort of bumping into each other as they walked, the tips of their cigarettes glowing at the ends of their lanky arms. I could see their long hair coming out from under baseball caps, their cargo shorts hanging on what existed of their skinny hips. A screen door slammed shut to my right and I saw Ken standing outside of the nurse's cabin. He stretched and scratched his stomach. He looked up at the farmhouse and I waved, but I could tell he didn't see me. I could hear him say something and I realized a couple other staff members were walking down the hill from where the cabins were. He was talking to them. They stopped in front of him, but by the time their voices got to me the words were muffled. When they walked away Ken was holding a beer. He looked back at the farmhouse, turned around and went back into his cabin. The screen door slammed behind him.

I waited until it was really dark, maybe another half hour. I started on my fourth beer, had a fifth one jammed in my pocket and was working on a healthy buzz when I slipped down the stairs of the farmhouse. It was eerily quiet in the dining rooms. Thankfully, no one had left any lights on so I didn't have to worry about being seen through the many windows. There was a door at the bottom of the stairs, but that opened to the front of the building, in full view of the road and the entire lower part of camp. I snuck through the kitchen and out the side door, on the opposite side from Ken's cabin and facing a wooded area. I crept to the edge of the trees, but it was dark and I could see that there was no one around. I walked along the edge of the woods and sprinted across the road, around the back of the office from where my father was called, and down into the lower field where I could confidently walk at the base of the hill where no one could see me from above. This was my best bet to get across camp and closer to the fire.

I heard voices coming from the building we called the playhouse. It was clear I couldn't crawl while carrying my beer, so I chugged the second half and jammed the empty bottle in my pocket. I crawled to where there was a bench next to a tree and looked up at the playhouse. I could make out two figures on the porch swing, which was up about fifteen feet from the ground and about thirty feet from where I hid.

Below the porch, I saw a lighted room where I had only ever seen a locked door. This door was the stuff of legends. Because the playhouse was on a hill, the 'basement' of the building, that is, the space under the porch, was only accessible by a single door along the outside of the building that no camper had ever seen unlocked, much less open. There were no windows, no cracks, no way to see into that space. The younger campers were told scary stories about what happened there long long ago, when this place was a farm and before that a campsite for the loggers who worked up on the mountain above camp. Terrifying tales of ghosts who haunted the buildings, of loggers who lost limbs and then their lives, of crazy relatives locked in that room. All the stories were different, all equally horrifying, and all completely successful at keeping most potentially wandering campers in their beds at night. As older campers, we heard rumors that staff members used the space to drink beer, smoke pot, or have sex, or all three at once. We longed for a glimpse of what was there, or at least to learn the truth of that room. What was it? What was behind that door?

And here it was. Through the open door, I could make out several seated figures and hear the commingled sound of laughter and loud talk. A cloud of smoke hovered in the harsh light that poured out of the open doorway. Nothing scary at all. It looked like fun. A male staff member stumbled out of the doorway and walked towards me. I froze up. He stopped about ten feet from me. I could see he was looking up at the sky, and then I could hear him whistling as he peed. I held back laughter, almost unsuccessfully. He turned and walked back through the door. I could recognize him by his silhouette.

I waited there a few minutes, hoping for something more interesting to happen. Nothing did. All that build up, and behind that mythical door was simply a few couches, a refrigerator and what looked like an old toilet that appeared to have been converted for use as an ottoman, or an ashtray, possibly both. I continued my creep. I was emboldened by the four beers I drank, barely making any efforts to conceal myself as I made my way across the open space to the woods on the far side of the playhouse. There was about fifty feet of sparse woods between where I was and the large bonfire, which loomed massive and bright through the trees. I stopped to pop open my fifth beer, and then made my way close to the edge of the trees on the side by the bonfire. The fire was about forty feet from where I stood, but I could feel its heat. I sat down on a fallen tree and concealed myself in the shadows.

The flames seemed to reach all the way up into the black night, the sparks twirling their way upwards joining the stars in the sky above. I had never seen such a large fire. The driftwood fires we enjoyed earlier that summer on the beach in Little Compton which seemed so impressive to us couldn't hold a candle to this one. Some counselors were sitting on a log near the flames, tending to a pipe they passed between them. A few stood in pairs talking or just staring into the huge pile of embers, where you could see thick tree trunks and branches and what seemed to be pieces of the frame of a shed or small cabin. One skinny counselor I remembered from my last summer as a camper was running and skipping around the fire, sweat pouring down his smiling face, his long curls flying out from under his ragged baseball hat.

I was almost done with my beer, and I was feeling drunk. I felt like I was a part of this group. I felt like I belonged here in this place, and I hadn't felt like that much lately at home. There were two counselors sharing a joint pretty close to where I was sitting. I could just saunter up to them and ask for a hit, why not? It couldn't be such a big deal. A popular camper comes up in a stolen car, and that guy knew me from last summer. And the girl smoking with him? She talked to me a bit earlier. What's to lose? Ken is asleep in his cabin by now, he'd never know.

Full of confidence, I stood up from the log and took an off-balance step, stumbled backwards and landed hard on my ass on the tree I was sitting on. Momentum carried me back and I flailed to grab something, spilling beer on my face as the bottle flew from my hand into the woods behind me. I struggled to get back into a sitting position, positive I'd been heard.

The only thing that appeared to have changed was that Ken had come down the road and was approaching the fire, walking almost directly towards me but some distance away. I panicked. I'm not sure how fast I ran, or if I took the best route, or if anyone saw me for that matter, but I soon found myself back in the cook's quarters. Out of breath and feeling a little bit nauseous. I pulled the empty beer bottle out of my pocket and put it in the six pack. I thought about having the final beer, and then thought better of it. I felt sick. I couldn't remember if I turned off the light before I left, or if it was turned off while I was on my excursion. Had Ken come to check on me? I couldn't remember about the light. My head was swimming. At fourteen, five beers was a lot for me. Although I was wearing some of the final beer, and the rest was stranded in the woods over by the bonfire. I grabbed the six pack, stuffed it under the bed and lay down.

Lying down didn't help. I could hear music in the distance, and I tried hard to listen to it, to latch onto it to keep the bed and the room from spinning. That didn't help either. I rolled onto my stomach, grabbing the metal bars of the headboard with my hands to steady the room. I pulled myself up until my back was along the metal headboard, my feet hanging off the edge of the bed. Somehow the uncomfortable metal bar along my back helped. This was better. I slowly slipped into an uncomfortable sleep until I was awoken by loud noises coming from downstairs.

I heard the yelling and cheering of a group of drunken staff members. My mouth felt like I'd been chewing on sawdust or like my tongue needed a shave. How long had I been sleeping? A roar of anticipation bellowed up the stairs and then a loud thump followed by a dull thud, a crash of things falling, hysterical laughter and more cheers. The room wasn't spinning anymore, I got into a more reasonable position and pulled the thin blanket over me. I was chilly. I heard the series of sounds again, the roar of cheers, the thump, thud, crash, laughter and cheers. And then again. The noises seemed to fade as I fell off to sleep. The next thing I knew it was morning.

There was no telling what time it was, but it felt early. It was completely quiet, as silent as things get, really. I sat up and immediately remembered the fear that Ken knew I'd been out. Had he checked on me again after I fell asleep? I reached under the bed, grabbed the six pack with the four empties and one full beer and tiptoed across the hall to stash it in one of the half full boxes of supplies I saw there the night before. I crept back into the room to get my stuff but realized I didn't have any stuff. I also realized I didn't need to tiptoe around. As I walked down the stairs I heard some noises coming from the kitchen, and when I walked in I saw Ken standing by the flat top grill. He was making eggs.

"You're up early," he said.

I tried to play it cool, positive my face would show a hangover. "So are you. What time is it?"

He nodded towards the clock behind him without looking. It was before eight. I couldn't tell if he knew about my adventure, or the beer. I'm still not sure. "You want some eggs?"

"Sure thing."

We ate together in relative silence. I tried to get some information about the noises I heard the night before. "Sounds mysterious," he said mysteriously.

After breakfast, I wandered around the camp. The skinny guy who I saw running around the fire was asleep face down on a van seat by the side of the dirt road. The fire was still smoldering fiercely, a mountainous nest of embers glowing hot beneath a shield of ash. I wondered how long it was going to take to cool down. I spent a minute or two trying to find the beer bottle I dropped in the woods but couldn't figure out where I'd been sitting. I wandered to the back of the playhouse and into the room behind the mythical door. The toilet in the middle of the room was filled with cigarette butts. Disgusting. The dingy couches, the old rattling fridge, the hundreds of bottle caps nailed to the ceiling. The room that alternately mystified and terrified me for half of my youth was basically a frat house basement. I wasn't bothered by it though, just more jealous that my friends and I didn't have such a cool place to chill out.

I sat on one of the couches and tried to imagine hanging out there. I already had boyhood crushes on several of the female staff at this camp. I imagined drinking and staying up late, hanging out with the pretty girls and having the time of my life. The morning passed like this for the next couple of hours. I slowly replaced all my childhood memories of camp with the hope of being there as a staff member. I wandered and envisioned myself working there, the wood shop, arts and crafts, the well houses where the camp's water supply was stored that were up the trails behind the cabins. It wasn't until late morning that camp started to show signs of life. And slowly the place became alive again with talking and laughing, the sharing of vague memories from the night before, scrambled eggs and bacon, gallons of coffee and even some hair of the dog, though Ken made sure no one who was driving later on was drinking that morning.

Yesterday I felt alternately included and on the outside. Now I felt on the fringe again, like an extra in someone else's movie. I just wanted to go home. The fantasies I spent the morning creating seemed dashed to pieces. Ken arranged for one of the counselors to drive my father's car home, and it turned out to be the guy who almost peed on me the night before. I went upstairs to get my stuff, but halfway up the stairs I remembered, again, that I had no stuff. I came back down the stairs and let the screen door slam behind me as I left the farmhouse. It wasn't the first time I walked down those stone steps towards a waiting ride. I felt certain it would be the last.

Ken was talking to the staff member, Jason, by the back of the car. I could see the keys in Jason's hand, and I could see his several bags in the back seat as I approached.

"You ready to hit the road, Why?" he asked.

I looked up at Ken and then at Jason, to whom I said, "yeah, I just have to say bye to Ken." Jason stood there awkwardly until he realized that I meant alone. I felt a little shocked at myself that I managed to be so subtle, yet somewhat direct, in dismissing him.

"Thanks for letting me stay last night." I was still uncertain if he knew about my jaunt to the campfire, but I was feeling slightly more confident that I got away with it. "So, no chance of me working next summer, huh?" He just smiled at me.

★★★

Looking back, if I had to think about one word to describe how he looked, it would be that he appeared wise. I realize that at the time, he was probably only a couple years older than I am now as I ride this little bike across Providence. I've never felt wise in my life, can't imagine I ever will. He still had that look when I saw him after my drive to camp a couple of years ago. Where does the appearance of wisdom come from? Does appearing so make you so?

I once heard a comedian say that it is impossible to look cool when drinking out of a straw. Well, I can add to that the fact that it is impossible to appear wise when riding a kid's dirt bike when you are over thirty. But I wasn't thinking about that as I pedaled along the boulevard in front of me. I was thinking about Ken. And I was thinking about camp. I took a long sweeping turn to my right. The road sloped down in front of me, pulling me downhill into the cemetery at the end of the boulevard.

Chapter 9

It had been a long time since I rode a bike. It had also been a long time since I was in this cemetery, but I remembered it like a nursery rhyme. It was familiar and unforgettable. As kids, we treated it like a backyard, from the koi pond nestled in the middle of the grounds to the spooky old shed in the woods down by the river. We rode bikes and played manhunt, and definitely didn't treat the place with the respect that it deserved. As teenagers, we'd get high and wander around, pondering the people's lives who were buried nearby. It never seemed odd to me to be there. Mark could never understand when I'd tell him how much time we used to spend in the cemetery. For him, that was something you just didn't do. It made me feel guilty. Thinking about it now, I wondered if I should even be here. But I saw someone else riding their bike in the distance and I felt less conspicuous. It got me thinking about Mark though.

For a pair of teenagers, we were in a pretty damn good situation. We were young and now we were both rich and restless. At least Mark was, and I followed suit. Because when Mark was restless, he found things to do. And when he found things to do, good times tended to follow. I never really plugged into any scene during my time in New York. I never really needed to. Mark created his own scene, and I managed to tag along. The things we did were not grand scale. I'd love to say that our youth, energy and money had us rubbing elbows with the rich and famous, that we went to classy places and ate classy food, or that we became venture capitalists and funded the next generation of youthful entrepreneurs. The things we did were nothing quite so interesting. In fact, the things we did were probably not interesting to anyone. Keep in mind, of course, that in the process of finding things to do that were interesting to us, we were also being bombarded with issues surrounding being landlords of the worst type. That is, we had absolutely no clue what we were doing. This annoying fact became abundantly clear during the weeks in which we were in search of the perfect sandwich. During our first winter of property ownership, we finally broke down and hired a property manager to deal with these issues. We headed into spring with one less care in the world. Which technically meant we had no cares whatsoever.

We had full wallets and no responsibilities, and the weather was getting warmer. For some, this would lead to high adventure. For us, we pursued the goal of becoming world class hacky sackers, if such a thing even exists. If you have ever been to Washington Square Park, you may have noticed a group of people who are incredibly skilled at playing hacky sack. You might even wonder if these guys are the best in the world, perhaps champions, again, if there is such a thing. Mark and I got it into our heads that we could practice enough to hang with these dudes. It wasn't just that we liked hacky sack. In fact, I can truthfully say that it is just about the most useless pursuit imaginable. It seemed to us that we had an opportunity to be among the best in the world at something that didn't seem all that difficult.

We were wrong. Dead wrong. Hacky sack is hard, and apparently there is an understood etiquette to the sport which we didn't understand at all. We practiced for weeks on the roof of our building. We perfected a few of the moves we saw performed in the park, and even felt like we made up a few of our own. In the end, all that effort didn't matter one bit. Despite the fact that the circle of folks who play hacky sack in Washington Square Park is relatively small, we stayed away from lower Manhattan for a couple of weeks after our first attempt to play with them. It was humiliating, to say the least. We didn't let it get us down though, and we began considering our next project.

I tell that story so that I can tell you this: we had begun to get bored. Our fast track knocked us off the normal track for people our age; we stopped doing other things that were meant to move at a slower pace. The type of things that a lot of young people go through. Typical development. The slow dissipation of financial reliance on family. The evolution of a sense of self outside of the place where you grew up. Developing friendships with people you didn't know your entire life. College. In the excitement generated by what amounted to incredible luck, we removed ourselves from just about everything. When the initial excitement settled, when our silly escapades wore out and what got us up in the morning was trying to perfect our ability to kick a bean bag around, we began to get bored.

Very few things continued as normal. The only usual event in my life was getting up routinely at seven o'clock and making myself tea and breakfast, usually a bowl of soup. It was summer, and it was hot. I was used to hearing Mark rise an hour or two or more after I finished eating, so I was surprised when around ten in the morning he came barging through the front door. I figured he was still sleeping. He looked like he was surprised to see me, which was strange since it was him who was out of the routine.

"Morning, shithead. I thought you were asleep. Where were you?"

"I got a bike." He seemed out of breath. When he was excited he always seemed out of breath.

"A bike."

"Yeah, a bike."

"Where is it?"

He looked behind him. "Oh," he jumped back into the hallway and came back in, rolling the bike beside him. I looked it over.

"That's sweet." I wondered why he decided to get a bike. It seemed strange to me that he did it without telling me. I can't say that I was upset, though. I couldn't imagine riding a bike in the city. Providence was nothing like New York. "Sweet bike," I said again, feeling awkward.

"Yeah. I've been thinking about this, wanting to get one. I see these guys in Manhattan. Those bike messenger dudes. I think I can ride like those guys."

"You want to be a messenger?"

"No, I just want to ride like those guys. It looks like fun. I saw one of them hanging on the side of a garbage truck going down Eighth Avenue. They must have been going like fifty. I swear the driver knew the guy was hanging on too." He was crouched down and fingering the derailleur by the back gear. "I never rode much as a kid, but I'm going to."

There is one detail about him that I don't think I've mentioned. He was fearless. He was not reckless and he didn't have a willful disregard for safety. He was just like one of those mules you hear about on the Grand Canyon who don't fall because they don't consider it an option. He just seemed immune to being afraid.

"You won't catch my ass on a bike in the city. I saw one of those dudes just about get killed by a cab by Union Square the other day."

"Did he get hit?"

"No, he almost got hit…"

"But he didn't." He grinned at me. That friggin grin. The one that I'm sure got him away with everything as a kid. The one that got him extended due dates on term papers. The one that got him the number of whatever girl he wanted to talk to.

"Hey, have fun my man."

"Don't be a sore sport, Arch, this one's yours." He grinned again and rolled the bike towards me. I grabbed it clumsily. He went out in the hall and came back in with a second bike. He hopped on it and swerved past me, turning around the couch and crashing into the table. He laughed hysterically from where he landed on the floor. "Ah fuck, I think I broke the chair. And my finger." He was quiet for a second. I looked at the bike I was holding. I knew I must have looked like I was carrying an alien I felt so awkward with the thing. "Oh shit," he yelped from the floor, "did you know it's been exactly a year since we bought this place?"

I tried to get on board with the whole bike riding thing, but I just couldn't get comfortable with it the way Mark did. If I could get myself to Flatbush, I could ride with traffic, in panic the entire time, to Prospect Park where I could ride more comfortably. He wanted to go the other direction, over the bridge and into Manhattan. I'd ride the Brooklyn Bridge with him and then watch him disappear into Chinatown before turning around to head home. I liked the bridge, even though it was sometimes too crowded for comfort. In the early morning on Sundays it was pretty quiet and I'd fly back towards Brooklyn. The air would sometimes feel salty and fresh, especially on the cooler summer mornings, and it reminded me of the morning air in Little Compton. With the second half of the bridge almost to myself and the river, deep and lazy, below me, I would ride fast and hard and let the wind push tears out of my eyes.

Faster and faster, and I'm pedaling in the cemetery again, along one of the long straight roadways towards the north end. The tears drying out in the corners of my eyes as the wind beats my face. The road ends ahead of me and I keep pedaling until it seems like there's not enough room to stop. I grab the brake hard and come to a skidding stop right in front of Quinn's gravestone.

I'm staring at his stone, but I'm not thinking about him. I'm not thinking about the news that brought me back from college just weeks after I left. Not thinking about the shock of hearing one of your best friends fell to his death from a second story porch during a college house party. Not thinking about the rain that poured during the weekend when we tried to figure out how to mourn that loss. The rain that drenched me just feet from where I now stood panting on this rusty old bike. I was thinking about Mark. I was thinking about him and his bike. I was thinking about the phone call from his parents, distraught on a Sunday morning calling me at home where I was relaxing after returning from escorting him over the Brooklyn Bridge that morning. The confusion over why they called me first. Why I had to be the one to go downtown. To the city morgue. To identify his body. Why me?

I looked down at the bike I was holding. It looked tiny in my adult hands. I never felt so old in my life. The details of why they called me were pretty simple. They were abroad, but I've blocked out where. The only relatives they had weren't local anymore. They explained to me when they got back to New York that Mark never had any good friends, and that made them feel like I was the most special person in the world to their only son. The son they would now never see again. The son they lost while he was riding his bike. That god damn bike. That was why they called me. That was why I had to be the one. That was why they asked me to speak at his funeral. That was why they gave me full ownership of the other half of the property we owned together. And that, I assume, was why I never heard from them again.

★★★

In many ways, my life has been very easy. I'm lucky to have money, the kind of money that doesn't really run out when you live like I do. That's one thing I've never had to worry about. I have a core group of close friends. I had a dad who didn't treat me poorly, and a mother who loved me and showed it for a number of years. No one ever beat me. I was never a victim. I got the long straw in a lot of ways, but life has been confusing for me nevertheless. I'm lucky to have had the time to think about it and to try and figure things out, and I'm privileged enough to have not bothered doing so for quite some time. You know what they say about the unexamined life. I was heading on that path for a long time. I'm doing better now.

Memory is funny, and sometimes a strong one just pops into your head for no discernible reason. It was just such a sudden memory that sparked me to drive north a couple years ago, once again to New Hampshire even though I wasn't really sure why. That day, before I had a chance to get out of bed, I was flooded with images from a specific trip with my mother. Those antiquing trips held days full of curiosity and adventure which were punctuated by periods of self amusement. My mother taught me as much by talking to me as by forcing me to be alone. It was the end one of those days that found me standing idly on the rickety porch of a small-town Maine antique shop. The sun was dropping low in the sky. From where I stood it was going to set behind the trees on the far side of a dusty lot across the street from the porch where I was standing. The store was really an old house, and I wondered if the man inside might live upstairs. I could remember him from our visit the year before. He was a large, round man, with thick hairy forearms, a dense mustache and gentle, deep, blue eyes.

I was instructed to wait on the porch, and while waiting, I found games to play to entertain myself. The floorboards on the porch ran perpendicular from the house. I walked sideways with my feet placed carefully along each floorboard until I found myself at the opposite side of the porch. I went back the other way. I placed my feet across the floorboards and carefully trod from one side of the porch to the other, placing one foot's heel just touching the toe of the other until I walked the length of the porch. Back and forth, I walked this way sideways, this way skipping a board between each step, then skipping two. I learned to keep myself busy with games like this.

At a final crossing, I stopped in the middle of the porch and turned to face the front door. My feet fitting evenly within one floorboard, I walked heel to toe towards my shadow ahead of me, balancing as if on a tightrope. It had been quiet on the porch, but it was when I walked through the open front door that the silence became louder. Looking up, I saw my mom and the proprietor looking at me. She with those chestnut eyes, he with those blues. It was the kind of silence that seems to provide its own gravity, the kind of silence that children know is for them. Feigning play, I about-faced and found myself back on the porch, sitting on the steps watching the golden sun disappear between the evergreens in the distance.

A group of children about my age were gathered in the lot across the street. I could tell without hearing them they were picking teams. One kid went to that side. One kid to the other. I watched until they got to the last pick. He was a skinny kid, dark hair poking out from under a blue cap. He shuffled to the team that didn't even need to call his name. I wondered if the team felt stuck with him, or if he felt stuck with them.

I hadn't thought about that day in a long time, but when the images poured into my mind, it all seemed to have happened just days before: the floorboards of the porch, the looks on their faces, the kid in his blue cap. It struck me kind of funny even after all those years, and so I got in the car and drove. After a couple hours of driving and a somewhat awkward roadside conversation, I found myself following Ken into the farmhouse. About six inches taller and some fifteen years older than the day I arrived in my father's stolen car.

The screen door of the farmhouse slapped shut behind me, and the stairs to the cook's quarters loomed ahead of me. I flashed back for a moment to my mad scramble up those stairs on my last impromptu visit to camp.

Once in the kitchen, Ken offered me a drink. We sat down at the dining table on the porch alongside the kitchen, each with a plastic cup of iced tea. The benches felt much lower than the last time I sat there. I remembered sitting right here eating eggs the morning after the staff party, the uncertain feeling that Ken knew I was traipsing around the night before, the transition from feeling like I belonged to feeling once again like an outsider. The excitement with which I greeted Ken's phone call the following spring, inviting me to work at camp a summer earlier than expected. I took a long gulp of iced tea. It was unsweetened and delicious, and it made me hungry when it got to my stomach. I hadn't eaten since early that morning.

"What brings you up here today? It's been a long time." He looked curious but not concerned.

"I guess I have a few things to take care of. Trying to put some things to rest, I suppose." I realized I sounded unsure of myself, noncommittal. I was tapping my fingers on the table, sort of uncomfortable.

"Something to do with this place?" He looked around at the dining room, but I knew what he meant.

"No, no. I don't know. Nothing to do with here." I looked at Ken, directly in the eyes. "I just woke up with the itch, I guess." He looked back at me calmly. That was one thing about Ken. If he was angry, concerned, amused, whatever, his expressions were always muted. He had aged a bit since the last time I saw him. The fine wrinkles around his eyes from long summers in the sun had grown deeper. His blondish hair appeared much lighter and seeing him closer showed that there were a number of gray strands responsible for that. His eyes, sometimes hazel sometimes green, were clear and that was where you could tell his emotions. That and his eyebrows, whose subtle movements betrayed his emotions if you knew how to read them. His face expressed a concern and confusion. The last time I showed up here so unexpectedly, I acted casual and then broke down to him. I'm sure he wondered what would happen this time.

It was over a decade since my last summer at this camp, and a million things had happened since then. Over iced tea and some sandwiches, I tried to explain to Ken what had been going on with me for the past ten years. I talked about Quinn and college, a little bit about the money, the buildings I'd owned and about Mark. I struggled to provide details for the years following his death, and my own realization that I missed out on participating in my own life. That I somehow hadn't heard the signal that it was time to start. I talked about my job and that I was trying to get life started and that it was hard to do. A lot happened, yet nothing was happening. I trailed off.

We moved into the kitchen during the conversation, and we were sitting on stools on opposite sides of the counter while we ate our sandwiches. Ken wore the same expression as when I started. But then he smiled.

"So you drove here," he said, again stressing the word here.

"Yup. Here." I smiled too, feeling more comfortable for some reason.

It was Ken's turn to talk, and he did. I don't think I ever heard him speak so much. He talked about the history of the property on which we sat. It had been a farm and then a summer home before his grandfather bought the property and turned it into a camp. He talked about growing up here in the summers, about what buildings were there originally and about which ones he had seen built. He talked about the decision to work at the camp as an adult and his decision to buy the camp from his father. He talked about kids and staff members who had come and gone, about his wife who he married a few years back, a teacher named Laurel who worked a few towns over. I looked down at his hand. I hadn't noticed the addition of a wedding ring.

"So we finished winterizing the nurse's cabin, and we are here full time now. The first winter was tough, but we've figured out how to make it work." With that, he was finished talking.

We walked out the back door of the kitchen to where an old hand pump was located. I asked if it still worked and he said it had been a while since he checked. I pumped the wooden handle up and down, up and down and felt the pressure building as I did so. A trickle started and then water gushed out of the pump onto the bed of rocks below. We both laughed. I cupped my hands under the water and splashed a double handful into my face. The water was freezing. I cursed and laughed again. Ken was smiling at me with his eyes, his expression once again muted. The handle moved up and down on its own a couple more times and the water decreased to a trickle, then a drop and then nothing. I pushed the water off my face with my hands and wiped them on my legs.

"Oh man, that's cold!" I said.

"It's deep down," he said. "It has been there a long time."

I didn't know if he meant the pump or the water. I just nodded.

"I should probably get on," I said, pulling my phone out of my pocket to see that it was very late in the afternoon.

"Put some things to rest." It was more of a statement than a question.

"I suppose that's right."

"Well good luck with that, Archer." He reached out to shake my hand, and I realized he didn't plan to walk me back to my car. Which was fine.

"Thanks," but I wasn't thanking him for the luck he wished me. "I mean, thanks for being here."

"I'm always here," he said, stressing *here* for the third time.

"Right. Well, thanks for the talk. I'm glad I came through."

"Me too, me too. Stay in touch, Archer, I'd like to know how things turn out." He was still grasping my hand, firmly. "I mean it. You always were in touch with this place," he said, gesturing with his left hand, "you should keep it that way."

I left camp along the dirt road going the opposite way from which I came. As I bumped along the rocky and rutted road I thought about what Ken said about being in touch, and I realized he was right in a way. Camp had been there all along, not much changing. It felt like a home base, untouched and unfazed by all the things that happened everywhere else. I decided I would make an effort to stay in touch with Ken, since staying in touch with the place didn't require much effort at all.

I felt myself getting further from the safe feeling afforded by camp. The dirt road changed to pavement and I was able to accelerate a bit. I knew I'd entered Maine when I saw the tattered wooden sign that read: You've just left Freedom.

★★★

It was a slow and peaceful ride out of the cemetery and back along the boulevard, but a long hard slog getting back up College Hill, as expected. Once arriving at the top, I was able to coast for a stretch before arriving at Prospect Park. This is one of my favorite places in Providence. It's a small park, and there is really nothing to do there but sit and enjoy the view. I used to sit here for hours and read or just watch the skyline. I coasted into the park and stopped alongside one of the benches. I hopped off the bike, leaned it against the bench and sat down.

The park is really just a big lawn, with a few trees, some crisscrossed paved pathways and a few benches facing a wrought iron fence. There is a large drop off on the other side of the fence, which gives you a vantage point over all of downtown Providence and beyond. Enjoying the view with you is a giant statue of Roger Williams. The founder of Rhode Island gazes west with one hand stretched forward and one foot in front of the other, seemingly in stride. I'm not sure the meaning of this statue, but I have heard that his remains are entombed below it. That always seemed odd to me, and I never really believed it.

A few benches over, maybe twenty feet away, three teenage looking boys were also sitting down. I could tell by their body language and their glances over at me that they were huddling together in the effort of rolling a joint without being seen. I found myself staring at them, remembering that as kids we discovered very early that this park was the worst for getting high. Once observed by any authority, there was simply no place to run. These guys hadn't learned that yet. They noticed I was looking at them, and I saw rapid movements that made me think they were trying to quickly pack up their efforts. I caught the glance of one of them and threw up a peace sign and smiled at him. I looked away to show him I wasn't interested in what they had going on.

I had been sweating at the top of the hill but I began to cool off. I kept my sweatshirt on, and stretched out my legs, which were tired. I hadn't ridden a bike in years. The sun was on its way down, but it still had time to go. I closed my eyes.

★★★

I have always had a way with directions, so it was no trouble making the proper turns, recognizing the landmarks and signs that brought me to the place I was going as I left Freedom after my long conversation with Ken. When I pulled up in front of the antique shop, my heart was pounding. When I saw the sign hanging that said *Open for Business*, my hands were shaking. I walked up the stairs, noticing my foot was now the width of a board and a half when I stepped up onto the porch. The screen door was closed and it squeaked when I opened it, the way screen doors squeak in northern New England. An old bell rang as I opened the door, and I helped the screen door close quietly behind me. My eyes slowly adjusted to the dimly lit interior. It was very quiet inside.

"I'll be right with you," someone called from somewhere in the house with a thick Maine accent.

I looked around the front room of the shop. It looked like nothing had moved in years. The tops of the tables and chairs were wiped clean, but the legs betrayed their time there with a layer of dust. I fingered the handles of a roll top desk I recognized as a reproduction. The work was of high quality. The place was piled high with items. Lanterns and mirrors hung on the walls. Old milk bottles, baskets and metal signs crowded the shelves. Narrow pathways twisted around chairs and tables, desks and sideboards. I wandered into the second room of the shop and then back to the front room when I saw that the proprietor had entered from the other direction.

He smiled from underneath his thick mustache, now pretty much all salt and no pepper. His thick forearms folded over his large stomach. I noticed the bottom edge of a tattoo on his upper arm poking out from under his shirt sleeve. His blue eyes were piercing.

"Can I help you with anything?"

My hands were sweating. Why the hell had I come here? What was this all about? "Oh, nothing, just looking." I pretended to be interested in the desk I was standing in front of.

"You've picked a newer piece," he said. I was glad he wasn't trying to pass it off as antique.

"I noticed that. It stands out in here," I waved my hand at all the other antiques.

"I had a desk like it when I was a boy. I built this one. Didn't come out as I remembered mine. So I'm selling it." He spoke in short sentences punctuated by hard pauses. His accent was textbook Maine.

"You made this?" He nodded. "It's really nice." I opened one of the drawers and pretended to look at the joint work. I wasn't lying about it being nice, but I felt like I was full of shit.

I looked back at him and he was staring at me, his arms still folded. We made brief eye contact. "I'm Oliver," he said. "Oliver Martin."

"Archer," I said. "Archer Why." We shook hands. My hand felt like a child's hand in his fist. My skin like a baby's in his rough palmed grasp.

"She hasn't been here." He said plainly as we released our handshake.

"What?" I looked him in the eyes. "What?" I was stunned.

"If you came here looking for Eloise. She hasn't been here. Not in years."

I was silent, completely floored.

163

"You remember me?" I finally asked.

"Oh yeah. I remember you out on that porch. Walking back and forth doing God knows what. I remember you." He gestured toward the door off behind me. He remembered?

"I didn't think she'd be here. Or been here." I stuttered. There was a long, solid pause.

"Why'd you come then?"

"I don't know." I shrugged, my eyes darting around.

There was a long pause. "Well, it's been some time since I've heard from her. Don't know where she is either."

"How did you know her?" I asked.

"She was a good customer." His eyes betrayed nothing. So that was it?

"A good customer."

"Yup." He folded his arms again. They nestled comfortably together over his belly.

"Oh." I didn't know what I'd come for, but it wasn't this. I hadn't let myself hope for more, so if this was it then so be it. She was a good customer. That was it. I looked him in the eye for as long as I felt comfortable. I looked back at the desk and closed the drawer. For some reason my head felt full of helium, as if it was going to pull the rest of my body off of the ground. The floating sensation was followed by a quick grip of panic that felt like the start of a bad acid trip. I took a deep breath. A good customer.

I wasn't worried about being rude when I left the store, allowing the screen door to smack the frame as it swung closed behind me, the bell ringing wildly. I looked across the street where the dusty lot once offered late day solace to bored kids all those years ago. A long low building was in its place. A narrow porch with a railing lined the front of the building. The several doors with several mailboxes provided evidence that it was an apartment building. The white paint peeled at the edges, a shutter hung slanted, the whole building looked dilapidated. An orange and black "For Rent" sign was hanging crooked in one of the windows. It didn't seem that long since I was here last. I wondered how this building could have been built and allowed to rot in such a short period of time.

Chapter 10

I could smell the pot from the guys a few benches down. It smelled sweet and it reminded me of being younger. I haven't smoked in a long time. It became an unnecessary escape, and besides that, it started making me too paranoid. I glanced over at them, but they were lost in their activity. I looked behind me, hoping the police weren't going to drive by. These guys were dead in the water if that happened. I was enjoying the smell while I watched the sun slowly approaching the horizon. I like a good sunset. The finality of it is very appealing. The mystery of an overcast morning is fine with me. I don't mind being unsure of when something begins, but I like knowing when it ends. The air was crisp, more like the air during autumn than spring.

I spent a month sitting around in a stupor after Mark was killed. I didn't know what to do with myself. Friends from home, acquaintances from college, people who we met a couple times, even my father, everyone was calling and calling. I'd stare at the numbers on the screen of my cell phone, and let it buzz and buzz. My voicemail box must have filled up, because after a while it stopped telling me I had new messages after the phone finished vibrating. And then the battery ran out, and it didn't tell me anything. I spent a month like that. Ordering food for delivery. Dumping my trash down the chute became my only venture out of the apartment, and that was only after I discovered a two-week-old container of egg drop soup on the floor next to the couch. Disgusting.

I was disgusted with myself. Disgusted that I hadn't showered in days. Disgusted that I owned this entire building, and the one next door. Disgusted at the memory of the morning he died. That I didn't have the stones to ride with him into the city. Things might have worked out differently.

I woke up one morning in the middle of August. It was rainy and dreary, and I happened to catch sight of myself in the mirror as I walked to the bathroom. I turned and looked at my reflection. I looked greasy. My hair stuck flat to one side of my head and stuck up in stringy clumps on the other. My boxer shorts were ill fitting, and my once white undershirt looked gray in the pits. I had a few weeks' worth of stubble on my face, which isn't much as my beard grew in pretty scrappy in those days. It was summer, but I was pale as a ghost. I looked a sight. I could almost hear Mark's voice. "What the fuck, Why? You look like a fucking pedophile or something. Get your shit together."

It wasn't like a bell went off. It wasn't like I heard him speak to me from the grave, or that I had some profound life changing moment. I simply realized that I was pathetic, and that it wasn't going to change unless I made it change. So I showered. Then I shaved. I cleaned out the fridge. I took all my dirty clothes and sheets and towels to the cleaners; the first time out of the apartment in weeks. I went to the grocery store on the way home and bought fruit and vegetables, some yogurt and milk. Mangos, bananas, broccoli, a few heads of lettuce and a pineapple. My insides needed cleaning too. I swept, mopped, scrubbed the bathroom, threw out bags and bags of trash, took another shower. I started to feel better.

I spent a week trying to figure out what to do next. For almost two years, Mark interested me in a steady stream of random activities and projects. I never had free time like the time I suddenly had, and my creativity was a distant, distant runner up to his. It hit me that I needed something to really keep me busy. Like full time busy. I had enough money coming in as a landlord, and I didn't have much to worry about in that department as I had essentially no housing costs, no car, no bills to speak of. But I remembered the day Mark pounced into our dorm room and announced he found us jobs. I became determined to find a job for myself. I couldn't think of anything else more creative than that. It didn't prove to be an easy task at all.

I had a year of liberal arts education. Four times that much and I'd still likely be unqualified for the vast majority of interesting jobs. Getting a call back for something as simple as bar backing seemed impossible. I spent my mornings with a phone and a newspaper, and the afternoons navigating websites that promised to connect me to employment. No luck. The few people I was able to speak to on the phone knew right away I had no direction. I was too curious about details, I can tell as I look back, and no drive for the job itself. I was no less pathetic than when I spent my days wandering my apartment in scrubby boxers and an old undershirt, but I certainly felt productive. At least I was showered.

On a crisp September morning, I settled down with a cup of coffee and a newspaper for my morning ritual. As an addendum to my efforts at job hunting, I was also trying to learn to brew a good pot of coffee. This morning's batch was better than the day before, but still gross. For some reason that I never figured out, when I make coffee it is either gritty and too strong or watery and flavorless. That morning was no exception. I was lying on the couch with my feet up, a paper expertly held in my left hand, my coffee in my right. Without really paying attention to what I was doing, I reached to my side to put the coffee down and managed to rest half of my mug in thin air off the edge of the coffee table. I realized what I did when I heard the mug land on the floor.

"Ah shit." I leaned off the couch and instinctively started to wipe up the coffee with the newspaper in my other hand. I looked at the mess I made of the classifieds.

"Ah shit!" I said again. "Dammit."

I jumped up, ran to the kitchen, realized I had no paper towels and ran to the bathroom for a towel. When I got back to the couch I pushed the table to the side, and started trying to clean up my mess. The coffee was pooling under the couch, so I pushed it back, unveiling the pool of awful coffee. And a hacky sack. I left the towel on the puddle of coffee and picked up the sack like it was some sort of foreign object. I rolled it in my palm and tossed it in the air. A short burst of laughter escaped, and I felt my eyes well up. I took a deep breath and sat on the couch, still looking at the object in my hand. I looked at the wad of coffee stained newspaper on the table and back at the sack. I can't believe anyone could get choked up on a hacky sack.

It had been months since our foolish attempt at hacky sack stardom, and it had been some time since I was on the roof of my building. The air that morning was clean and still. It was still early, before nine o'clock. It was a beautiful morning, not a cloud in the sky. This was years before determining that I prefer rainy mornings, and I was happy I found the hacky sack and happy it was nice out. I tossed the sack up into the air and kicked it out of control away from me. I laughed out loud.

Running across the roof to where it landed, I tried again, this time managing to keep it in the air for a few kicks. I started trying some of the tricks Mark and I managed to perfect. I paused the sack on the top of my foot and then tossed it back up into the air to myself, I jumped up and kicked the ball with the inside of my foot from under my opposite thigh. I hit it with the outside of my foot in a giant arc over my head to the outside of my other foot. I was on a roll. I was laughing out loud, out of breath. After a particularly disastrous attempt at a trick move, I found myself on my hands and knees reaching under the rooftop air conditioning unit when I heard a far-off rumble that sounded like thunder. It was sunny. It didn't make sense.

There are no words to describe the feeling that pulsed through my body when I stood up and turned around. There were no thoughts, there was no awareness of self. Time seemed to stop. It wasn't until the second plane hit that I noticed the smell that surrounded me and that there was smoke burning my nose and throat. That hot chunks of ash were falling all around me. I'm not sure if I was crying before, but tears burned my eyes and slid down my cheeks.

I snapped out of my momentary reverie. It had been a long time since I thought about that morning. The sweet smell of burning marijuana was gone, and a warm late summer morning was now a warm spring evening. The sun in the clearest of skies was halfway below the horizon. The three boys, now stoned, were playing Frisbee on the lawn behind me. Given its position in the sky, I could look directly at the sun. But it was only when I looked away and then back at it that I could track its progress. I was happy no tall buildings were in the way. I was happy there were few tall buildings at all. I was thinking about the day, thinking about the night and thinking about the night before. Courtney's party was a lot of fun. I leaned forward on the bench and looked down through the railing. I could see the roof of his building, where Pete and I enjoyed a couple of beers earlier that morning, and where he shocked me with admission that there were, in fact, things that worried him. That he was always worried.

I was surprised I wasn't more tired given I lost an hour of sleep. But then I remembered that I didn't change my clock, and therefore didn't lose an hour. The sun was setting, so I had to be at work in about fifteen minutes, for six o'clock. Something was off though. I'd been getting to work right after the sunset, and the sun was setting. What was wrong with that? The time changed; that's what was wrong.

I jumped up and turned around. The Frisbee boys were the only ones there. I raised my hand to get the attention of one of them to ask the time. The one with the ponytail looked over at me, his eyes glazed. He smiled and threw the Frisbee to me. The four of us watched as it floated over my head, over the fence behind me and down to the street far below. I looked back at them.

"Sorry, I just needed the time." I smiled sort of sheepishly, pulled my cell phone out of my pocket to confirm to myself that I was about forty-five minutes late for work. "Sorry." I repeated. I hopped on my bike and took off as fast as I could go on that little dirt bike, leaving the three boys idle and Frisbeeless.

★★★

Of all the useless pursuits that I've engaged in throughout my life, Frisbee is not one of them. Hacky sack, we covered that. Doodling. Air guitar solos. Engaging in a pastime that doesn't require your brain gives it the time off necessary to focus more clearly on meaningful things, such as analyzing every detail of your life to figure out exactly where you went wrong. Or remembering where you left your keys. I suppose that means, technically speaking, that a useless hobby is actually useful. But whatever.

There is one such hobby which I've had throughout my life. It isn't one which I pursue with great passion, but it is one which holds quite a fond place in my heart. Bowling. And not just any type of bowling. Duckpin bowling. This is a rarity, it turns out, in the grand scheme of the sport. Duckpin bowling apparently doesn't exist throughout the country as other, more ubiquitous forms of bowling do. Alleys offering duckpin are pretty much only found in the northeast, with a few random outposts here and there. The ball is small, the size of a shotput, sort of like the ball in candlepin bowling. But the pins are shorter and squatter. You get three turns to knock all the pins down, instead of two. The rumor I've heard is that no one has ever officially documented a perfect game of duckpin bowling. There aren't many games in this world that can be played perfectly but have never been. I enjoy knowing that. It keeps the dream alive.

Having grown up just a few miles from a duckpin bowling alley meant that I didn't realize this was such a rare treat. We went regularly as kids, our parents taking turns bringing us before we could get to places ourselves. Later we would ride bikes there to play occasionally, and once driving we would go there for laughs and to have an excuse for reeking like smoke. This was a bowling alley like none I have ever seen anywhere else.

From the street, it was a tiny building. I'd guess it is about twenty feet by twenty feet, and that is a generous estimate. How does one fit a bowling alley in such a small building, you might wonder when seeing the sign out front? Well, when you walk in the back door from the large parking lot, you are greeted with nothing but a simple staircase, which you will descend. While making your way down these stairs, you are welcomed by a cloud of smoke, the strong smell of a deep fryer, and the familiar and calming sound of bowling balls rolling smooth over polished hardwood followed by the thunderous crash of the ball smacking wooden pins. The grind of gears, and the sound of metal rubbing metal as the ancient equipment arranges pins, clears deadwood, and sends the balls rolling almost silently back along metal and rubber tracks to the bowlers. You have entered the Bowl-a-rama.

Of course, nowadays the smoke is gone, the remaining smokers banished to the parking lot. And the deep fryer smell isn't quite so strong. But the effect is the same. And what is still there are the sounds of bowling, familiar, predictable and comforting. Almost sedating. In addition, this alley still has the original scoring tables, where you are required to manually enter your score on a piece of thin paper resting over the glass table top, which is then projected on a screen above your lane. None of that automatic scoring, no animated pins on a plasma screen above your head. This was the real thing. Nothing silly about it. And then there was the sponge.

Built into each scoring table was a rectangular dish made of metal. It was the shape and size of a standard sponge. Each table had a sponge, and each sponge was kept wet. The purpose of the sponge is to wet your palm. After doing so, you hold your hand over the small vent by the ball return that was always blowing a stream of air. The air would dry the wetness, leaving your palm slightly sticky, allowing you a better grip on the ball, and therefore more speed and more control. I always imagine that these sponges were here for years, perhaps since the alley opened. That would mean that every person who ever bowled here had rested their hands on this sponge. This sponge which was kept moist and at room temperature, possibly for decades.

I have very distinct memories of coming here as a child, and the handful of times I was here with my mother I recall her making sure that I washed my hands thoroughly before eating, never allowing me to pick at a basket of fries or to eat popcorn or anything while in the middle of a game. I suspect that she, as I do now, considered those sponges a festering pool of germs and funk. Possibly infected with the plague or worse. But man, could you ever get a grip on those balls with such a nicely sticky palm.

As a bowler, I'm no fanatic. If I had to compare myself to anything, it is sort of like the religious person who goes to church once a year, to pray or confess or whatever. It isn't that this person doesn't have faith, it just isn't his routine to attend all the time. I bowl once or twice a year, and I get something out of it in a weird way. Like I said, it frees up your mind for more valuable pursuits.

So, naturally, I had to introduce Chance to the sport. It had been a long winter, and the evening I chose was a cold one. Daylight savings time would be starting in just a few weeks, and Chance and I met the last time it ended. We spent a lot of time with one another over the course of the winter, which was unreasonably cold and snowy. Since our unseasonably warm visit to the beach the previous fall, it was rare for more than a day to go by where we didn't speak or see each other. I wouldn't say things moved fast. That isn't typically my style when it comes to getting to know people, and she was busy with school. But things were progressing, and progressing well.

And so that is how it was when we went bowling together for the first time. We slogged our way through the slushy parking lot, into the tiny building at the front of the lot, and down the time worn stairs. The threadbare carpet soaked with melted snow and etched with the white lines of dissolved road salt. We entered the alley.

"We're under the parking lot," Chance remarked, ever the architect, wide eyed at the sight of this hidden relic.

"Weird, right?"

We walked up to the counter, where perhaps the only person who had been here longer than the sponges was stationed. Jimmy, the manager and owner, stood solemnly behind the register. It was one of two places you might find him. The other being behind the long low counter that kept patrons separated from the wall of tiny cubbyholes holding the rental shoes, where he would spray the inside of each shoe with some sort of chemical that killed whatever foot funk might be left behind. Frankly, worrying about the shoes seemed a little arbitrary, given the petri dish of a sponge at every lane, but whatever. It gave the semblance of a health code.

"Hi Jimmy," I said. We weren't on a mutual first name basis, but he wears a name tag, so it always seems appropriate to use his name. Jimmy always made you feel like he remembered you, but he didn't. "One lane, please. Not sure how many games we'll play." If you didn't tell him up front, he'd charge you after. It was sort of an honor code. Only on weekend nights did you have to pay up front, and that was just because you paid for the lane, not per game. "I'm a size ten and a half," we slid down a few feet to the shoe counter, where the aerosol can rested alongside a long row of shoes, lined up like soldiers ready for the shower. I turned to Chance, "six and a half?" She nodded. "Six and a half," I said to Jimmy.

His hands shook slightly as he pulled the shoes out of their cubbies and placed them on the counter in front of us.

I wondered if it was from some specific physical reason, or from breathing in that spray for so many years. That can't be good for you. I kicked off my right shoe, reached down for it and handed it to him. He turned and placed it in my cubby.

"She's wearing boots, can I just give you my other shoe?" I asked.

"Sure," he smiled wearily, but with kindness.

I handed him my other shoe and he put it in the now empty cubby from where Chance's shoes had come.

"Lane seven," he said.

We walked over to the lane, and sat down on the long plastic bench, 1960's style, with curves like a Windstream camper. The light came on at the end of the lane as we sat, and the mechanism cleared off the pins and reset them as I was putting on my shoes. "Leaving your shoes is like a deposit, in case you want to make off with the bowling shoes." I stated the obvious while I looked down at them, their patchwork blue and red leather just retro enough that they didn't look like absolute clown shoes. "You could see why someone would want to steal these babies."

Chance picked the knots apart on her laces and pried her boots off, then slipped her feet into the shoes. She has dainty feet. No other word for it.

I forgot a scoring sheet, so I grabbed one from the counter and made my way back to the lane, the soles of my shoes felt slick on the carpet as I walked. Chance bowled before, but never duckpin. The concept was the same, but she didn't know how to score manually, nor did she realize that she'd get three balls per turn.

"And what's that?" She asked, pointing to the button on the ball return.

"Deadwood. You push that if you want the machine to clear the pins you knocked down."

"You have the choice? It doesn't do it for you?"

"No, it's not automatic, so I think you can leave it if you want to. I guess if the fallen pins could help you then you can leave it. Your choice. That's how we always did it." I never questioned that before. I wasn't sure if it was an official rule, so I just went with it.

"And this is the sponge." I explained the purpose and showed her the vent you used to dry your hand. I explained the stickiness. I handed her a ball after she tried it. "See what I mean?"

She nodded. "That's gross," she said. "But this place is awesome. It's as if time is frozen down here. It's like a bomb shelter where everyone has been bowling since 1962."

"Yeah, things don't change much down here." I was sitting down in a chair in front of the scoring sheet, and I picked up a tiny, green, eraser-less pencil from the lip in the table where several of them rested. I wrote our names on the paper in the space for bowlers, Chance first. "You're up," I said.

"These balls are so light. No finger holes." She passed the ball from one hand to the other to illustrate her point. "So I just throw it down there?" It didn't make sense that she was asking, since I knew she'd bowled before.

"Maybe just roll it. Don't pitch it or anything"

She rolled her eyes, "thanks, boss." She turned around and steadied herself for a second. Taking a few awkward steps and swinging her arm back, she rolled the ball as if she perfectly aimed a shot straight towards the gutter.

"Nice angle," I said, as the ball made its long journey down the gutter to the end of the lane. I put a zero in the first tiny box on the scoring sheet. "Or, did you want to be the one to record this for posterity?" I teased.

"Jerk. I'm just getting warmed up." She picked up another ball, did the same awkward approach and sent the ball straight down the middle of the lane. A perfect hit at the center pin, knocking down all the pins but the furthest to each side.

"The dreaded seven-ten split," I said, recording her score. "Nice shot though."

We went back and forth for several turns, offering advice, teasing each other and bragging about our shots. It was fun. Chance was fun. And she brought out a fun side of me that I missed about myself. Dating is difficult, and relationships are tricky. Maybe for everyone, but these things always seem especially so for me. The fact of the matter was that I liked myself better when I was with Chance. That felt selfish in way, even though my feelings for her were stronger than my improved self image. I never had anyone to teach me what's normal in these situations, so I never feel normal. And don't get me wrong about one thing. There were still a lot of things that I didn't like about myself, even when I was with her. We all have those things, if we aren't afraid to admit them.

I once heard life described as a structure similar to a whirlpool that forms when water flows down a drain. This sort of structure is kept stable by a constant input and output. It is destroyed if there is a powerful enough disruption to either the input, the output or the structure itself. No more water, no whirlpool. Drain clogged up, no whirlpool. Stick your finger in it, you get the idea. It descends into chaos, and it's gone. Game over. You could say that my whirlpool had been a little slowed up for a while. Less going in, and less going out. Things were starting to flow better at this point.

I began to feel very, very comfortable around her. There were still choppy moments though, which I suppose isn't so out of the ordinary. The most likely cause is my occasional lack of comfort with myself. Those uncomfortable moments were most often only recognizable to me. But there were those times when it was quite clear to both of us.

I was walking back toward the lane from the bar area, and I could see that Chance was leaning over the scoring sheet, studying it. It turned out they served hard cider, so I picked one up for Chance thinking she might like it, her not being a beer person. She took it happily when I offered it.

"I think I figured out this scoring thing," she said after taking a sip, "and I think I see a way that I can still kick your ass. I just need at least a spare in this frame. Or maybe if I get one in the last frame, but I don't get what happens if you get a spare or a strike on your last turn."

I was quiet for a second.

"What happens then?"

I let out a little laugh. "That's so funny, you just totally sent me back into a memory of when my dad taught me how to score bowling." I thought about it for a second, racking my brain to quickly figure out if this was the only memory I have of him teaching me anything. Seemed so.

"Oh yeah?" She smiled and seemed interested. Her elbow was resting on the table and she leaned her head sideways onto her hand. She looked at me, no longer interested in how to score the final frame. I'd understand later that she enjoyed hearing me talk about my past in this way. I never did that.

"Yeah," I thought for a minute. "I guess it isn't anything much more specific than that. I just remember him explaining it to me and the feeling of getting it." I paused again. "I didn't really remember that he taught me that. Or that he ever came here with me. I feel like I can even picture that we were in one of the lanes on the other side, over by the stairs."

Chance had a faraway look in her eyes. She lifted her head up from her hand and picked up her cider, taking a long sip and sitting back in her chair. She looked down the lane.

I went on. "I really only remember my mom bringing me here. She would take me and the guys down here on the weekends when we were kids. She hated that it was so smoky then, but I guess no one really did anything to avoid that type of thing in those days." It sounded hokey to say *in those days*. But it was true. "My mom was so out of place in a bowling alley, but she must have been a good sport about it, because I remember her here more than any of the other moms."

"What was she like?"

Difficult question. "That's hard to say. She was peaceful, but hard to read. You couldn't really tell what was on her mind, but you could tell something usually was. She didn't really do games, or activities. She was really into her antiques." I stopped. Chance remained silent. "She'd sit right over there," I pointed to the snack bar area, "and read a book or watch us. It was usually me and Courtney or Jonas, sometimes Quinn and Pete. We'd have so much fun and get so competitive with each other. I think she got a kick out of that."

Chance was looking at me again. "I've never seen you look like that when you're talking about something."

"Like what?"

"Don't know. I guess I've never seen what you look like when you speak warmly about your mother. You never talk about her."

"What's there to say?"

"I know, I know. You aren't *in touch with her*," she did air quotes with her fingers. "But there must be some things to say about her. She's your mother. You have things to say about your dad, and you aren't really in touch with him all that much either."

She was right, even though there wasn't so much to say about my dad, I did talk about him more often than my mother. And I hadn't told Chance about what happened with my mom. Saying that I wasn't in touch with her was certainly true, but a version of the truth that didn't reveal all that much. At this point in my life, almost everyone who knew about my mom knew the story because they'd been through it with me, at least on some level. And there hadn't been any new people in my life in a long time with whom I was close enough to feel like it was important to tell, until now. But I was out of practice. The sharing reflex seemed dead. Or at least in a deep sleep.

You tell someone about something like that, about your mom leaving you, you let go of all control. They can do whatever they want with it. It's not about them telling someone else. It's more that you leave it up to them to make sense of it, especially when you can't make sense of it for them. I've never been good about letting go of that kind of control.

"I just don't know what to say about her," I felt stumped.

"You could say anything, but it just feels like you clam up when she's the topic. And you brought her up this time."

"It's complicated."

She laughed. The conversation didn't feel quite as heavy as it might seem. "Of course it is. How could you not be in touch with your mom and it not be complicated? I'm sure your friends know more about it."

Of course, in some ways it was complicated. In other ways, not at all. She left. It's really as simple as that. But not so simple to say. "I guess I'm just not that good with telling new people about it."

"That's the problem, Arch. You need to stop thinking of me as new people." She looked a little sad, and it made my chest hurt. I just couldn't open my mouth to say anything useful. "I just think you could just let people in a little bit more. Or at least let me in a little bit. Be more of an open book."

"I'm just not that way. Not open." It didn't feel true, though, the second the words were out of my mouth. It wasn't a lie. I just don't think I knew myself well enough when it comes to things like this to be accurate. "I don't get how people can live life like that. Like an open book. It's just not me." I was being stubborn.

"You know, being an open book doesn't mean you have to tell everything to everyone." She stood up and walked to the ball return. She turned around after picking one up. "It just means letting people read you a bit. That's all." She turned around and whipped the ball down the lane, knocking the shit out of the pins.

"Strike!" I said, in spite of the awkward turn of conversation. "Nice shot!"

She smiled. "Told you I was going to kick your ass." She walked around to my side of the table, shadow boxing as she came over to me. Bending down, she put her face right in mine, locking eyes with me, the smile vanished from her face. She looked me in the eyes, and whispered, "I'm here." She kept her deep brown eyes locked with mine for a few seconds, then used the tip of her nose to brush against the tip of mine, kissed my forehead, smiled and said, "your turn, sucker."

I reached up to touch her cheek, but she pulled her head back. "Seriously, you want to touch my face after putting your hand on that nasty sponge all night? Go wash them if you want to touch me. That's disgusting."

I couldn't help but laugh. She sounded just like my mother.

Chapter 11

She did not end up kicking my ass, in our first game or the next. We played out the final couple frames of the second game in the spirit of pure competition. It was still relatively early, but it was Tuesday and Chance had class the next day. I had nothing to do, but that is typical for me. We settled up with Jimmy, returned our shoes and retrieved mine from the cubbies where Jimmy stored them as collateral for the sweet shoes we paid three bucks each to rent.

Chance thanked me when I paid, which she always did even though I told her to stop. Money is such an awkward thing when you are dating, or maybe it just feels that way to me. At this point, I didn't really consider us dating anymore, we were past that in my opinion. But I didn't really know what to call it. Another thing that I'm not very good at, I suppose. I had at least convinced her that she didn't need to keep offering to pay or to split things. It isn't that I'm so chivalrous or anything like that. I just figure if I'm not worried about money, then I'd just as soon have the people I'm around not worrying about it either, when possible.

It had gotten a lot colder out while we were inside, and the slush in the parking lot was frozen solid. We made our way carefully across the parking lot to the car. It never really occurred to me that this parking lot was a little shady at night. Like, the kind of place where you might stop if you needed to drop a dead body somewhere. It didn't seem like that when I was a kid, but the stores on either side of the parking lot were boarded up, closed and empty with little hope of new tenants. The lighting was minimal, with only the far off streetlights casting a dull glow back to where we were parked. We made it to the car just fine though, and I opened the passenger door for Chance and held her hand as she climbed in.

We let the car warm up for a minute, and Chance busied herself finding something on the radio. She left it on a country station and turned it down low. I put my hand, which I washed before leaving, on her thigh and leaned my head towards her. "Sorry I had to beat you like that, but I couldn't have you sully my reputation at the Bowl-a-rama. I have a profile to manage around here."

She rolled her eyes, "just be glad I let you win. Next time you won't be so lucky."

"Glad you'll want to come back. I guess you like duckpin then?"

"It might be that I like the place better than the bowling." She said, looking back at the tiny building across the parking lot. "But yeah, I like it."

"Good." I put the car in gear, the tires crunched over the ice as we made our way out to the street.

The drive back over to Chance's place was a straight shot, about two miles and only one turn. In five minutes we were back by her place, stopped alongside the garden that led to her steps. "You sure you don't want to come sleep at my place?" I asked.

"I'm beat," she said. "Let's talk tomorrow."

I looked at her.

"What?" She could tell there was something on my mind, and she was right. It was like all the blood in my body was trapped in my torso. Like I had no pulse. My chest felt like a water balloon. My nerves felt numb. If I didn't say it now, I might never be able to. I just had to get the first few words out.

"She left, you know." I said. A wave of relief swept over me. I could feel the blood rush to every part of my body, warm and flowing.

She looked at me quizzically. Her eyebrows and forehead furrowed. "What?"

"She left." I said it again. "My mom. She just left."

Her forehead and eyebrows softened, but the look of concern came on stronger. It looked like her eyes moistened, but maybe it was just mine. "She left?" She was a little confused.

I looked out the windshield and put the car in park. The car rocked forward a couple inches when I took my foot off the brake pedal, the parking brake catching. "I came home from school, and she was just gone. I never heard from her again. Never saw her again."

There was a moment of silence between us, the country station playing softly in the background. "Oh, Archer. Jesus. I didn't know. I didn't mean." She didn't know what to say. How could she? Who would? "You didn't have to tell me. I didn't mean for you to feel like you had to." She was really feeling badly.

I turned back to her. "No, no. You didn't make me tell you. I wanted to. I have wanted to." I licked my lips, not really sure what else to say. "It's a hard thing to say out loud. I feel like it has been a long time since I said it out loud."

She was at a loss for words. She bit her lip, looking like she might cry.

"Pretty much everyone else who knows about my mom, they've known me since before it happened. I know where I stand with each of them. I guess, I don't know, I guess it's hard to know what someone will make of it."

"What do you mean?"

"My mom left me. She's never tried to contact me again. More than half my life. What does that say about me?" It was my turn to bite my lip. I looked back out the windshield.

"How old were you?"

"Fourteen." I said.

"Hey," she put her hand on my stomach and pulled on my jacket a little bit. I turned to her. "It doesn't say anything about you."

It took me a long time to answer, not only because I didn't want my voice to catch, but also because I just didn't know how to respond. It was easy for anyone else to say it didn't mean anything. Not always so easy to feel that way. I spent a long time being mad at my father, and then a long time being indifferent to him. I've felt confusion, and hurt, but I don't think I've ever really been mad at my mom. That might have been the place that most people would start.

"That's fucked up." Chance stated in a matter of fact tone. "Who does something like that?"

There was a time in my life when hearing someone say something like that would probably have made me mad at them. But Chance was right, and I knew it. Thinking about all this was a lot for me. Too much for what was supposed to be a night for bowling. I nodded.

"Come inside, would you?" She still had her hand on my jacket, and she pulled on it again. "Look over here, Why." I complied. "Come on, just come in." She looked into my eyes, and now I could tell they were a little teary.

"No, it's cool. You're tired, you have class in the morning. I'm fine."

"Archer, just come the fuck inside." She smiled at me. At this sort of a moment, it would typically be me whose job it was to break the tension. That's one of the things I love about Chance, she's fine taking things like that into her own hands. "It's not pity, in case that's what you think. I'm going to bed. Just stay over tonight."

"Fine, sheesh. I'll come in." I feigned resistance. I actually did want to come in. I like Chance's place. I put the car in reverse and pulled back about ten feet up the hill to avoid blocking the fire hydrant. We got out of the car, and she was waiting for me when I reached the sidewalk. She reached her arms up over my shoulders and gave me a big, warm kiss on the lips.

I leaned my head back and looked down at her face, her arms still draped over my shoulders. "What was that for?" I asked.

"Pity kiss. Don't question it. Last one you are getting."

I gave her a big hug, bending over slightly so I could bury my head in the scarf she had around her neck, my arms so far around her that each hand was touching the other arm's elbow. My breath made it feel warm and humid for my face nestled in her neck. "Let's go inside," I said, my voice muffled by the knitted wool.

My apartment feels like home, but Chance's place feels homey. It is small, with a tiny entrance vestibule that opens up into a small kitchen that has enough space for anything you'd expect in a kitchen as well as a tall table with two stools at it. When we have cooked there together, it provides enough space for two people who like each other a lot to cook and then eat. That room opens to a cozy living room, with a couch facing a television and a large drafting table that Chance uses for her work. Through that room is the bedroom, which is actually as big as the rest of place put together. There is a small bathroom off the bedroom, also accessible from the living room area.

It isn't so much the space itself that feels so comfortable, though it does have good energy, if you subscribe to that sort of thinking. More so, it is all the stuff she has that makes it feel like such a home. You would never know that she hadn't been living here for years. There are ceramic lamps, candles, hanging artwork, throw pillows, various knick knacks like nesting dolls and wrought iron puzzles. Lots of books. Nothing corny or hokey, just lots of interesting things to look at, to pick up and manipulate and ask questions about. Pictures of family events, friends having fun. Pieces of artwork that make you want to ask, "did you do this?" Yet somehow, with all that chaos and the limited space, it doesn't feel crowded. It always seems warm in there, but never uncomfortably so.

I opened the fridge and looked around as if I lived there. I spotted a half bottle of wine that I recognized from a takeout dinner a few days prior, and I pulled it out. "You mind?" I asked.

"Course not."

"Thanks," I pulled out a tall glass from the wooden cabinet and held it out to her. She shook her head no, so I closed the cabinet and pulled out the cork. I poured myself a generous glass, leaned against the counter next to the fridge, and faced Chance who was leaning against the stove. We were only about five feet apart.

"Did you want to talk more?" She asked in an unnecessarily cautious voice.

"I don't think so," I said after thinking a moment between two sips of wine. It was cold and sweet. "I don't know what else there is to say. Just wanted you to know, I guess."

She looked at me, her lips slightly pursed.

"I'm sure there'll be more to say another time."

"Your call," she said, not wanting to press me, I could tell.

"Why don't you get ready for bed? You have class, I'm going to watch TV for a few and relax." It always sounded funny to me when I said I was going to relax. My life affords a lot of time for that.

She yawned. Chance is highly suggestible when it comes to yawning. Reference that it is late, tell her she has to get up in the morning, mention bed, she yawns. She nodded, said something unintelligible but clearly affirmative, and then disappeared into the bathroom.

When she came back out a few minutes later to say goodnight, I was lounging on the couch, flipping channels. I don't have a television at my place, so I only flip channels when I'm somewhere else, like here. I enjoy the mindlessness of watching whatever appears while flipping around like this.

Chance leaned over and gave me a kiss. Her skin smelled like the soap she uses to wash her face.

"You okay?" She asked, truly curious.

"Yeah, I'm fine. Really, it was a long time ago. Hard to bring up, but it's been brought up now. You now have carte blanche to bring it up when you want." I raised my eyebrows and gave a grin. "I'm fine," I repeated.

"Good night, Arch."

"Good night, babe."

She closed the door to her bedroom behind her.

I pulled my feet up onto the couch and grabbed a blanket off the top of it. I adjusted the pillows behind me and covered myself up to the midsection with the blanket. My wine in one hand, remote in the other I searched for something to watch. I can't really explain why it was so nerve wracking to discuss something that happened so long ago, nor can I explain the relief of having gotten it out. There was a part of me that still felt nervous that Chance knew, but at the end of the day, I knew it was safe with her. I can't say why I never realized before that it would be so.

Lying on a couch, all covered in blankets and warm, it reminded me of a sick day, home from school as a kid. There is a very clear line in my life for days like that. The days before my mom left, when I knew she was there to take care of me, and the days after, when I was there to take care of myself. I was glad that Chance asked me to stay over. It was comforting to know that if I needed her, she was right there. Even though I knew I wouldn't.

I was scrolling back down through the channels, having made my way up to where they put all the less interesting stations, when I landed on an old movie from when I was a kid. I remembered watching this with my friends, probably before we were teenagers. Not a timeless classic, but nostalgic and familiar. I swallowed in one gulp what was left of the wine and put the glass on the floor. It was cozy and warm on the couch in the flickering glow of the television. My eyes felt heavy, and it seemed like I had slept for hours by the time I opened them.

The movie was finished, and there was some sort of infomercial on the television. A helpless woman attempting to pick up leaves with a traditional rake. But wait, there was a solution for her and anyone else with such an incapacity. I sat up on the couch, my foot knocking the now empty glass over onto the carpet. It fell silently. I shut off the TV, put the glass in the kitchen sink and made my way to the bathroom in the near dark.

Being as quiet as I could, I brushed my teeth with the extra toothbrush Chance procured for me a few weeks before. Chance rustled a little under the covers when I slid silently into bed next to her. She was on her side facing away from me, and I reached my hand over and rested it on her hip. She stirred again. I closed my eyes. Sleep was not far off, but in that moment I knew without any shadow of a doubt that I was in love with her. I'm pretty sure I woke up with the same smile on my face as when I dropped off to sleep. Fucking bowling.

★★★

After leaving the park, the ride was pretty much all downhill. I was riding quickly now in an effort to get to work. Benefit Street was mostly empty, so I rode fast down the middle of the street toward the large intersection with Wickenden Street. From where I was now, I was less than five minutes from work. I wasn't worried about the boss, and I wasn't worried about Chrissy, who was bartending. But I knew that the cook on the shift before me was going to be pissed that I was late. Carl never liked me for some reason. Sometimes I felt that he knew I didn't really need to work, so it bothered him I had shifts he could have worked. What he didn't know, and what I did know, is that he was only employed there as a favor. He couldn't cook a cheeseburger to save his life, and his pants looked like they could get up and walk away on their own they were so dirty. It was like he only wore one pair to work and never washed them. I sort of felt bad for the guy. He was only working there one shift at this point, and he blamed everyone else for that. He always gave me shit for coming late, but not directly. There would be three loads of dirty dishes waiting for me, and several orders that people would have been waiting on for quite a while.

Why. Me.

I was flying down the hill, actually making myself a little nervous, although it felt sort of freeing. Why did I ever bother driving when I could do this? I got to the intersection, where I slowed down despite my green light. I turned right and headed toward the underpass. This was where I made my first mistake. Instead of just sticking with the lane, I hopped the curb and rode the island under the bridge. I needed to go left after the underpass, but I knew the traffic light would screw me. I thought I had space to make a move so I jumped off the island into the oncoming lane and pedaled my ass off. That was my second mistake.

What I didn't see was the car turning into this lane from the opposite direction. With no time to react, I jerked the bike sideways between two parked cars, making a hairpin turn I'm still not sure was humanly possible. There was no time to be impressed with myself, and there was no time to lift the front wheel to hop the curb in front of me. The bike stopped in a split second when it slammed into the curb, but I didn't. I flew ass over elbow over the handlebars and onto the pavement. I found myself in a seated position on the ground, numb with shock. I barely heard the brakes squealing behind me or the voice of the driver yelling at me, "What the fuck, man!?"

It's fucked up how the world works. I lose a friend, I get everything he owned. A country loses its sense of safety, and within a month the real estate values in Brooklyn just about doubled. When I sold my buildings that winter, I walked away with more money than I knew what to do with. And I was left feeling guiltier than ever. It took me ten years to stop wallowing in that puddle of crap.

Sitting there on the pavement, though oblivious to the present, I was abundantly clear of what had just happened. In my head, I had pictured over and over the scene that was described to me when I went to the city morgue to identify Mark. The yellow cab, the twisted metal, the woman whose life he saved. People say that New Yorkers don't pay attention to what is happening around them, that they don't consider others. No less than a dozen witnesses saw exactly what happened that morning, and they stuck around to describe it. The cab was going to hit that lady, and to the people there it seemed as if the entire block froze in anticipation as Mark swerved from his lane directly towards her, yelling his fool head off and making her jump back. Seconds before he was killed by a speeding cab that ran its red light. But as I sat there I wasn't thinking about that damn cab driver. I wasn't thinking about Mark dying a hero just a month before the country finally began to really appreciate them. I was wondering what went through his mind the second before he died, which was instantaneous, the coroner assured me as I bawled into my hands at the morgue, my emotional response just about enough to vouch for his identity.

Was he thinking about the lady who he was trying to save? Was he thinking about death? Was he thinking about lunch? Me? I am no hero, and I probably wasn't close to death in the moments before I was sitting on the sidewalk under that bridge. But I know what was going through my mind when I looked up to see that car headed straight towards me. It was Chance. Funny how that works.

"Dude, what the fuck, are you okay?" The driver was out of his car now, his tone a combination of anger and concern. I looked up to see him approaching me between the two parked cars I had swerved between. He looked cautious, like he was the one going the wrong way down a one-way street.

Why. Me.

For some reason, I got goofy when I saw him. "Hey, don't I know you?"

He looked puzzled. "Ah, what?" He looked over his shoulder and back at me. "What?"

"Seriously man, didn't we have homeroom together? I know we did. In high school, you don't remember me?" I didn't get up, just sat there on my butt with my arms resting on my knees. "What's your name again?"

Still confused, "um, it's Rice. Simon Rice." This guy was probably eight years younger than me, minimum. There was no way we went to school together. He looked at me like I was crazy. "Are you okay?"

I just looked at him with a deadpan look on my face. "Never better, man. It was great running in to you. Don't worry about me." I got up from the pavement slowly. When I put my hands down to rise, I realized I skinned my left elbow pretty good. I stretched my limbs to check how I was doing, and I was feeling okay. Nothing broken. My head was fine. "I'm okay," I said, but not really to anyone in particular. A couple walked past who obviously witnessed the whole affair. They seemed to be giving us some privacy. "Have a nice night," I said to them, "don't worry about me. I'm here all week."

"So you're okay?" Simon seemed to want to get back in his car and get out of here.

I turned to him. "I'm fine, you run along. It was good seeing you after all these years, brother. Say hi to your mom for me."

He was looking at me, but not at my eyes. I'd guess he was looking for head trauma and didn't see any. His expression changed from concern, to confusion and then jumped straight past anger at my ridiculousness to resignation. "Okay, you too." He walked back to his car and drove off. I watched him go, no longer worried much about being late.

I picked up my bike and pulled it onto the sidewalk. Straddling the seat, I first noticed that the front tire was out of alignment with the handlebars. I remembered how to fix that, and spun around with the tire between my legs to twist it back straight. That was when I realized the rim was totally dented and the tire completely flat. The bar was only a block or so away at this point, so I resigned myself to walking. I tried to roll the bike beside me with one hand but since it wouldn't roll on the front tire, I needed to balance it on the back tire and walk it in front of me. It was a little bit awkward. The shock wore off and my hands and body were shaky. Walking now, it was clear I also hurt my leg. My pants were shredded a bit on my right knee and you could see a little blood there by the rip. I had a moment of panic when I felt something warm on my cheek, worried that maybe there was blood dripping down my face. I had to pause a second when I pulled my hand away from my cheek. It took me a moment to realize that what was on my fingers were tears. I must have looked crazy to Simon Rice. Bloody, disheveled, tears on my face, asking about homeroom.

I was pushing the bike awkwardly in front of me and approaching the bar. I could see Carl standing out front. Even before I could see his face I could tell he was pissed. He went back inside. When I was about twenty feet from the front door, he came back out. "Thanks a lot, asshole."

"Sorry Carl," I had the readymade excuse, "I had a little accident and it held me up." I let the bike bounce down on the lame front tire and showed him my elbow like a little kid on the schoolyard.

Why. Me.

He looked at the bike, at my face and at my elbow.
"Bitchin' bike, Why. There are a few orders up for you."
He said the last couple words as he was walking away from
me towards his car. He flipped me the finger over his
shoulder. For some reason, I always wanted to smack his
face when I saw it. And the back of his dirty blond head
made me feel the same way. At times, as I mentioned, I felt
bad for the guy. For the most part, though, he was such a
jerk. Of course, I was technically lying about why I was late,
but he didn't know that. I shrugged it off and walked
through the front door.

I learned to feel pretty much at home in this place. The
bartenders, bouncers, the regulars, everyone seemed to have
their niche here. The place is called the Charter Club,
which makes it sound awfully classy. It is decidedly not.
Don't get me wrong, it isn't a dive either. It's just not a club
in any sense of the word, and nothing about it screams
"charter." It is right on the mouth of the Providence River,
at essentially the top of the Narragansett Bay which nearly
splits Rhode Island in half. It is just inside the so-called
hurricane barrier, with its three giant doors that are meant
to prevent floods during big storms. I remember as a kid
being shown the plaques on the side of some downtown
buildings showing how high the water rose during floods in
the early 1900's. They were over my head then, and still are
now. The barrier prevents that. It's a useful thing, a barrier
like that.

The Charter Club, or, as we all call it, the Club, is really
just a bar. A bar in the truest sense. And a lot of people go
there because it is just that. A place to sit, to drink, to look
at the water and to meet up with people who you may or
may not know. It is family owned and family run; it is
neither old school nor modern. It has no expectations of its

patrons other than to be nice and to have fun. It is an easy place to be.

Sunday nights were my favorite. It was quiet and two of my favorite people were there, Chrissy, who I ran into that morning, and the bouncer, Frank. Chrissy, as was mentioned, has a head of wildly curly, flaming red hair, a loud mouth and uses foul language. She also had a string of loser, borderline abusive boyfriends and a wicked Rhode Island accent. She was absolutely nothing like anyone I ever met, much less became friends with. You just can't help but love her. She has a bachelor's degree in computer science but is content to bartend on weekends while working the desk at a hair salon during the week. She never talks about the fact that she went to college. She reads romance novels, smokes menthol cigarettes and is bitingly sarcastic.

Frank is equally unlike anyone else I've ever met or anyone else in the entire universe, I'm sure. Standing about six foot eight, with broad shoulders and hands like a lumberjack, he is about the calmest person in a crisis I've ever seen. When troublemakers who have a different idea of what a "club" should be like make their way in, Frank just walks up and gives his trademark, "what seems to be the issue here?" His height, his meat hooks and his overall size tend to take care of the rest. He's a pure diplomat. He finished a semester of community college but decided it wasn't for him. He works in the corrections department part-time and bounces at several local bars. He tells wild stories that have no point and that most people believe to be untrue, which earned him the nickname of Frankie Fable. He loves to play cards, he loves to curse and he loves to laugh.

Why. Me.

Frank was sitting at the booth by the front door. I could hear Chrissy's shrill voice from the front bar area. I felt at home and relieved to be here.

"What's with the bike, toolbag?" Frankie said without looking up. He was shuffling a deck of cards. It looked like a miniature set in his hands.

"I stole it from your mom." I said as I walked past him. I wheeled the bike awkwardly through the front barroom. I could have taken the long way, but I think I was looking for some attention from Chrissy and the regulars up front. *Hey, look at my band aid. I got a boo-boo.* Good thing I wasn't holding my breath for that.

"Hey Arch. I got your dinner" (hear: *dinnah*). "You want one slice or two?"

I didn't recognize the sarcasm for a split second and almost got pissed off. I really hate pizza. Then I remembered who I was talking to. "Where's my fucking spinach pie, Chrissy?"

★★★

"Order up, Arch." Chrissy's voice rang from around the corner.

"Coming." I yelled without taking my eyes from my cards.

I had stashed the bike in the back by the dumpsters and caught up on no less than four loads of dirty glasses and three small orders that Carl left for me. I had also tossed all the rolls, lettuce and tomatoes that I suspected he handled during his shift, questioning the cleanliness of his hands. Then I settled into a series of card games with Frankie. Recently, we'd been playing cribbage. I think the clientele of the Club enjoyed seeing two relatively young guys playing cribbage like two old men at the front booth of the bar. On Sundays, it was mostly a regular crowd, and slow enough that we could sit most of the evening playing cards and relaxing. It had been close to an hour since I did any real work, and about half an hour since I sat at the bar eating my spinach pie and chatting with Chrissy, who was now flirting with two of her Sunday night regulars. These were good guys. Big drinkers. Anesthesiologists.

"I've got an eight hand." I said, quickly counting my hand before running up to check the order.

Frankie was finishing up one of his long, pointless stories, and didn't appear to have heard me.

"... so he just reaches in to the back seat and grabs the dog by the balls."

I stared at him blankly. I hadn't really been listening.

"Just grabs him by the balls." He repeated.

"Huh. Wow." I replied, knowing he wouldn't count his hand if I didn't acknowledge his story. "Crazy."

"Yeah, right?" he said, smiling brightly and looking at his cards. He laid them down, and said, "eight hand, too." He moved his piece ten spaces.

"Frank, that's ten spaces. Back it up kid." He placed his hand palm down over the pieces. It covered the entire board.

"You miscounted your hand. I'm taking your extra two." I didn't even realize he looked at my cards what with the dog testicle story and everything. I looked again at my cards. He was right. I missed two points when counting off. Shit.

I went into the front barroom and looked at the order over the grill. Two cheeseburgers and a grilled zucchini. Simple. I tossed two patties on the grill, sliced a zucchini lengthwise, brushed some olive oil on it, dusted it with the spice blend and put those on the grill as well. I saw a pack of cigarettes and a plastic lighter on the edge of the countertop. Carl. I put his lighter in my pocket. I spread out the coals under the grill and leaned against the post by my station. Chrissy was looking at me.

"Let me see that elbow, Arch." She said. I walked over to her and awkwardly showed her my elbow. It really hurt at this point. When she held my arm under the triceps she was surprisingly gentle. She frowned and lifted my arm up a little higher and looked closer. "Go wash that off again, Archer. And get your ass back to my bar when you're done." In the bathroom, I looked at my elbow in the mirror. I hadn't done a very good job cleaning it out, and despite the bright red abrasion, you could see bruising underneath. It was going to really hurt tomorrow. My shoulder was also starting to feel sore. The cuts on the elbow looked a little dirty. It didn't look good. When I got back out to the bar, Chrissy was sitting on a stool with a clean, wet bar towel and an open first aid kit.

"This is going to hurt," she said a few seconds after she started scrubbing my elbow roughly with the towel. Her left hand had a firm grip on the back of my arm, but I wasn't going to pull away. It's not hard to imagine how long it was since I felt mothered like this.

"That fucking stings. Sheesh."

"It's got vodka on it, quit whining." She smeared some sort of cream on the cut, pressed a gauze pad onto it, "hold here" she ordered, and began sticking it to me with a series of band aids. "No tape in the kit," she said. When she was finished I awkwardly attempted to look at the back of my elbow, not the easiest task, and straightened and bent my arm a few times. It was very sore, but I was impressed with Chrissy's work on the bandage job.

"Thanks Chrissy. You're a real expert at that, huh?"

"Yeah, and you're a fucking loser. What makes you think you should be riding a bike like some friggin kid. Stupid ass." She flung the now bloodied bar rag into the garbage as she walked back behind the bar. Despite her words, she looked at me with a tender smile and a wink as she washed her hands. "Have a coffee with me?"

"You know it." I said, turning my back to finish the grill order. I looked at the bandage again, impressed that it seemed to stay in place even as I bent my elbow. I reached in to flip the burgers and to move the zucchini to a cooler part of the grill where it wouldn't get overcooked. I tried to use the heat and the movement to keep my elbow from tightening up.

It's funny what Chrissy said about the bike, and she was right. It was sort of ridiculous to be tooling around on that little old dirt bike. But it was fun until the underpass, that's for sure. It's also funny that when I thought of Chance at the moment when I realized the car was about to hit me, it wasn't that an image of her appeared in front of me in some grand realization that she was the meaning of my life. It was just that I wondered what time she'd come by the bar. I guess even in the face of impending doom, my creativity is pretty weak. If my life flashed before my eyes, it would probably be all the boring parts.

As I was arranging the order onto wax paper in two little plastic baskets, Chrissy set a white porcelain mug down in front of me. "Thanks, babe, here's your order." I took a sip from the mug she left for me. Our typical routine of having "coffee" with each other during our Sunday night shift meant splitting a couple of beers disguised in coffee mugs, a practice overlooked to an extent by the owner of the bar. I straightened up my materials at the cooking station, sliding the knives to one side, wiping off the cutting board and tied off the now half empty bag of rolls with a knot and tossed it in the cabinet below the counter. I picked up the plastic tag from the bread bag and rotated it absently between my fingers. I slipped it into my pocket.

From the front of the bar, I heard an impatient voice. "Why, get your dumb ass up here to finish this game." I almost forgot about Frankie.

Chapter 12

You could tell from where we sat in the booth that it had gotten colder outside. When folks came in and out through the door the coolness from outside either followed them in or trailed back in their wake. A nice April evening.

"Nice night to kick your ass, Why." Frankie was saying. We split games to this point, and he was indeed beating me in this game. It was early yet, and I hoped to get the better of him. I'm not the most competitive guy, but Frank's shit talking was enough to make me want to shut him up most nights. He brought out that side of me.

I welcomed the respite when Chrissy came out from behind her bar to tell me she needed a couple bottles from upstairs, which was where all the hard liquor was kept. "No problem," I said, slapping my cards down on the table, face down, and giving Frank the finger. I turned my finger downwards and tapped the cards, looking him squarely in the eye. "Touch these and I'm going to kick your ass." He raised one eyebrow. Naturally I was kidding, and naturally there was no chance I'd ever be able to kick Frank's ass. Two can join in trash talking though.

There is a ladder at one end of the front bar that heads to the upstairs storage. It is the only way to get up there, and none of the bartenders really like doing it. I happen to enjoy it.

"I'll get the light for you."

"Nope, leave it. I'm fine." I said. This was my favorite part.

I shimmied up the ladder and swung myself onto the floorboards. They creaked. Even though this storage area is open to the downstairs, it is always oddly quiet and very dark. During the day, the light streams in from skylights, but at night there is no source of light and unless you stay up there for a while it is hard for your eyes to adjust. I could hear Chrissy faintly from downstairs, which meant she was talking loudly for my benefit. She said something about me and what I like to do by myself upstairs. I couldn't really make it out.

For my part, I was exercising my habit of trying to find what I was looking for in the dark. I knew where the vodka Chrissy needed was, top shelf, about halfway down the row. I recognized by touch the squat bottle and the straight neck of it. I took one bottle and tucked it under my arm, heading further down the row for the brandy, a less usual destination, but one I was confident I could find as I felt my way along through the dark. And that's when it hit me.

"I just remembered it," I stated, sitting back down in the booth.

"Remembered what?" Frankie said.

"My dream." I said flatly, as if he should have known. "From last night, I've been trying to remember it all day."

He looked at me in silence. I looked back at him.

"Okay, so spill it. Do I have to wait all night? What the fuck?"

It was a weird one, but not of the truly bizarre type. It was a silent dream, and mostly dark. I was standing still, but only because I couldn't move. I couldn't talk. I was just sort of stuck there, and all these people from my life kept coming and standing in front of me and just looking at me. And I couldn't do anything but look at them. They would stand there and stare at me, but it was like they were looking at something just behind me. It felt like they wanted something from me, but I couldn't figure it out. There was a steady procession. All these people I knew from growing up, from when I lived in the city, from Providence, from camp. Even really random people I only met a couple of times. "I felt like I was some sort of spectacle. They'd just stare and I'd stare back. Then they'd walk away and it would be dark until the next person came along to look at me."

"Except they weren't really looking at you." Frank said flatly, looking at his cards.

"I guess. It seemed like they were looking at me, but it was like they were looking through me."

"They were looking at themselves." Frank said.

I stared at him. "What are you talking about?"

"They weren't really looking at you. They were looking at themselves." He finally looked up from his cards.

"I heard you the first time, what are you talking about?" For some reason, this was making me angry, but I was trying to hide it.

"Your dream. You were a mirror. See? They were looking at you, sort of. But they were looking at themselves. That's why you couldn't talk or move or anything. You were a mirror. You didn't have to say anything, you were just showing them back to themselves."

My anger vanished instantly. "Hm." I thought about it for a minute. That hadn't occurred to me. I thought about it for another minute. Frankie was staring at me. I finally said resignedly, "well that's a pretty shallow dream. All I can do for others is to show them a reflection of themselves? I guess that doesn't say much about what I bring to the relationship."

"Nope, you got it wrong, Archer. That dream is deep. I mean, what are any of us if we aren't a reflection of every person we've ever met? Yeah, we bring something to the table, right? But we get all these bits and pieces from other people, we reflect things back to them, they take a piece of us and we all grow and change. That's a deep dream, kid."

I stared at Frankie. I was stunned. It wasn't just that he said all that, or that he was so clearly right. I was equally stunned by the fact he managed to say all of it without uttering a single curse. "The mind walks a golder forest," I stated matter of factly.

"You're fuckin-a right it does."

That was more like it. I picked up my cards and couldn't help but smile.

★★★

Standing outside by the water, I flexed my arm a few times, a little annoyed with myself about the bike accident. Frankie and I played four games of cribbage, splitting them back and forth each time. We were both bored by the fourth game and decided to call it a tie for the night. It was getting close to the time to close the kitchen, and there hadn't been an order in almost an hour even though it was busier than usual for a Sunday night at the bar. After loading the dishwasher full of glasses, I stepped out onto the deck overlooking the river.

There were a few couples sitting at tables out here, and another guy sitting quietly, drinking and smoking a cigar by himself. It was early in the season for the deck to be busy, but it was a pleasant evening. I watched the lights flicker on the rippling water. The current was running swiftly out into the bay. Across from the bar is the electric company, and three tall smokestacks shot straight up into the sky, lit from underneath as if to make them more striking. For an industrial building, it is beautiful. I found myself staring at it blankly.

I enjoy being by the river, but it bothers me that you can't really take a walk near the water here, which would be nice. When I lived in New York, there was no shortage of places to walk along the rivers flowing around the city. I'd find myself taking such walks quite a bit when I was still living there, even occasionally after Mark died. After I found a buyer for my buildings and was waiting for the sale to close, I took one long walk that stood out among the others. I'd just left a midtown meeting with my broker and attorney. I walked west, finding the river just north of the Intrepid Museum. I turned right and headed north towards the upper west side.

It was freezing outside, and I wasn't dressed well for the cold at all. My hands were jammed in my pockets and I tried to walk quicker to keep warm. The wind was whipping across the water and slicing through my clothes. My so-called insulated work coat was no match, and the warm-up pants I was wearing, despite their fleece lining, might as well have been track shorts. I was impressed by the joggers that came along every so often, steam bursting out of their mouths and noses, looking like ninjas in black pajamas as they swiftly overtook and weaved around me. Who were these people out running in the middle of the day? Then again, who the hell was I? I guess none of us had anything better to do on a weekday.

I was about to make a shit ton of money selling my properties, but I was in a foul mood. I was almost getting off on walking right down the middle of the pathway so people had to avoid me. I began only looking at the ground about three feet in front of my steps, not caring who was coming from the other direction, making it their problem that I wasn't looking where I was going. Past the boat basin and the dog walk and then the cold got to be too much, so

I turned right and headed back into the rumble of the city blocks. Once I got a block or two deep into the city, the wind was less powerful, and I found myself winding along a few random streets until I realized that I was on one that was familiar.

I didn't last long in college, and I didn't get that much out of it. There was one professor I really liked, though, and I thought of her often. I found myself actually wanting to impress her, and I liked for her to comment on my work. I listened when she spoke. It was a literature course, and we were reading some poetry by a woman who was going to be doing a reading during the semester. She told the class about it when it was coming closer. I signed myself up.

I can't say I got much out of the event. Poetry tends to be a little over my head. Sometimes I try to read poems and see if I can find anything there. I rarely do. It makes me feel dense. Sometimes they make me think, though. Maybe that is the point. Refrigerator magnet poetry is about my limit. So, on this morning things were no different, and after the reading and a question and answer period, Jill, the professor, told me and the other two students that we were welcome to come to her apartment for tea and to discuss the morning.

It ended up being just me and one other student, a girl with striking tattoos on the back of each calf visible through her black stockings. Each one was of a simple star with a thick black edge, about the size of my palm. Pow. One on each calf. I wondered what I'd add to the conversation as I stared at her calves while we trudged across Central Park, following Jill to her upper west side apartment. I also wondered about the judgment to wear a skirt given how cold it was that day, but she seemed less fazed about the temperature than I was.

I found myself at the same place, standing in front of Jill's building, once again unsure why I was there. My warm-ups flapped against my legs, they were almost numb, which would have been a blessing. Could she be home? I stared up at the building. The tea had been a warm welcome after that morning of poetry, and I remembered feeling sort of out of place while Jill and the other student talked fluently about poetry and metaphor and other things. I focused on my tea and nodded a lot. I still can't remember that girl's name. The one with the calf tattoos.

I looked at the bank of doorbells and Jill's name immediately jumped out at me. Jill Larsen - 10D. Impulsively, I rang her buzzer. I looked over my shoulder like I was doing something suspicious. No answer.

Pushing the button longer now, I shivered. I was really freezing. Turning away, I heard a crackle behind me.

"Hello?"

...

"Hello?" A slight annoyance in her voice betrayed that she believed someone was ringing random buzzers in an effort to gain entrance.

I turned back around and pushed the intercom. "Jill, it's me. It's Archer. Archer Why." *It's me?!? Why would you say that?*

There was a long pause. I pushed the intercom again. "From your class. From the poetry reading." I was floundering. Why did I ring the bell? I considered running. What was *wrong* with me? "I'm sorry to just ring the bell." I released the button, fully expecting her to simply ignore me. She couldn't possibly remember me.

The crackle. "Archer. Did you want to come up?"

"Yes." It was all I could come up with.

210

There was a short pause and the door buzzed. I yanked it open, leapt up the short staircase, pulled open the second door and found myself in the polished stone lobby. It was perhaps the quickest I moved in months, up those five steps, and I could feel my heart pounding. I jumped up and down a few times to get my blood moving. It was warm in the lobby, but I was chilled to my bones. The elevator door opened and a teenage boy exited and went out the door to the street, never taking his eyes off the floor. Before the doors closed I slipped in and pushed ten. When the doors opened and I stepped out, I realized I was out of breath. I also realized I had no idea why I came here. As the doors closed behind me and the door to Jill's apartment opened, it was clear there was no escape.

Would there be an awkward moment when Jill greeted me at the door? Should I hug her, shake her hand, go in for the cheek kiss? New York is so confusing. Jill solved the problem by simply opening the door, standing to the side and gesturing for me to enter. Very gracious. She smiled, but beneath it there was a question. Which was sort of the same question I was asking myself. "Why am I here?"

"What brings you here?" Jill asked. And there it was.

A simple version of honesty prevailed. "I was on a walk and I stayed out a little longer than I should have. I realized I was on your block, in front of your building, and I was freezing. I guess I just rang the bell and here I am." It sounded like total bullshit as it came out of my mouth. Was that really the truth? I could feel the warm blood pumping to my toes now. I was not looking forward to leaving.

I looked at Jill as she looked at me, standing there uncomfortably in the hallway of her apartment. She looked a little bit older than I remembered, though it was only a couple years since I saw her last. She still looked younger than her age though, which I put at about sixty. She smiled at me. "I have to admit, it is unusual for past students just to stop by. Here it is, the middle of a weekday. Happens to be a day I'm not teaching." She looked at me searchingly, as if there was something to figure out by looking at me. I smiled at her, having no idea what to say.

"Well, come on in then," she said, and sort of shooed me ahead of her into the living room. It was a crowded space, with a small sofa, a couple arm chairs, a coffee table and a wall of built in bookshelves, jam packed with books and knick knacks. The living room opened off the hallway to the left and to the right was a small galley kitchen. Straight ahead was a dining nook. Something about the kitchen told me that some serious cooking happened in there. The house smelled good, and felt lived in. It felt like a home.

"Nice coffee table," I said. I leaned down and took one hand out of my coat pocket for the first time, running my fingers along the edge of it.

"Now don't comment on the dust," she said laughingly. I continued to look at the table, bending lower to look at the legs. I felt under the table with my freed hand, touching where the leg joined to the table. It was a nice piece. She looked at me with curiosity, another question in her eye.

"Antiques are sort of my thing. Or, they were." I trailed off and stood up again. I was very conscious of my hands, both of which were now out of my pockets. I let them hang limply by my sides.

"Let me take your coat, have a seat. Can I get you something?" Such hospitality. I slipped out of my coat and handed it to her, thankful for something to do with my hands. She took my jacket, and, realizing how thin it was, looked at me again. "You must have been freezing out there, Archer. I'll be right back."

I sat on the couch, which was firm and not super comfortable. I leaned way back and then felt like it was too casual. I sat forward, sort of perched on the edge of the seat. The coffee table in front of me had lots to occupy my time. There was a large glass ashtray filled with various items. Several glass marbles, a set of keys, a number of shells and small stones. Two large knitting needles and a ball of yarn. And there was a pile of large hardcover books as well. The one on top was some sort of collection of engravings. I opened it and leafed through it listlessly and then let it close. I picked up a marble and rolled it between my fingers. I picked up a second one. Jill disappeared into the kitchen and I could hear her voice faintly despite the fact that she wasn't so far away. It sounded like she was on the phone. I could only hear a few words. Student. Unexpected. Postpone.

She came back into the room. "Jill, you had plans. I should go." I stood up.

"No please, it's fine. You are here and my plans can change. It was nothing important." She looked sincere. I really didn't want to leave. "I'm heating you some soup. You must be freezing with that thin coat. And what are you wearing, a flannel shirt? You should have dressed more warmly." I looked down at myself. Not the best winter outfit. Jill was right about that. Not the most fashionable outfit either, but then that is never my goal. I sat back down on the couch and rested my hands on my knees.

"You've lived here a long time." I said to her. It was more of a statement than a question.

She smiled and looked around. "We moved here in the seventies and raised both our sons here. You could say we've been here a long time."

I saw framed pictures interspersed with the books on the shelves. Her sons in shirts with little alligators on their chests, posing for grade school pictures. A graduation shot, caps and gowns. One that looked like it was taken at a wedding. I took it in with a quick scan. Then found myself staring at the coffee table again. Jill got up and excused herself to the kitchen.

I rubbed my hands slowly on my knees. My eardrums were aching dully as they warmed up. It was uncomfortable. I stuck my fingers in my ears and tried to make myself yawn to see if they would pop. It didn't help. Jill came in with a steaming bowl of soup and put it in front of me. She left and came back with another one for herself and two spoons.

"You make a quick soup," I attempted a joke.

"Hush, it was in the fridge." She smiled at me.

She handed me a spoon and we ate in silence for a few minutes.

"This is really good. What kind of soup is this?" I couldn't recognize any of the flavors. But then, I'm no gourmet.

"Potato leek. You like it? I've been experimenting with soups. This weather is a good motivator." She put her half empty bowl down on the table and looked at me. "You sure there isn't some reason you came by today, Archer?"

"No, really." I raised my eyebrows, and even though I was pretty sure there was no reason, I felt like I was lying. I could tell it looked that way too. "I had a meeting in midtown and I just started walking up Riverside. I like walking along the water. I just didn't realize it was so cold today. I guess I could have stopped in a restaurant or something, but I just got walking and here I was. I recognized your building from when me and that other student came here. That time after the poetry reading." I was rambling.

"You had a meeting?" She smiled curiously. "What sort of meeting?"

"It was a real estate thing." I wasn't sure why I wasn't more forthcoming.

"So you left school to go into real estate? Did you decide to get your real estate license?" I could tell she was genuinely curious. She is a writer after all. I guess they like to ask questions, to figure people out. Sort of like therapists.

"Not really. I guess, I..." my eyes back to the coffee table again. I looked her in the eyes. "Do you remember Mark Rush?"

"Yes. You two were together a lot when you were at school. You left at the same time." I was impressed by her memory; we'd been there less than a year. And then, "I heard what happened to him. You two were still close?"

"The closest," I said. "The closest." I was impressed I kept my voice steady, but I felt the welling inside.

"Oh dear. I'm so sorry, Archer. That's terrible."

She wasn't asking me to tell anything else, but her eyes were searching me. So, I told her just about everything. I told her about the adventures, about the internet startup, the stock options, the building, the hacky sack, the bikes. She listened intently. I hadn't talked to anyone this much since Mark died. I hadn't told anyone this whole story start to finish. I was almost out of breath. "And then this whole thing happened with the planes and all." I gestured the direction I thought was south, towards where the towers had been. I took a deep breath and exhaled. The soup was in front of me, almost finished. I lifted up the handle of the spoon with one finger and let it drop back down with a clink.

"So I'm selling the building. Both buildings. I own both of them now, just me. His parents wanted it that way. That was the meeting. That brings us to the meeting, today. It's almost done." I stood up and walked over to the bookshelves. My back was to her now. My eyes felt hot. I tried to focus on the bindings of the books. There were knickknacks on the space between the edge of the shelves and the books. A ceramic figurine of a horse. An old postcard. More marbles. There were streaks in the dust that told me which books were recently removed from the shelf. I remember seeing James Baldwin. And Moby Dick.

Jill was talking. My ears were burning now, and I felt like I could hear static in them. Her voice was calm and even. I could barely hear her. I placed my fingers on the shelf in front of me and then looked at the finger marks I left in the thin layer of dust there. My eyes blinked back tears. She was talking about the city and how things changed so much since this past September. She was talking about making meaning of these things. "It will be up to your generation to make sense of all this."

I didn't want to make sense of anything. I felt the hot tears pour down my face and a sob racked my body. I wanted my friend back. I felt Jill's hands on my shoulders and I turned around quickly. She put her arms around me and we held each other. We stood there, embracing, for what seemed like an eternity. Both of us crying but for different reasons. The next thing I knew we were sitting on the couch, and with tears and tissues we both settled ourselves down. By the end of it, I was spent. She left the room at some point and returned with tea. I was finishing the final sip when Jill excused herself from the room again.

Why. Me.

I don't know how long I'd been sleeping on the couch when I felt her laying a blanket over me. I don't even remember laying down. "Hush," she said as I stirred. "You just rest."

Sometime later I heard muted voices from down the hall. I sensed that the front door had opened. I could hear Jill talking to someone. I opened my eyes to the dusk light in the apartment. Jill's voice carried down the hallway. "He's a former student... I think he needed to talk... Said he was at a meeting nearby." I guessed it was her husband she was speaking with, his voice was too deep for me to make out any words.

I sat up on the couch. Jill had cleared our tea cups and soup bowls. I must have slept hard. Unsure what to do, I sat there and rubbed my knees. Jill came around the corner from the hallway and I jumped up. "Jill, I should go. You weren't expecting me. Your family..." I didn't know what to say.

"My husband just came home. You are welcome to stay for dinner."

"I've overstayed. I'm sorry. I don't know what's wrong with me."

"Nothing wrong with you, Archer. At least nothing wrong with you that isn't wrong with all the rest of us." She said with a smile that told me she meant it.

As usual, I had no idea what to say. My hands felt sweaty and my mouth tasted like it does after a hard nap. My lips were chapped. I pressed them together. "I'm going to go. Jill you've been so... um." I smiled. "Thank you. I should really go."

Jill's husband introduced himself as I stood by the door while Jill got my coat. He gave me a firm but gentle handshake. "I really don't feel right sending you back out in this little jacket."

"It's okay, I'll get a cab."

"Where are you going?"

"I guess I'm figuring that out." I wasn't thinking she meant geographically. They both looked at me. "Well, tonight I'm going to Brooklyn. And then I'll figure out where to go next." Jill opened the door to me.

"A taxi to Brooklyn, that could cost a fortune. It's rush hour." Jill looked at her husband expectantly. They must have discussed this already.

"No worries there." I said with a smile. "Money is the one thing I've got."

★★★

Standing on the deck, looking out at the river and the electric company, I wondered why I was thinking of that day. It only took me a second to remember that Jill's was one of the faces that appeared out of the darkness in my dream the night before. I started to think about what Frankie said about my dream when I felt a tickle on my neck. I twitched and then smiled. "Hey you."

"Hey Why."

I turned around and gave Chance a big squeeze. Leaning back, I looked her in the eyes, my arms still tight around her waist. I gave her a big, loud kiss on the lips. "You look good enough to eat."

She pushed me back. "Don't get your hopes up, sucker." She smiled, pretending to be coy, and smacked herself on the butt. "You wish you could get this." She laughed in spite of herself.

"You just get here?" I looked over her shoulder through the windows, but I could only see silhouettes there.

"Yeah, me and Stacey and Chris. We ate already," she said, almost apologetically, as if I'd be offended they didn't ask me to cook for them. That was fine by me. "Going to have a drink. Or a couple." She smiled again. "Chrissy told me you hurt yourself. What happened?" She leaned over and tried to arch around me, looking at the bandage on my arm, a concerned look. "Jeez, what'd you do?" She grabbed my arm and spun me half around trying to look at my elbow, though she could only see the bandage.

"I took a spill, nothing major."

"A spill off what?"

"My bike." I said.

"Bike?" She looked at me quizzically. "Bike?" She asked again.

"Yeah, sort of a long story. I'm okay, don't worry about it. It's just a flesh wound."

She looked at me with curiosity. It was one of those moments I knew she wanted me to explain something more. I knew I wasn't always very good at explaining things at the level of detail she wanted. She shrugged, seemingly unphased at this example of it. "Maybe someday you'll tell me."

"Sure." I felt sort of frustrated with myself for not explaining it all. "Maybe later. Go get a drink, I'm going to close down the kitchen. What time is it?"

"Almost eleven," she said as she pulled her phone out of her back pocket to check, "a quarter to."

The kitchen is supposed to close at midnight, but it is sort of an unwritten policy that you can close at eleven if you've had no orders for an hour or so. It was over an hour since my last order. I didn't think it would be a big deal to

219

close a bit early tonight. Chrissy wouldn't care, or the other bartenders at the second bar.

The ritual of shutting down the grill area is one I really enjoy. There is something satisfying and final about it. My routine starts with running all the utensils and cutting boards through the dishwasher, which usually first requires emptying the glasses and other barware already in the machine. Once the washer is running, I wrap up all the lettuce and tomatoes that will still be good the next day in a couple layers of cellophane. I leave the large roll of plastic wrap on the counter because I will use it to seal up all the containers of uncooked ground beef, hot dogs, chicken and sausage once I've checked to make sure there's enough life in it. I'm a little over cautious with things like that, but when someone like Carl is working the shift before you, you can never be too careful. That guy would serve decomposing chicken and gray hamburger meat just out of laziness. Everything that needs to stay cold I carry to the back of the bar and put it on the shelves of the walk-in fridge. This part isn't necessary, but I like to wipe out the inside of the small fridge in the cooking area, possibly overkill, but then, there's Carl to consider. I thought about how he came back into the bar a couple hours into my shift. He walked right in and said nothing to me or Frankie while we played cards. Ten seconds later he came back to where we sat with a pack of smokes in his hand, asking where his lighter was. I told him I didn't know. He cursed at me and stormed out. What a jerk.

After wiping out the fridge, I take the bags of rolls out of the cabinet and toss them in the fridge for the night. I tighten the lids on the jars of spice mix, wrap the olive oil spout with wax paper and a rubber band, and put those and the other condiments into the fridge as well. I've usually got the water running to a nice hot temperature by that point, and I take a clean bar towel from behind Chrissy's bar and get it very hot and soapy, wiping down the counter until it is a soapy mess. Then I rinse the towel, wipe the counter, rinse the towel, wipe the counter and repeat until the counter is just wet, no soap.

I empty the cutting boards and utensils out of the dishwasher and dry them meticulously with another of Chrissy's bar towels. The utensils and cutting boards go in the cabinet, and the towels go in the bin behind the bar. The small broom is used to quickly sweep up the floor in the grill area, and a dustpan to scoop up the various crumbs and stuff, which I dump in the empty case of beer by my feet that I use as a garbage can.

The last step is the grill itself. Usually, especially on a slow night like this, I've got all the coals pushed to the back corner of the grill, so they will stay hot. I spread them out evenly, watching as the rush of air being drawn up the flue makes ripples of deep red and orange. There aren't that many hot coals left, at least, not as many as there could be. I stare at them, watching as the light breeze fans them slightly. I'm aware of how much cooler my back is than my chest, and my face feels warm and tight. I drop the piece of rebar we have there to stir the coals, and I put my hands in my pockets. Carl's lighter ends up in my hand. I smiled to myself as I took it from my pocket, pulling the metal child proof thing off with my fingernail and popping out the wheel of the lighter. I put the wheel back in my pocket and drop the remains of the lighter into the garbage box without looking. By my knees there are resting two large metal doors, which are meant to block the opening to the grill, hanging by two large hinges on each side of the brick fireplace. I hung one and then the other, closing them almost all the way and letting the draft pull them closed, making a mental note to close the flue before leaving for the night.

As expected, I feel calm and relaxed by the end of the ritual. I turn around, satisfied, and lean against the post, arms crossed. Behind Chrissy's bar there are shelves and shelves of glasses, a beer bottle display, and countless bottles of hard liquor. Just behind these shelves are windows, on the other side of which are booths that are served by the so-called "outside" bar. It isn't really outside, but in the warm months the doors along the outside of the building slide out so it is open to the air along the river. So we call it outside, even though the deck is really the only outside area.

In any case, sitting in the center booth were Chance and her friends Chris and Stacey. I saw them laughing about something, and Chance had a huge smile on her face. Sometimes when someone lets go and smiles because they really feel it and they are totally unaware of themselves for a moment, they show the side of themselves that usually only kids can show. And you can sort of see what they must have looked like as a child. Chance had that smile on her face right at that moment. It was the smile she wore when seeing the beach for the first time and when nailing a strike at the bowling alley. It's the smile I picture when it occurs to me just how in love with her I am. You can't hide behind anything when you are smiling like that.

Chapter 13

About six years ago, I freaked out. I had been reading the newspaper quite a bit, which wasn't the most usual thing for me. It was a phase. For some reason, I decided to subscribe to a handful of newspapers, The New York Times, Washington Post, USA Today, and a couple of others. I felt out of touch with the world, and for some reason this was my solution to that. It didn't really work. The news was depressing at best, but when I found myself reading the business sections, that was what did it to me. I had plenty of money, and I didn't spend a whole lot on living. But I was feeling very aware of the fact that I wasn't earning any money. I typically spent less than what my investments brought in. The news was making me nervous about that. Nervous is actually an understatement. Like I said, I freaked out.

My money has been a major source of guilt for me. The fact that I was living off of that money and that money alone made my entire life a source of guilt, and I was a little swamped in all of that. That didn't change the fact that I needed that money, as I had no work experience, no education after high school to speak of, and little to no motivation to actually *do* anything. I called the guy in New York who was managing my money. He was a close friend of the Rush family. They introduced me before we lost touch. I trusted him because I trusted them, but I didn't really know him.

I was reading things that I didn't really understand, which was not good for me. I was nervous because other people were writing things that they were nervous about. "Should I be nervous too?" I asked him.

He explained and re-explained about risk and how markets go up and down. He said some stuff about expectations and earnings. Something else about valuation and the long-term horizon. He was making me more nervous.

"Is my money safe?" I asked him.

He went on about what was safe and what wasn't safe. Levels of safety and about risk and about returns. My head was swimming. I called him because I was freaked out. He was freaking me out even more.

"Sell it."

"Sell what?"

"Sell whatever I have. You said cash is safe, right? Sell it. I want my money in cash. I want it in a bank account. I want to see it." This is when I got stubborn. I didn't understand it. I was told what to do if I didn't understand something. What he was talking about sounded like smoke and mirrors to me. He explained how much money I had in these investments. He explained how well I'd done. He started talking about taxes and that I should talk to my accountant.

No one ever taught me about any of this, so I started to talk to a couple people, but my stubborn unwillingness to understand led me the same direction where I started. I sold it all. Everything. I put everything in cash accounts and CDs, which someone explained as being very similar to cash. That part made sense to me, nothing else did. I ended up paying a big tax bill, but as I saw it, I was still ahead. I only paid taxes because I made money. That seemed fair to me.

Cash is much more real than an investment account, and I found myself looking at my balances every day. Sometimes I would withdraw several thousand dollars and walk around with it stuffed in my pockets. I even started to become a little nervous about my money being in banks. I read an article about inflation. And I started looking around on the web, finding myself on websites promoting gold as the single safest investment for avoiding inflation. The arguments seemed rational. I started buying gold from local dealers. An ounce here, and an ounce there. It was sort of like a hobby, but it became an addiction.

It was clear to me that my financial advisor and my accountant both thought I was a complete idiot. In the process of selling everything and moving money out of places where it was making money and moving it to accounts where it would make so much less, I found myself talking with them a lot. I'd taken up the interest in gold before I finished unloading my other investments. They worked for me, and they were making money from me, but that didn't keep them from essentially telling me I was a dumb ass. "You are selling investments that will make you money. You are buying metal that is overpriced. It's a bubble that's going to burst," they told me.

It was only a year or two later when I found myself wanting to call and ask them "how do you like me now?" A series of decisions based on fear. A series of decisions that seemed pretty unintelligent at the time. I looked like a genius when all the shit hit the fan. Keep it simple, stupid. That's why people say that kind of thing. Of course, I was only lucky.

★★★

About two years ago, I freaked out again. I came home one day and my front door was open. I looked down the hallway, for some reason, and then walked into the apartment, petrified about what I might see. Nothing looked disturbed. I walked cautiously around the corner and peered into the kitchen. There was nothing to see. I went over to the bathroom and opened the door quickly. Nervous now, I went back over to the front door, locked it, which was probably not the best choice if there actually was an intruder, and walked over to the spiral staircase.

"Hey." I shouted, really loud.

Nothing.

After creeping up the spiral stairs and searching though the bedroom, I took a deep breath and walked to the corner of the room that functioned like a closet. I got on my hands and knees and pushed a few shoeboxes to the side to reveal a small wooden chest. It was nothing fancy. I bought it at a discount store, I just thought it looked like a treasure chest. I opened it up and sighed in relief, even though I was sure by this point that I'd simply left my door open. No one had been inside. And no one had touched, because no one knew about, the box in my closet that housed the hundreds of ounces of gold bullion that I bought a few years before.

I sat on my butt in the closet and said out loud, "I have to get rid of this shit."

And so I did. I went back to the places where I bought it in the first place. Having run through the phase of reading newspapers, and having not purchased any gold for some time, I didn't realize that it was worth more than I expected. I had too much to sell to these dealers. They didn't want to buy it all, couldn't afford to. I got my so called advisors on the phone and figured out the best way to get rid of all of it. To sell it all off. I somehow made a large amount of money as a result of buying this stuff. Guilty, guilty, guilty. Everyone else thought I was smart. I just felt like a jerk.

Why. Me.

★★★

About six months ago, we went for a drive.

"C'mon, Chance! What are you doing up there? Let's go."

Chance's head appeared over the edge of the bedroom loft. "What is your rush, Archer? You've been acting like a nut all morning. Sheesh." She shook her head as she turned around, her incredible curly hair bobbing around her head.

She was right. I was excited for this trip. She didn't even know where we were going, but she knew me well enough to know that getting there on time wasn't super important. She knew I didn't have tickets to something or anything like that. Trying to be patient, I picked up my bags and moved them a few feet closer to the door. I went into the kitchen and dried an empty bowl and put it in the cabinet. There was a puddle of water on the counter so I grabbed a dishtowel and wiped it up, tossed it on the counter by the sink. I fought the urge to ask Chance if she was almost ready. She was still fussing around upstairs. A drawer closed, and then another one opened. What could she be doing up there?

Less than five minutes later she came down the spiral staircase, carefully and slowly like always. I jumped up from where I sat down on the couch in the middle of the room. She was wearing tight jeans and a white turtleneck under a thin wool sweater the color of rust. She wore small silver dangling earrings, and her hair was more curly than usual. She was carrying a green nylon duffle bag over one shoulder and a pair of speckled gray wool socks in the opposite hand. The bag hit the floor at the same time she hit the armchair. With one leg crossed over the other, she pulled on a sock,

227

and then switched and did the other one. She was looking at me, so I sat back down.

"Where are you taking me, Why?"

"Is that what took you so long to pack? I said we'd be gone a night, maybe two, totally casual and..."

"I know what you said," she interrupted me. "Did I take longer than twenty minutes to get ready this morning? You are off the wall today, boy." She laughed and shook her head and stood up. "Do I have to wait for you now? Get my bag, would you?" She walked toward the door and took a jacket off the hook but didn't put it on.

Outside, it was cool and dry. There were leaves blowing around the parking lot. It wasn't cold out, but I'd told Chance to pack for cold weather, since we were going north. I just didn't tell her the north part. She tossed her jacket in the back seat while I put the bags in the trunk. It looked like I packed more than her, but I think it is because her clothes are smaller than mine. She is pretty small.

We'd been driving about twenty minutes when Chance asked me, "would it ruin something if you just told me where we were going?" She was pretending not to be excited about having a surprise. I think she was also excited we were going somewhere. We had sort of a low-key summer, as she was really busy with classes. She was hoping to be done with school at the end of this academic year. She was in the middle of a semester now, but I think she needed a little break.

"It wouldn't ruin anything. Did you want me to tell you? I thought you liked surprises." I didn't take my eyes off the road, but I could see out of the corner of my eye that she was looking at me. "I was actually thinking it's sort of pointless not to tell you where we're going. It's nothing amazing, really."

"You don't have to tell me. I like the suspense. I'm just excited." She turned her head and looked out the window. I did feel sort of silly not telling her. For months, I'd been wanting to bring her up to New Hampshire and for her to meet Ken and his wife Laurel. I've been visiting him occasionally, and we've stayed in touch, slowly becoming friends along the way. I also thought Chance would love seeing the camp. I spoke about it with her, here and there. She would look at me, interested, but with that look of someone who is trying to share in someone else's fond memory. Hard to pull off. For some reason, I wanted to share it with her. I hoped it might become a place where we would have memories together. That, and the fact that the place is simply beautiful this time of year. There are entire industries created just to bring people to places far less beautiful than this spot. October up there is perfect.

Chance was asleep for over an hour when I took the exit for Route 16. We were really close now. She dozed off sometime after Boston, we'd been chatting here and there but I could tell she was sleepy. She always gets tired in the car. I saw a sign for Freedom approaching, and I didn't realize she was awake until she said, "Oh, camp. You're taking me to camp." I could tell she was still waking up when she said it. She yawned and turned over to me. "You brought me to camp." She rested her hand on my forearm and her forehead where my bicep met my shoulder. I was always amazed how little she looked when she was in the front seat of a car. She could sit there all crossed legged in the seat like a kid in an armchair.

I put my hand on her knee. "Surprise, kid." I said quietly. I took the left onto Route 153 and turned right into a gravel parking lot. "You wanna stretch your legs a minute?" I was eager to get up to camp and show Chance around, but I was thirsty and I wanted to give her a chance to wake up. We were really almost there, but I stopped at the little package store at the edge of town. The air was just as dry and crisp as when we left Providence, but it was a few degrees colder, even though it was now the middle of the day and the sun was about as high as it would get. I stretched up and walked around to the other side of the car to give Chance a squeeze. She was stretching when I got over there, and she draped her arms over my shoulders and fell limp against me. I wasn't really ready for it, but I snatched her up and swung her around. "Let's get a drink," I said loudly, swinging my head back.

Inside, the store was exactly the same as the first time I set foot in there, about fifteen years ago. Except instead of the old guy behind the counter, there was a young guy wearing a knit cap and drinking an energy drink. The place was dusty and smelled like old wood, the floor creaked and you could hear country music playing somewhere faintly. We walked over to the cooler and each found a drink we were happy with. I suggested to Chance she find a bottle of wine to bring with us. She agreed and went a row over to look. "Red or white, you think?" She asked. I gave her a clueless look. Wine is not my thing.

I wandered to the back of the store, which wasn't all that large, and found myself in the whiskey section. For a small town, there was a pretty decent selection of booze in this place. I was impressed when I saw a bottle of Oban on the rack, an 18-year-old single malt. Not a huge drinker when I was younger, working at the Club gave me some knowledge of these things. And I'd developed a little bit of a taste for scotch. I'm no expert, but this is pretty decent stuff. I snatched the bottle off the rack, thinking Ken might appreciate it, and walked over to Chance.

"What is this all about?" She said, looking at the label on the bottle of red wine in her hand.

I glanced at the label. It was in English. That's when it occurred to me that she wasn't talking about the bottle. "What about, about what?" I stumbled on the words.

"Why didn't you tell me we were coming here? Why this... why a surprise to come here?" I didn't answer right away. "Not that I'm not glad you wanted me to come up here. You talk about Ken. He... it always seems like this is your place. With him. Like it's something you have just for you. Or something."

I shrugged. "I guess I wanted to share it with you."

She touched her hair and looked down at her jeans. "I look like a bum."

"It's okay, he's not my mom." Which was a weird thing to say for a lot of reasons. I tried to recover. "A bum? Please, you look awesome. Don't sweat it. Ken's as easy as Sunday morning. His wife too."

"Laurel, right?"

I nodded. "You getting that one? We getting that one?" I corrected myself, pointing to the bottle in her hand.

"Sure. What do I know?" She handed it to me, noticing the other bottle I was carrying.

At the checkout counter, the young guy put his phone down to get our stuff. "That it?" He asked to the beverages.

"Yup." I didn't recognize the insignia on his knit cap. "What's that?" I asked, pointing at his head. He must have thought I was talking to Chance. I looked at her but she was focused on the kid's hat too. She didn't look at me. He was looking at the bottle of scotch I handed him, rotating it, looking for a price. He pulled a book out from under the counter. His head rotated back and forth from the bottle to the book, flipping the pages slowly. *L, m, n, O.* I thought

231

to myself. This kid was cracking me up. Isn't it in alphabetical order? He put the book back under the counter and excused himself to walk over to the racks. "It was the only one there," I said when I realized what he was looking for.

"Of course it was," he muttered. Back behind the counter, he finally looked at my face. "How much is this?"

He was asking me how much it cost. "You're asking me?"

"Is it like thirty bucks or something?" He looked at the label again for a clue. He seemed unsure of himself. Nervous.

I never bought a bottle of this before, so I had no idea, but I really didn't want the kid to get in trouble if he under charged me. Chance was looking at me. I reached into my pocket and pulled out a billfold. "How much is the wine?" I asked him. "And these?" pointing to our cold drinks.

"Wine is fourteen ninety-nine. These are each a buck fifty."

I pulled five twenties off the billfold, thought about it, and pulled off another twenty. "I'm sure this'll do it."

"You sure?" he said, looking at the bills I was handing to him. Chance was still looking at me, her chestnut eyes gone a little bit rounder than usual, mouth open.

"Not really, but this is good stuff."

"Okay, you say so." I wondered if he'd pocket some of the money. Not my problem.

The three of us stood there in silence.

"You think I could get a bag for these?" I finally asked.

The screen door slammed shut behind us, and Chance swung around and walked backwards in front of me. "Is that really a hundred-dollar bottle of scotch?" She asked.

"It is now," I said, shrugging. "I've got no clue, but I'd guess about sixty or seventy. They overcharge on everything around here."

"Except you overcharged yourself, sucker." She poked me in the stomach and turned around. I would have snatched her up, but my hands were full.

The last bit of the drive was only about ten minutes, maybe less. Chance was pretty quiet most of the way, just looking out the window. As we made our way up the final hill, she asked me something.

"Arch, should I be nervous about this?"

"Why would you say that?"

"I don't know. You never do surprises. Just makes me wonder if you've got something up your sleeve."

"Nope, nothing up there." I pushed my sweatshirt up to prove the point. I reached over and put my hand on her knee. "You got nothing to worry about, babe. This is just fun. These are our friends." I leaned over and gave her a quick kiss on the lips, kind of sideways.

"They're your friends."

"Soon to be ours, okay?" I could see her staring at me out of the corner of my eye.

The tires rumbled on the dirt road as we made the final turn. The road was sloped, and I coasted down, easing off the road to the parking area on the left. We arrived.

Suddenly I was nervous for some reason, too. I'd never been nervous here before. At least not since I was a kid, showing up in my father's car at fourteen. Even then not so much. Maybe I just hadn't really thought what it would be like to introduce Chance to someone. I never did a formal introduction like that with her. Or, with anyone really. I should have known nothing would be difficult with Ken.

He came strolling down the hill as we were getting out of the car.

He gave me a signature bear hug, which he'd taken to doing with me every time I saw him lately. "Farmer Why," he bellowed, plopping me back on my feet. I couldn't help but smile. He never explained why he started calling me that. I never really asked.

"This is Chance." I gestured towards her, which was unnecessary. Her hand went out for a shake, but I don't think Ken really noticed. He pulled her in too and gave her a hug. She had a big smile on her face when he put her down. I could tell she wasn't nervous anymore.

We exchanged the typical pleasantries while Laurel made her way down the hill, taking the same route Ken took just a few minutes before. She gave me a lingering hug and one for Chance too. It is hard to explain, but Ken and Laurel are special folks, if only in that they are both just real people. Honest, kind, relaxed. Neither were married before they met in their forties, which is hard for me to understand for the simple reason that they are both such awesome people. They seemed made for each other. Their life together was, simply put, a pure expression of love. I can't think of any other way to explain it. Whenever I want to get myself choked up with sentiment, I only have to think about them together.

After a few minutes of chatting, Ken said, "well, I'm sure you want to show Chance around," he winked at Chance, adding, "and I'm sure Chance can't wait. Come on up to the house when you are done. We can have lunch then." The last few words were over his shoulder as he started back walking across the road.

"Really nice meeting you, Chance. See you in a bit." Laurel turned to me. "So glad you are here, Archer." She followed Ken up the hill.

For the next forty-five minutes or so, Chance followed me around the grounds of the camp. We walked through the old farmhouse and the playhouse. We went up by the cabins where the campers would sleep, which were all boarded up for the impending winter. I showed her inside the arts and crafts room that was up behind the maintenance shop, and past the empty goat pen to the wood working area. I pointed out the shower house, the so called "tripping" shed where all the equipment for camping and canoeing trips was kept. I even showed her the woodshed I helped build one summer when I worked there. All through the walk, I tried to tell stories about the different places in camp. The time the camper caught his thigh on the swing set and needed stitches. The time when I fell backwards through the fence into the goat pen and how it took us half an hour to coax the goat back in there. She smiled with forced interest while I spoke. I knew it was hard for her to get excited about all these stories. They were my memories. I was being a little selfish, this wasn't why I brought her here.

We were back down below the road, on the porch of the playhouse. "You're being a good sport." I said, giving her a hug.

"What do you mean?" She left her head against my chest.

"This is boring for you, the stories and stuff."

"No, I like it. I like seeing you here."

"Thanks, babe. But I'll try to cut the stories out. This place stands on its own," I looked out over the porch railing, where miles of gold, red and orange leaved trees spread out to the horizon past where the lawns of the lower fields of camp ended. "Let's get some lunch."

"It really is beautiful." I think it was the first chance I gave her to see that.

★★★

Ken and Laurel live in what is technically the infirmary. There is a small nursing office in the front where kids get their medications or a bandage applied during the summer. During the off months, that becomes a small sitting room. There is a larger L-shaped room which sort of wraps around that sitting area, where sick kids would nap during the day if they needed a rest away from their peers. This became a dining room and living room of sorts, with a small wood burning stove at one end of it. Just past that is the small kitchen. Then there are two small rooms in the back of the cabin; a bedroom and an office. They call it their family room. It is a small and very cozy home.

It wasn't always a year-round house, but after they were married, they decided to fully winterize the building. A wood burning stove, a propane heater for the bedroom, a boat load of insulation and fresh drywall later, and they were in business. There was only one other structure on the grounds that could even conceivably be called year-round, and it was at the far corner of camp, right by the trailhead that leads up to the well house and then to the mountain above camp beyond that. It was aptly called the Red Shed, it being red and about the size of a shed. But, for some reason, a wood burning stove was installed there decades earlier when it was built. So even though it was not insulated, it could be kept warm if necessary. It was one of the older buildings there, probably only younger than the farmhouse and the playhouse. That's where Chance and I were going to sleep.

Lunch was a tasty treat, with a great big spinach salad full of dried cranberries, goat cheese and sunflower seeds, a platter of fresh mozzarella, slices of tomato, and fresh basil, some grainy fresh bread and a pitcher of iced tea. It was nice clean food. Delicious.

After lunch, Chance and I grabbed our bags from the car and went up to the shed to settle in. They'd made the bed up with lots of pillows and a stack of blankets. There was a pile of wood and newspapers outside the front door, with a book of matches on the top like a mint on a pillow. It probably wouldn't be cold enough for a fire, but it might be romantic. We'd have to see what the night would bring.

This cabin is small, especially when it is set up with two mattresses side by side. There was one small dresser wedged into the corner, blocking almost half of the entrance to the tiny bathroom, toilet and sink only, opposite the door. There was about two feet between the foot of the bed and the stove. It was tight, but we didn't need much space. We pulled a couple things out of the bags and put them in the dresser, but mostly opted to leave the bulk of our stuff in the bags, jammed in the corner opposite the dresser.

"Lunch was good." Chance said, laying down on the bed.

"You got that right." I stretched out next to her on the bed, looking up at the wood roof of the shed.

Chance propped herself up on one elbow. "Do they always treat you so well?"

"Always." I said towards the roof.

"I like it here already." She curled up a little and nuzzled her forehead into my armpit. She threw her left arm over my chest. I could tell she was going to fall asleep. I listened closely to her breathing, her breaths coming slower and deeper. I felt her arm go slightly limp. Chance could always fall asleep so quickly when she was comfortable. She really must have felt at home. I could relate to that.

When I woke up it was with a start. For a split second I didn't know where I was. The Red Shed. Chance was now on her left side, facing away from me. I lifted my legs over the side of the bed and got up slowly. Chance didn't move at all. So the screen door wouldn't slam, I held it all the way till it was closed. I sat on the three cinderblocks that made up the front step of the cabin, wondering what time it was. My cell phone wasn't in my pocket, where it usually is. It must have fallen out onto the bed. I didn't feel like I slept long, but the light had a late afternoon quality to it. Maybe I slept about an hour or so, hard to tell.

I heard a slight creak behind me and felt a gentle tap on my lower back. "Hey, move over." Chance was opening the screen door into my back. I leaned forward enough for her to get out of the door. She closed the screen door gently, same as I had, like she didn't want to disturb anyone. She sat down next to me. "You were going to leave me in there?" She said with a yawn. She leaned her head against my shoulder and tucked her arms between her knees.

"You kidding me? I'm just out here protecting you. Gotta watch out for bears and stuff." I put my arm over her shoulders and pulled her in tight.

"Yeah right. You'd wet your pants if a bear came up here. Tough guy." She made herself laugh whenever she talked about what a wimp I am. It's true, though. I'm pretty much a wimp.

"I guess you're wide awake, already making fun of me." I mocked up a little hurt feeling, and then, "I'd let the

238

bear eat you first, of course, while I made my getaway. But then, you'd just be a little snack for him."

We sat quietly for a few minutes, just looking at the grass, the leaves, the trees. I turned and put my lips against her head and took a deep inhale through my nose. Damn, she smells so good.

"So what do you do around here?"

"We could go for a walk. Drive down to the lake for a swim. Nap. Sit here. Whatever you want."

"No expectations?"

"Nope. What do you want to do?"

"You brought me up here with no plans? What would you do if I wasn't here?"

"Probably just sit around. Maybe play cards with Ken or Laurel. Sometimes go for a swim."

"Let's do that."

"What, cards? Sit?"

"No, swim. Can we do that?" She was so earnest. She really wasn't sure if that was okay.

"Whatever you like."

We got our suits from our bags inside the cabin. I realized we didn't have any towels, but we'd find some around somewhere. Ken was sitting outside on the steps of the farmhouse, reading. He liked to read out there on the concrete steps. It always seemed so uncomfortable to me. "Ken, you guys want to hit the lake?"

"I'm good. Laurel is sleeping, so I think she's all set." He barely looked up from his book. He said something else.

"What's that?" I asked.

"The dock is still in, and the raft. Have fun," he looked up and smiled at us.

It was only about ten minutes to the lake. Chance had her feet up on the dashboard, which always made me nervous, but less so up here on these country roads. Not so many cars coming from the other way, I guess. I missed the turn to the camp's lakefront driveway the first time, but after a quick U-turn we were home free. I pulled past the parking area and parked right behind the bench at the top of the beach. We both got out. Chance looked so excited. She loves being outside. I couldn't believe I never brought her up here before.

Throwing modesty to the wind, Chance dropped her bathing suit on the ground, and stripped naked. Despite my expectation that she'd pick up the bathing suit, the next thing I knew she was sprinting full speed down the beach and running into the lake. She disappeared under the water, and then her curly head bobbed up about fifteen feet further out. Ripples spread out in concentric circles from her head. They disappeared under the deck that was parallel to the shoreline and then appeared, somewhat smoother, on the other side.

"Get on out here, Why!" she yelled, giggling. She disappeared under the water again.

I had never been skinny dipping in this lake before, and for some reason I felt bashful about it. But I didn't let that get the better of me. Stripping down and dropping my clothes on top of my bathing suit, I felt a little goofy running naked into the lake. I didn't feel like I could get in the water fast enough, that someone might see me just flopping around like that.

★★★

By the end of dinner, we all had quite a buzz. After the bottle of red that Chance and I brought, we went through another, and then opened another, the first round of which was in our glasses when we were finally clearing our plates away from the table. Another amazing meal by Laurel and Ken, who zipped around the kitchen together when they cooked, creating a meal the way two old friends create a conversation, effortlessly and enviably. Ken came back to the table carrying the bottle of scotch I brought him. He was looking at the label.

"So what did you bring me here?"

"Just a bottle. Thought you'd like it."

"Well, I guess we will have to see." He smiled wide, his teeth slightly purpled by the wine.

"Why don't you boys go on out and have a drink. Chance and I are going to watch a movie here." Laurel came out of the kitchen, where she and Chance were putting things into the sink. I wasn't really sure what to do. Before answering I slipped out of my seat and went into the kitchen.

"Hey babe, you doing okay?" I whispered in her ear, giving her a squeeze from behind.

"I'm great," she swiftly rotated in my arms and popped one on my lips. "You guys should go have a drink. Laurel and I were just saying we could watch a movie for a bit. I'm too tired to drink more, but you should go out with Ken. You never see him.

I really wanted to make sure that she was comfortable, not just saying so. "You sure you're good? We could just go to bed."

"Go have your scotch, just come check on me in a bit, okay?" She leaned back. Her eyes were sleepy and a little red from the drinking. She was tired, but I could tell she was relaxed and happy.

"Okay, kid. I'll see you in a bit."

Ken and I walked in silence down the hill and across the road to the playhouse porch, the only sounds were our footsteps and the tinkling of ice in our empty glasses. The steps creaked as we made our way onto the porch. Ken leaned against the railing and I sat on the porch swing, where a couple of hours previously Chance and I watched the sun set after our swim in the lake, like a drop of gold melting on the horizon. It was a good one.

The sound of the cork popping out of the bottle was satisfying, and Ken poured us each a couple fingers. I swirled it in my glass to speed its cooling. I took a sip. It was smooth and slightly smoky. Delicious. I took another. Ken let out a long low whistle.

The moon was high in the sky, and I could make out the silvery tops of the trees in the distance behind Ken. He was silhouetted against them. We got to talking about various things. He spoke about getting ready for winter. I spoke about how things were going at the Club. He talked awhile about how he and Laurel were considering taking in a kid from foster care. I mentioned that my father was about to put the Providence house on the market, that he had pretty much officially relocated to Florida.

We were a couple of glasses into the bottle, and Ken was now sitting next to me on the swing, our feet on the railing of the porch. "There was a fire down the road at the end of the summer." He said in a matter of fact tone.

"While the kids were here? That must have been scary. Forest fire or something?" It seemed odd it hadn't come up earlier. His tone of voice seemed odd, too.

"No, after the session. Late August. No, early September," he corrected himself.

There was a moment of silence.

"No, not a forest fire. The house. The family next door, you remember, the Pelletiers? The ones you kids always had the stories about."

"No shit, really? Everyone okay?"

"No. No, not at all." He said flatly. "No one is okay. Not really."

I got up and leaned against the railing. The moon had dropped slightly, so I could see a slight shadow in front of me. My eyes were adjusted, and I could see Ken's face pretty clearly now. "What do you mean?"

He went on to tell a crazy story, about how the fire started in a shed on their property. One of the sons of the family came running over to Ken's house, about three in the morning, banging on the door and yelling. "They had no phone," Ken explained, "he wanted me to call someone. So I did. I'll never figure out why."

I didn't know what he meant by that, but it didn't register to me to ask. "So then what?"

After making the call, Ken went down the road with the Pelletier kid, a lanky tattooed guy, thinking maybe he could help. The kid was jumpy and nervous. Their house was up a steep driveway from the road, and when they got closer to the top of the driveway, he just ran up into the house, leaving Ken standing there. The shed was near the house, but not so near that the house would necessarily be in danger, Ken described. Weighing his options of what to do, it took him by total surprise when the shed simply exploded. Ken said he dove onto the ground, and when he looked up there were a couple of trees up in flames. He could see the kid and a couple others running out of the house with armfuls of something and heading up the hill behind the house. The flames gave him enough light to see a little, but their property was a mess with no particularly large open spaces.

"I figured the explosion was a propane tank or something like that. It was loud as hell, and the fire was really hot. I wasn't sure why I was there. Nothing I could really do. All the years here, and none of us ever really knew the family. I didn't even know how many people lived up there, just that they'd always be coming and going on their motorcycles and pickups. I remember thinking that the fire could spread to camp. But the wind was going the other direction. It was crazy."

A fire department in a town like Freedom doesn't have a huge capacity. In a case like this, volunteers from several neighboring towns would come out to help fight a fire. This one took quite a while to put out, from the story Ken described. But it wasn't until daylight that the real story would get told.

"Turns out that their property was basically a meth lab. The Pelletiers were neck deep in producing and trafficking the stuff. The whole family is basically in jail at this point. The numskulls were running up the hill trying to hide stuff away before anyone could get there to help them put the fire out."

"So the fire was a meth lab exploding or something?" I was out of my element on this topic. I have no idea if meth labs explode.

"Nope. A cigarette. Some idiot left a cigarette burning in the shed. But I guess there was a fair amount of accelerant around. Tough fire to put out. Spread to the house and everything before they got it under control. Real mess."

"That's some story." I took a deep breath.

He let out another long whistle. "Pour us a splash more, would you? Let me tell you the rest."

Chapter 14

After Ken finished the story, we sat in silence for a few minutes, looking out over the moon drenched countryside. Side by side on the porch swing, more than half drunk at this point. At least I was. I stood up a little bit too fast and snatched the bottle off the railing. I steadied myself and raised my glass at the moon as if to toast it, but I had nothing to say. I sat back down, poured a splash into my empty glass, and took a sip. The bottle was about a third full at this point. Or two thirds empty. I swirled the contents and looked at the moon through the bottle, which was now visible through the limbs of the tree in front of the porch. I poured another inch of scotch into my tumbler.

"Let's go for a walk," I said at long last. I felt a little like I was on display, but Ken didn't seem to notice. I'm not sure exactly why I felt that way. "C'mon. Get up." It is possible I had the hiccups at this point. The scotch was getting to me.

"Yup." Ken said. I think he was pretty drunk too, but he knew where I wanted to go. He stood up slowly and held out his glass. I gave him a heavy pour.

"Let's go check on the girls first." I was feeling guilty that I hadn't done so earlier like I promised Chance.

"Yup."

The road looked almost like it was broad daylight. Even the small rocks seemed to have defined shadows. The moon gave off almost enough light to see things in color, but everything was in sepia tones. I could tell it was cold outside, but I wasn't cold. As I approached the front door, I felt a tap on my shoulder. Ken was gesturing for me to come over to the window. "Don't go inside," he whispered, almost like a little kid. "Let's peep in on them."

We crept over to the window, where you could see the telltale flicker of a television. It took only a moment for my eyes to adjust to what I was seeing through the window. Laurel and Chance were lying on the couch, head to foot, completely asleep.

"C'mon," Ken whispered. "They're out."

I stood there for a minute, transfixed. I could hear Ken's footsteps walking away, but I was mesmerized by Chance's face. Sleeping there in the cool iridescent light of the television, she looked simply beautiful to me. Her skin seemed soft and pearly, glowing. She looked like a woman and a child all at the same time, so pure and perfect. Maybe I was drunk, but what a sight. I found it hard to look away. Thinking back on that moment, I wonder how I never knew until that point quite how deeply I'd fallen for that girl. What a nice thing to realize, even in a drunken stupor.

★★★

Looking at her through the windows behind Chrissy's bar, her smile as pure as a child's, I remembered that night and smiled in spite of myself. I can be such a cheeseball about stuff like that when I let myself. I can't be sure how long I was standing there with a goofy smile, reminiscing, when I realized Chance was looking back at me through the window. *Hey you*, I read her lips while she waved at me. She gestured for me to come around to where they were sitting. I nodded and smiled, a normal smile, not the half glazed one I was wearing a moment before.

I turned around to see what else I needed to do to shut down the grill area, but there was nothing. I was done for the night.

Why. Me.

I sidled up to Chrissy's bar and picked up my mug from where I left it by the napkins and straws. Chrissy turned to look at me. I smiled, tapped my mug on the bar and held it up. She smiled back, reached into the cooler, pulled out a beer and opened it for me. She slid it down the bar and said, "quit fucking smiling at me you stupid shit. All you do is stand around here and bother everybody. What the fuck is wrong with you?" She wasn't even looking at me anymore, walking back to talk with her regulars at the other end of the bar.

"I love you too, sweet thing." I hurled down the bar at her. She gave me a flirty grin over her shoulder and swung her head back around, her flaming hair swinging wildly about her shoulders.

I joined Chance and her friends in the booth on the other side of the bar, but they were deep in a conversation about something to do with their big project. Nothing I could help out with. On any other day, I'd try to get involved in the conversation, but I felt like I was in a daze. My body was aching, and it felt a little worse to be sitting down now, like I wouldn't be able to get up. Chance had her hand on my thigh under the table. It was about the only thing that kept me sitting there for as long as I did. I excused myself and went over to the juke box, which wasn't really a juke box. It was one of those wall mounted things, but it served the same purpose. I slid a dollar in the slot and chose a few songs, sort of uninspired by the selection. I wandered to the windows that overlooked the river, put my beer on the ledge and stretched my arms and pulled my knees up to my stomach one by one. I took a long draw off my beer.

"Hey stranger." Chance slid up next to me and rested her elbows on the ledge, her face on her hands. She looked out at the water.

"Hey," I replied. I looked over my shoulder, over the bar to the now empty booth. "Everyone left?"

"Yeah, we just wanted to have a quick drink. I'm glad you could close early." She turned around and rested her elbows on the ledge behind her. She looked up at me. "You ready to go, Why? I'm pooped. You kept me out too late last night."

"And we lost an hour." I said quietly, yawning so that the word hour came out in three syllables. I was pretty tired too. I put my hand on her stomach. "Let's go."

I said goodbyes to Chrissy, a couple regulars and Frankie as we made our way out of the Club. Chance was parked on the street rather than in the parking lot. I opened her door for her and was about to get in the passenger side when I realized I forgot my bike. "Hey, I'll be back in a second. I want to grab my bike." I figured I could get it in the trunk, even if I couldn't close it. The drive wasn't all that far.

Frankie didn't look up when I came in, intently reading something in some sort of men's magazine. I walked around past the booths and the walk-in cooler to the back deck, where I left my bike leaning by the dumpster. It only took a second of trying to push it to remember how messed up the front wheel was. I leaned the bike against the fence and stepped back to take a look at it. A part of me wanted to bring it home, fix it up, and hold onto it. A far larger part did not.

I picked the bike up and tried to throw it into the dumpster. But the thing was too full and the bike was sticking up out of the top. The manager was a cool guy, but I could see that leaving the bike there might piss him off. The deck on this side of the bar was narrow, and it ran from the dumpster area all the way along the side of the building to the water. I rolled the bike awkwardly to the edge, picked it up by the seat and the top tube, and flung it into the river. Or at least I tried to. I heard a thump and a crash below me. I only managed to toss the thing onto the walkway that led to the marina just next door. It was sitting down there on the dock.

"Fuck." I said to myself. "Dammit all." I hopped over the fence, shimmied down the ladder to the dock below, picked up the bike and hurled it as far as I could in the river, which was only about ten feet. I watched it sink quickly into the water. Climbing back up the ladder, I wasn't really sure why I wanted to get rid of the bike like that. I don't even litter.

As I passed Frankie on my way to the door, I heard him say to my back, "where's the bike?"

"I'll pick it up tomorrow, don't think I can get it in the car." I said without turning around as I opened the door and walked back to the car where Chance was waiting for me.

"Where's this bike?" she asked as well.

"I threw it in the river."

She shrugged and put the car in gear, heading home. I'm sure she thought I was joking.

Driving over the Point Street Bridge, I looked across the water, the final resting place of that stupid bike, and thought about what Frankie said. What he said about my dream. He was onto something. When you meet people and when you get to know them, you end up keeping a piece of them. I suppose that means they end up with a part of you as well. I think that's why when someone leaves it hurts so much. You become incomplete. And when they are gone forever, so is that piece of you. You're left with what you've got of them, though. That helps. So we're all just walking around, it seems, with bits of ourselves scattered around. And in those empty places we hold the pieces of everyone else. We risk losing bits of ourselves, but we are made whole by what we get in return.

"What are you thinking about over there?" Chance put her hand on my leg. We were driving alongside downtown, which was off to our right. I was looking at all the lights. It actually looked like a busy place, even on a Sunday. But I knew they were just lights.

"I was just thinking about Frankie."

"Did he beat you at cards or something?" She teased. She knows how competitive I can get with him.

"No, we tied tonight. Just something he said. It was nothing." But I could feel my heart beating a little faster for some reason.

★★★

I took off my shoes when I entered my apartment. Just sitting in the car for ten minutes made my body feel tight. I peeled off my sweatshirt and hung it on one of the hooks under the mirror. The bag Jonas left was sitting there near the wall, I gave it a kick and then slid it with my foot till it was up against the bricks. I told Chance that I was going to rinse off in the shower before bed and tend to my wounds. I made it sound more dramatic than necessary, just to get a little more sympathy, but it wasn't so forthcoming. That isn't always Chance's style, which I like.

"Let me shower first, I hate it when you are ready for bed before me." That was true, she did hate that.

"You showered this morning, that's not very green of you."

Why. Me.

"I just want to go to bed as fresh as you. Wait your turn." She crept up the stairs to get some items for her shower. I flopped myself down on the couch and instantly regretted it when my elbow landed before my body. That shit hurt. I groaned and rolled to my other side. Damn bike. I heard Chance coming back down the spiral stairs and the bathroom door closing. The water started running in the shower.

I rolled slowly onto my back and looked up at the lights above, which were dimmed very low. The whole apartment was bathed in a gentle light. With the lights like this it is reminiscent of the moonlight up in New Hampshire on a real clear night, like the night when Ken and I were headed down the road for a little walk, nearly half a bottle of scotch in each of us, while Chance and Laurel were sacked out in the infirmary.

After Ken called me out of my reverie, gazing at a sleeping Chance on the couch, we made our way down to the road. I only suggested a walk, but like I said, Ken knew where it was I wanted to go. We turned up the driveway at the Pelletier property.

"You sure there's no one here?" I was whispering, which was probably unnecessary. But this had all the makings of a horror movie. I could almost hear the audience saying *don't go up there, are you crazy?!*

"There's nobody here." Ken said, also whispering, but much louder than me. We continued to head up the steep and curving driveway. After about fifty yards, the trees were noticeably less close to the driveway. After another fifty or so, the driveway was curving through a wide yard. In the moonlight, you could see the area was overgrown and strewn with various items. Broken flowerpots, tires, mounds of dirt, five gallon buckets, a pile of rope. There

251

was an old pickup on cinderblocks. Even the moonlight couldn't make it pretty. The driveway sloped up to an old outbuilding that looked like a small barn. Or half of a small barn. The half that was closest to the house looked like something had taken a giant bite out of it. The house, which sat alongside but further up the hill was more than half burned, and you could see even more rubble up behind the barn looking building. We stopped walking when we got even with the barn, but not quite as far up as the house.

"Holy shit." I said.

I looked at Ken and he was looking at the house. He was standing there with an empty glass in one hand and a bottle in the other. I looked down at my glass, which I carried dutifully the whole walk to where we stood. I drained the last mouthful. It went down smooth as molasses. Not one demon shook through me.

"Hand me that bottle." Ken handed it over. "Let me see that glass." In the moonlight, I was able to pour the rest of the bottle into both of our glasses, about an inch and a half each. Maybe two.

I took another sip as we both surveyed the sight in front of us. I rocked myself from heel to toe, testing my stability. The scotch had gotten to my body, but my head felt remarkably clear.

"So. The Pelletiers. They all in jail?"

"No. Not really all of them. But the ones who actually owned this place. They are the ones who are going down. That's what I'm hearing anyway."

"So why doesn't the rest of the family want this place? Why are they selling it?"

"Can't afford it. Can't afford the taxes on it. Can't afford to rebuild it."

"They didn't have insurance? Homeowners or whatever?"

Ken looked at me. The moonlight was bright as day, so I could see eyebrows up and his eyes sort of rolling. "These guys? Not a chance."

"That's crazy." Another sip. Delicious.

"Besides, the family, they need to sell. They need the money for their lawyers. They are trying to beat this thing in court. They can't even post bail. They need to cash out."

"All that drug dealing and everything, don't they have piles of cash somewhere?"

"Even if they did, they couldn't use it, so they better not let anyone know where it is. It'll be sitting there when they get out of jail. If they get out of jail." Ken looked down and swirled the contents of his glass. I'm not even sure who started walking again, but we wound ourselves around the house and past a rather large pile of charred something or other, which I assumed was once the shed where the fire started. We walked another fifty feet or so up the hill and past where the fire burned. Ken stopped and turned around. We looked at the scene from above in silence for a few minutes before he spoke.

"I guess I always assumed their property ended somewhere back up here, up behind their house."

"Uh huh." I wasn't really sure where he was going with this.

"You know, these guys, they're country boys. Old country boys, I just never assumed they'd be sitting on a whole lot." No response seemed necessary, I just let him continue. I was looking uphill at him, and the moon shone right in his face. I could see every detail of his face clear as day. He bent down and put his glass on a flat piece of earth. He pulled a rubber band off his wrist and pulled his hair back into a ponytail, then picked his glass back up. "When my dad sold me this place, I never really paid attention to who owned the property back here," he gestured over his shoulder, "behind the Pelletiers. And behind camp."

He was silent for a moment. "Go on."

"It wasn't so long back. I just never really thought about it. I knew I'd look into it someday, but it didn't seem to matter. Why would it matter?"

I started to answer, but I didn't need to. There wasn't much to say. I knew what he was going to say even before he said it.

"It's all theirs. All the way up to the top of the mountain. Coming all the way back around pretty much to the cemetery at the top of the hill. Every trail we hike up, it belongs to them. They literally have camp surrounded." He seemed as sad as I ever saw him. Sadder. I wondered why he didn't tell me all this before.

I tried to be optimistic, and I didn't see why it wouldn't make sense to say, "but if it never mattered before, why would it now? If they didn't mind camp using the trails, why would someone else?"

"Because it won't be some meth dealing bunch of losers buying this place. It's going to be a timber company. Every big parcel of land that's come to market around here gets bought by the loggers. They'll take the trees they want; they won't cut them all down. But there will be new roads. And noise. It won't be this year. It won't be next year. But it's coming. That's just what's been happening." He tipped his glass back and emptied it.

There wasn't a whole lot I could think to say, but my mind started working. I looked at Ken's face, but he was looking over my head. I turned around and stood next to him and looked up at the moon, which was getting lower but still visible over the tops of the trees below us. We'd walked far enough up the property that we were almost even with the tops of the trees at the bottom of the clearing below the house, where the driveway ended. When you looked up at the trees and the moon you could ignore the disgusting mess of a property they'd left behind. And if you focused on how beautiful the moon looked and how delicate the tops of the trees looked, painted silver by its light, you could almost ignore Ken's pain, the pain of a guy who felt that everything he had was being ripped away.

"Fuck it." I said.

"What?" I saw his head whip towards me, and I knew right away from his tone that Ken thought I was dismissing his concern. Like I meant he should just forget it, let go. But that's not what I meant.

"Fuck it," I said again, this time finishing my thought. "I'll buy this place."

Ken laughed. "You're nuts, Archer. You couldn't buy this place."

I turned my head to face Ken. "Don't you know I'm rich?" I deadpanned. Ken did know I was comfortable, but he didn't know the half of it. I turned back and faced the ruins below us. The last mouthful of scotch went down smooth, and I looked at the bottle in my hand and back down at the house. I reared back and flung the bottle towards the house.

"I christen thee the Archer Why!" I shouted, my voice echoing around us. The bottle landed with a thud about ten feet shy of the house. Ken started laughing beside me.

"The bottle is supposed to break when you do that."

"Doesn't matter to me. We'll make the rules when I buy this shithole."

It took me about ten minutes to help Ken understand that I wasn't joking. And it took about another twenty for me to convince myself that I could make it happen. I'm sure Ken thought that the morning would come and I'd have either forgotten what I said or come to my senses. But the morning did come, and I was still clear about it, but I didn't get a chance to speak with Ken about it then. The conversation would surprise him about a week later, though.

The morning came with a hangover for all four of us. Chance and Laurel split the final bottle of red wine, it turns out, before passing out on the couch. When Ken and I got back from our walk, we roused Laurel who followed Ken sleepily to their bedroom. Chance and I woke up on the couch where I'd joined her. We enjoyed a quiet and peaceful breakfast of buckwheat pancakes, eggs and bacon, fresh strawberries and many cups of strong coffee. Everyone felt much better after that, but none of us felt great.

Bags packed and after a quick morning dunk in the lake, Chance and I said our goodbyes to Ken and Laurel in the late morning.

"Sure you won't stay for lunch?" Laurel asked without any pressure over Chance's shoulder as she gave her a long hug goodbye.

"No thanks, we'll get something on the road." I replied quickly.

Laurel pulled me into a tight squeeze and whispered in my ear so no one else could hear, "she's a keeper. Don't let that one go."

"No worries there," I whispered back.

She held me out at arm's length and gave me a serious look, despite her smile. She winked at me. I winked back.

"Love you guys." I said, surprised at the words as they came out of my mouth.

"We love you too, Archer." She said back without hesitation. Ken put his arm over her shoulder. A New Hampshire man's way of agreeing, I suppose.

Chance hopped in the car while I held her door. Ken and Laurel were still standing there, his arm over her shoulder, her arms around his middle, watching me from atop the railroad tie retaining wall above the road as I walked around the rear of the car. I backed out of the spot and pulled out into the road, going the opposite direction from where we came. Driving, it was less than a minute to the Pelletier property. I looked as we drove by, but because of the curve of the driveway, you couldn't see up to the house and definitely not up to where Ken and I sat the night before. I arched my neck as we drove by, almost leaning into Chance's lap.

She looked to her right at the unidentified driveway. "What's that?" She looked at me as I turned back to face the road.

"Nothing." I said. "The neighbors' place."

A few minutes passed and Chance asked, "what's on your mind over there?"

"Nothing," I lied, "just trying to will away this headache."

"You guys drank that whole bottle?"

I nodded.

"Sheesh. No wonder." After a few more moments along the dirt road, she noticed, "hey, why are we going the other way? Is this another way out of here?"

"Nope." I smiled slyly.

"Then where are we going?'

"I booked a night at a spa up in the White Mountains. You think I'd just surprise you with a night at this old dump?" I laughed and grabbed her thigh with a squeeze I knew would tickle her.

"Shut up!" she said, pushing my hand away. "What, really?"

"For really. Take a nap. It's like an hour away, I think." But she spent the whole time just looking out the window.

★★★

The shower was off now, and Chance told me to go ahead in. I think she thought I was asleep, but I wasn't. I peeled myself off the couch and made my way to the bathroom. Stripping down, I fully assessed my injuries for the first time. The leg was a little worse than I expected. I tried to take the wad of bandages off of my elbow slowly, but it hurt. So I pulled it off in one fell swoop, wincing more in anticipation than at the removal itself. My elbow was raw. I looked around for anything else I hadn't noticed, but there was nothing to speak of. I figured I'd survive.

I looked at myself in the mirror, leaning over the sink and putting my face very close to it. I brushed my hair back and looked at my hairline, opened my mouth and looked at my tongue and then my teeth. I finished by looking very closely at the skin around my eyes, which had begun, I noticed, to develop more fine wrinkles than were there earlier in life. I was going to have to try and stop smiling so much. Either that or moisturize, if I hoped to avoid looking any older. I turned the water on and stepped into the shower.

I wasn't really prepared for the stinging on my leg and elbow when the water hit it. I winced again, but I was going to have to bite the bullet, so I soaped up a washcloth and just went at it. Got everything nice and clean. I turned the water up really hot, telling myself it would help the soreness in my limbs that was now approaching my back. I leaned my head down and let the water run over my head and down my back, my eyes closed.

The process of buying the Pelletier property was simpler than I thought it would be. I assumed that going against a timber company in a real estate purchase would be a losing effort. Ken thought so too when I called him a week after our scotch induced conversation. But we were both wrong. Turns out there are plenty of wooded properties these companies could buy up in those parts. They didn't want to compete with anyone it seemed, which worked out well for me. The closing happened just after the new year began, and I found myself the proud owner of a couple hundred acres of New Hampshire forest, a small mountain peak, and a handful of charred buildings. Having a girlfriend working on a master's degree in architecture was an added bonus. A little frosting on the cake, which meant I could have a small group of soon-to-be professional architects working on designing the new house I planned to break ground on in the coming summer. It was nice for me, and nice for them since they'd actually see their class project come to fruition, though I'd most likely need it approved by someone with a license or something before we really got started. Permits and all, or so I was learning.

The first few weeks they were working on it, I made myself somewhat of a pain, and I knew it might not work out if I kept it up. So, I decided to just completely back off. They knew what I wanted, in general terms as well as a couple specific things I preferred, and I hired a firm to assess the land so they knew what they were working with in

Eric Toth

terms of terrain, slope of the land, and all that. I hadn't seen any details for a couple months or so. Despite the fact that I was itching to see what they were coming up with, I never asked a word. There was something nice about the anticipation. Chance is one of the smartest and hardest working people I've ever known. If she had something to do with it, it was going to be better than I could have envisioned. The money I'd be spending was a bit of a concern to me, in addition to all that I already dropped on the land purchase. I wouldn't call it a drop in the bucket, but I'd still be okay. I have enough insight to recognize that I don't have much earning potential, and if I didn't figure something out for myself... let's just say I probably shouldn't keep spending money indiscriminately and indefinitely. Thinking about all that may just be where my wrinkles were coming from.

I put my face right under the shower head and let the hot water pummel my mouth and cheeks. It had to be getting close to midnight at this point, but it didn't feel that late, probably because of the time change. Without looking down I shut off the water, I gave myself a quick once over with my hands to push the dripping water off my body and grabbed a towel off the bar as I stepped out of the shower. The mirror was completely fogged over. Using my hand, I made a quick swipe so I could see my face and quickly flossed and brushed, realizing as I finished that I was staring at myself the whole time, deep in a thought that I couldn't quite access. My reflection was blurred by the steam which started to fill in where I wiped the mirror with my hand. I gave it another swipe and leaned in again, looking at myself in the mirror, real close.

With a towel around my waist I walked out into the living space of my apartment. I went back in the bathroom and picked up my pants. I tossed them onto one of the armchairs and went into the kitchen and over to the counter on the left, which was sort of my junk area. Some people have a junk drawer, I have a junk area that includes a cabinet with several drawers and the upper cabinets as well. Not to mention the old spice rack that sits on the back of the counter. The one I put all my useless stuff into. I slid it away from the wall out to the front of the counter. The top of it was covered in a layer of dust. Old spice racks like this one don't really look like what we use now. It is really just a small chest of drawers, four rows of four, with little knobs on each one and a small slot for labels. There was only one label on mine, second from the top all the way to the right. It said nutmeg. All the rest of the labels were empty. I picked it up and carried it across the room to the coffee table and set it down gently.

My pants were on the back of the armchair. I pulled them onto my lap and reached into the pockets, emptying the contents onto the table in front of me. The cell phone and the billfold I pushed to the side. There were two lighter wheels, a bread tie, a rubber band, a key, a quarter, three dimes and two pennies. More than usual for one day. Opening specific drawers one by one, I put the items in their corresponding places, gently closing each drawer ceremoniously. The same ritual I did once or twice a week for years. I wiped the top of the chest absentmindedly with my hand and then wiped the dust off on the towel I was wearing.

I sat and stared at the small chest for a couple of minutes. Each drawer looked basically the same at first glance. But the wood of each one was faded differently, and the unique grain made the small chest look like a patchwork the longer I stared at it. Almost like a quilt. I stood up suddenly.

In the kitchen, I opened the cabinets under the sink, but I knew I was in the wrong place. I stood up and looked around, not totally aware of the fact that I was only wearing a towel until I stretched to reach in the cabinets above the counter and it fell to my ankles. I pulled a jar down from the shelf and carrying it in one hand, I picked up the towel with the other and walked back to the table. I wrapped myself up, sat down and unscrewed the top of the oversized mason jar.

One by one, I pulled out the drawers and began emptying the contents into the jar, making layers as I went. A thin layer of flint wheels became buried under a pile of rubber bands. On top of that, a pile of loose change. Another layer and another. Guitar picks. Pencils down to the nub. When I got to the bottom of the second column of drawers, I pulled out two envelopes. I was stumped for a second, but then just folded them into quarters and dropped them in the half full jar. They flattened out underneath a layer of marbles. Atop that, a single perfect skipping stone. From the final drawer came a handful of bread ties, and the jar was nearly full. I transported the now empty rack to the counter where it came from and walked back towards the table to sit. I screwed the top on the jar and tightened it, feeling satisfied. Seeing the key still resting on the table, I opened the jar and dropped it on top, then secured the lid again.

I held the jar up in front of me and looked at the layers of random objects. It was heavy. I gave it a little shake, but it only rattled. The layers held firm. I placed it down in the middle of the table.

"That's better," I said to myself. I went to the kitchen and washed my hands, picked my pants up off the chair and tossed them into the bathroom hamper. I slid quickly up the spiral stairs. Chance was sitting on the edge of the bed.

"What were you up to down there? What was all that rattling about?" Chance asked me, genuinely curious.

"Nothing really," I said. I wasn't really up to nothing, I suppose, but it didn't feel entirely like a lie.

"Sounded like something." She said.

I went over to the closet area, but I didn't really have anything to do over there.

"You are so secretive sometimes, Archer." She was looking at her feet. She looked up, "you don't have to be, you know."

This was a little more serious of a conversation than I was ready for at this point, but I felt it wasn't cool to play the *c'mon I fell off my bike and I'm tired* card. Even if there was a card like that. Chance deserved me being honest. But I couldn't really explain the jar, and it didn't seem like such a big deal. I turned back around from the closet and leaned against the dresser that was across from the foot of the bed, my elbow resting on the top, my cheek resting on my palm.

"It's no secret, babe. I'm just tired. I'll tell you in the morning. I'll show you." I said, thinking about the jar she'd see down there.

She looked down at her feet again, which she pulled up onto the bed, sitting cross legged now. The answer didn't seem to impress her. I couldn't really read her mood, it seemed off. "Okay, top secret. We'll see." She didn't look up. I could tell this wasn't exactly about whatever she heard downstairs. There had been a few moments like these lately, always to do with me and mostly to do with me not talking about things. And once when the future came up, but only in vague terms, which was probably the issue. I realized that we weren't talking about the noise she heard downstairs. Eventually, I tend to come around on these things. I'm just not always so quick on the uptake.

I looked at Chance where she sat and took her all in for a second. She always seemed a little tan, with a rich olive like complexion, I think they call it. Her curls were drying out now from her shower. Her mouth had a little pout to it, but that wasn't from her mood. That was just a resting expression. Her looks were one thing, but her way was something else. I never met someone so true and so honest. She expected the best from people and seemed to really have faith in the goodness of people. It was a nice quality. If there was someone who could always be expected to do the right thing and to be there if someone needed her, it was Chance. I thought about her and what a special person she was. I thought about how lucky I was to have her. I thought about the ring that was in the drawer under my elbow. And I thought about how I'd never be able to wait till the summer to give it to her.

But not tonight.

"Listen, kid. I was just playing around with some of my junk downstairs. I filled up a jar with it. I don't know why exactly, but I'll figure it out by morning and I'll tell you all about it while you eat the soup I'm making you for breakfast." She didn't look up but she was smiling.

"Now. Can. I. Please. Get. In. Bed?" I walked over like a robot and pushed her back on the bed, climbing and then rolling over her like a steamroller. My towel fell off again.

She giggled, "get off me" and pushed me to the side.

I groaned. "Oh, fuck. My body." I rolled over onto my back, kicking the towel onto the floor.

Why. Me.

"Shit, Archer, you're bleeding on the bed."

"It's nothing. I'm okay." I didn't even bother looking, I just shimmied my way up the bed and slid my naked body under the covers. "I need to let my wounds breath for the night. Can you get the lights? I'm being selfish."

She hit the lights and slid into the bed next to me.

"I guess I can't have my way with you tonight, then?" She teased me.

"Maybe in the morning."

I was on my back with my arms above my head, feeling somewhat out of breath. Chance slid alongside me and curled up on her side, one leg flung over my thighs, one arm across my body, just below my sternum. She managed to get into the position without touching any of my sore spots. Her limbs felt warm resting on me, and the weight of them was stabilizing. My breath started to slow and I could feel my eyes getting heavy, so I let them close. Chance's face was close enough that I could feel her breathing on my shoulder. I could smell her damp hair.

Between the beers, the hot shower, the spill off the bike and Chance cuddling up next to me, it wasn't hard to start dozing off quickly. I felt myself drop down and twitched slightly, my breath catching, and then I slipped off.

I was sitting on a porch, and I could tell by the light that it was late in the day. There were a lot of voices around me, and from where I sat in my Adirondack chair I could hear kids yelling from behind the house. I wasn't looking at the faces, but I knew who was there. Chance was somewhere inside, behind the screen doors, and I could hear her voice over the clinking of kitchen activities. Jill was there on the porch, talking with Mark and Frankie. Quinn was leaning over the railing and speaking to someone's kid down below. Ken was there, I could hear his laugh.

Over the cacophony of voices, I heard a car rumbling up the driveway. I stood up from where I sat and walked along the porch that wrapped around the side of the house to the front. The sun was settling down over the trees, and it was blazing bright even as it started to sink on the horizon, painting the treetops of the forest golden. It was almost too bright to keep my eyes open. Shielding my eyes and trying to focus, I saw a dark green sedan pull up the driveway down below, where a dozen or so cars were parked along the driveway that approached the house. It stopped in the middle of the driveway, and a plume of dust pulled up along the side of the car and then settled back down.

As the door of the car opened, I saw a woman stand up, her long dark hair was graying in streaks. I squinted hard against the sun, glowing golder now through the forest of trees, my hand tight above my eyes. A mosquito or something tickled my neck and I tried to swat it away. It tickled me again and I started, suddenly opening my eyes.

Chance let out a small moan. "I fell asleep," she whispered.

"Mmmm. Me too," I said quietly. I tried to get back to sleep, to the dream, but I knew it was gone. I looked up at the skylight, my eyes were adjusted to the dark. I let them close again, near sleep. "How is our house coming?" I asked Chance sleepily.

She lifted up her head slightly, and I could feel her looking at me. It was the first time I used the word *our* about the house they were working on. It just came out. I kept my eyes closed.

Her head rested back down on my shoulder, and she moved another inch or so closer. "Good, Arch," she said. "It's good."

I brought my right arm down around her back, my hand on her ribs. Without intending to, I let out a small sigh. "That's good, babe. Can't wait."

"Me either," she whispered.

My dream from the night before flashed by me. The darkness. The faces. And then the entire day played itself out in my head. The bike ride, my rooftop conversation, cribbage. The morning felt like years ago. It was one of those days. One of those days when it seems like nothing really happens, which then, in a breath, is over.

About the Author

Eric Toth is a lucky man. He is married to a remarkable woman, whose creative and considerate spirit brings joy, direction and often hysterical laughter to his daily life. He also has three extraordinary daughters, whose curiosity, honesty and humor keep him in awe and in check. Most days, Eric works as an executive in the behavioral health nonprofit sector. It also turns out that he is a writer with a penchant for amassing fictional events in his head before ever getting around to putting them on paper.

Among the beliefs that drive his writing are the following: time is not linear; we become who we are through our interactions with others; reading should be an active and intentional pursuit; and music is the best way to describe emotions when there are no relevant words or descriptive phrases available.

A New Englander by birth and by nature, Eric lives in the Lower Hudson Valley of New York. He enjoys spending time with his family (naturally), home improvement (by default) and conceiving fiction (he just can't help it.) He gets uncomfortable when people put their feet on the dashboard. Most of his inspiration to write comes by way of listening to music, usually Bob Dylan.

Made in the USA
Las Vegas, NV
16 July 2022

51704806R10154